HER LAST CRY

PAUL J. TEAGUE

Storm
PUBLISHING

Ebook ISBN: 978-1-80508-490-7
Paperback ISBN: 978-1-80508-492-1

Cover design: Lisa Horton
Cover images: Shutterstock

Published by Storm Publishing.
For further information, visit:
www.stormpublishing.co

ALSO BY PAUL J. TEAGUE

The Fallen Girls

Her Last Cry

The Fifth Girl

ONE

'You've got to be joking.'

Hollie steadied herself on the wooden platform as the water surged up at her feet once again.

'I know, right?' DC Jenni Langdon replied. 'She walked in, just like that, according to the desk sergeant. Calm as a cucumber, he said. What's all that noise? Where are you?'

Not thinking it through, Hollie's immediate reaction was to scan her surroundings. It was a mistake. She could barely maintain her balance with the grey torrents swirling around her in a thousand different patterns. The fierce rush of water towards the tidal barrier almost carried her away, just looking at it. She couldn't recall a time she'd seen a river as ferocious as this. She had to focus. One loss of footing and she'd be swept away.

'I've just been making a house call on Gilly Hodges—' she began.

'Well, at my end of the phone it sounds wild, wherever you are.'

Hollie might have got annoyed with Jenni if she wasn't quite so scared. She felt the need to justify herself.

'Oh, I've just left now. I'm walking to my car. It's terrible out here.'

'What do you want to do about the suspect?' DC Langdon continued. Hollie was thankful she didn't push the issue further. It would take some explaining, her being in the middle of the River Hull, standing on a flimsy wooden structure underneath the flyover next to the city's tidal barrier. Without backup, too. And without mentioning to anybody what she was up to.

Hollie steadied herself with her free hand and looked for the man she'd been pursuing. There was no sign of him. But there were two young men now standing on the safe side of the river's fencing, phones out, no doubt making videos of the tumultuous water. They seemed to be shouting over to her, but she couldn't hear a thing; the wind was too wild and the roar of the water almost deafening.

There was nothing Hollie wanted more than to drive directly over to where Mandy Tyson was being held and interview her there and then. No way was that happening. She was sodden, her clothes heavy and weighed down with cold water. Her shoes squelched as she moved, and her hair clung across her face where the gale had pulled strands out of her hairband. She was shivering, too; she'd only just realised how cold she was.

'Go over to Clough Road with DS Anderson, once she's been transferred, and make sure the preliminaries are done. I want to speak to her with DS Anderson first thing tomorrow morning at HQ. I'll be in early. I want to question her before the morning briefing. Has she got legal representation yet?'

'I don't know, ma'am. This is hot off the press. We'll get her booked into the custody suite and processed, and I'll prep things for tomorrow.'

'Okay, great, thanks very much for letting me know—'

Hollie was about to sign off, eager to give her full attention to more immediate problems.

'Just so long as you're sure everything's okay. I'm happy to drive round if you're in need of help.'

A sudden gust of wind caught Hollie unawares and she finished the call, thanking Jenni for her concern. She stepped back, expecting there to be a solid surface on which to place her foot, but there was none, and she stumbled. Stupidly, her first priority was her phone rather than her own preservation. As her arms shot out in front of her to steady herself, she let the phone drop onto the sodden wooden planks of the walkway, before reaching out for the flimsy barrier. Her body lost its fight for stability, and instead of managing a lurch towards safety, she toppled backwards, her waist striking the barrier on the other side as her foot dropped into the water below. Hollie felt the shock of adrenaline gripping her chest as she cast her hands around, searching for anything to hold on to. She slipped and felt herself falling, heavy and stiff, the deadly waters just below her. As her other foot entered the water, she was able to grasp the barrier at the edge of the walkway, first with her left hand, then with her right. Half-submerged now, she felt the phenomenal forward motion of the water; it wrenched her towards the tidal barrier with a force she could barely believe.

If one of the young guys hadn't grasped her arm at that moment, she was certain she'd have been torn away and washed out to sea. The second youth grabbed her other hand.

'Don't do it, luv. It's not worth it,' the first lad said as he pulled on her right arm to bring her back to the safety of the wooden floor.

These kids thought she was suicidal, though she didn't care much at that moment about correcting them – they'd saved her life. Shane Hardy's face flashed in front of her momentarily, she hadn't a clue why. Perhaps it was because these lads were about the same age as him. Instead of messing around on illegal motorcycles, they were out rescuing what they thought was a depressed middle-aged woman. She thanked her lucky stars she'd been fortunate and had got the classier end of the teenager spectrum. They were strong, lifting her out of the water with seemingly little effort. She could have kissed them both, she was so relieved. Hollie had been seconds away from going on a fare-free trip across the Humber Estuary and out into the North Sea. She'd rather pay the price of a ticket and take the ferry. As her feet touched the soaking wooden platform, the two young men held their grip on her arms, like they expected her to make a dash for it at any moment.

'Are you all right?' the other young man asked. 'You'd have been a goner if you'd fallen in there.'

'I'm fine, thank you so much,' Hollie replied, grateful for the help but embarrassed by the fuss. She fought back the tears of relief; that had been a close call and she knew it.

'Let's get you off here. It's scary as hell,' he continued.

'My phone,' Hollie spluttered. 'I need my phone.'

'I'll get it,' the first lad said, releasing her arm. She hadn't realised how weak her legs were. As he let go of his grip, she felt herself dropping. The other young man rushed to support her.

'Whoa, you've had a fright. Careful.'

Hollie hoped her own son would turn out like these two. If there was one thing she had to force herself to remember in her job, it was that the shits and dickheads were in the minority. Most people were like these kids. They did the right thing.

She'd almost forgotten about the man she was chasing. As the young guy helped her over to the safety of the railings that ran along the river, she felt a blissful sense of relief at being off the wooden platform at last. Gilly was there, too, waiting for her, her face ashen with worry and cold.

'Are you all right, DI Turner? I was concerned about you,' Gilly shouted as Hollie awkwardly made her way over the metal fencing.

'He got away,' Hollie cursed, annoyed with her failure but delighted to be standing on firm ground once again.

'Do you know her?' the young guy asked.

'Yes, she's... a friend,' Gilly replied.

'Well, best not let her out of your sight,' he continued. 'She must have been pretty desperate to jump in the river. Doesn't she know how much shit is in there?'

He gave a cheeky smile.

'I know you, don't I?' he added as his friend returned, clutching Hollie's mobile phone. He was looking at Gilly.

'Maybe. I'm a local councillor. You might have seen me in the papers.'

'Yeah, I know you. You saved my granddad's allotment from being turned into a housing estate. He loves you, he does. He says you're his pin-up girl, after that.'

'Well, tell him you've more than returned the favour,' Gilly said, flinching as a gust of wind shook them all where they were standing in the gravel car park.

Hollie had never felt so grateful to be on solid ground. She took her phone from the second youth.

'Thank you both so much,' she just about managed. The cold water had gripped her to such an extent she could barely form the words.

'We need to get you back to my place and warmed up.'

Gilly was taking the lead now, and Hollie could have hugged her.

'Lads, you've done a brilliant thing here today. Just tap your contact numbers into my phone. There has to be some citizen award or something we can organise for you. I can't thank you enough.'

They both shrugged, embarrassed at Gilly's attention.

'So long as your friend is okay.'

Gilly placed her arm around Hollie's shoulders and pulled her in tight as the boys shared their contact details, then resumed their filming of the river.

'You must be freezing—'

Hollie couldn't stop shivering now. Her lips were trembling and her fingers stiff from the cold. Her hands looked blue under the radiated light of the streetlamps.

Gilly looked up and pointed into the distance.

'Isn't that our man?'

Hollie followed Gilly's gaze across the car park. She was right. It was the man she'd been chasing. He'd made it across the length of the walkway to the other side. Thank God.

He held his hand up, a signal that he'd seen she was okay.

Hollie tensed immediately and turned to run after him.

'He's not getting away from me this time—'

Gilly reached out and firmly grasped the top of her arm. For one moment, Hollie fought it.

'You're freezing, DI Turner, and you've just had a fright. Leave it now or call your colleagues. You need to sit this one out.'

Hollie stopped and watched the man heading for a footbridge at the far end of the car park.

'Where does that lead?' she asked.

'That's the Scale Lane swing bridge. He'll be away into the Old Town and the city centre once he's over there—'

Hollie reached for her phone.

'He's away now,' Gilly reassured her. 'Leave it now, you need to warm up and get dry.'

Hollie knew she was right, though every bit of her wanted to give chase. She could see he was gone, and there was no decent description she could give that would enable a patrol car to locate him. He'd slipped through her fingers for now.

She was about to walk off with Gilly when she stopped dead and felt in her pocket. It was cold and wet and felt horrible to touch.

'Wait.' Hollie stopped, pushing her hand into her pocket. 'He dropped something. He seemed pissed off that I had it.'

She drew out the small Ziplock bag that she'd picked up after their struggle in the underground parking area. She opened it up to find a paper bag from Willis Ludlow inside.

'I haven't seen one of those bags in a long time,' Gilly exclaimed. 'That department store closed years ago.'

The paper bag had remained dry, as had its contents. Hollie pulled out a black and white photograph showing a school netball team. It was just a sea of faces to her, but Gilly was immediately interested in one of them.

'Here, let me look at that near the streetlight over there.'

She walked over and held out the photograph, studying it intently.

Gilly looked like the ghost of a loved one had just brushed by her on the street. Her face was pale, and she was gently shaking her head, seemingly in disbelief.

'I haven't seen that face in years. That's the girl who took the photograph on my wall. It's exactly how I remember her. That's the same girl whose name is blanked out on that list of yours from the mother and baby home.'

TWO

Hollie examined the notes that had been handed to her about Mandy Tyson. It didn't look like the profile of a killer. Mandy had no police record, everything about her pointed to a quiet, normal, unassuming life. She lived in a small, terraced property close to the city centre and had a part-time job working for an office cleaning company.

Her body language was reserved and tense, her voice soft and almost apologetic. Mandy dressed in a way that suggested she was happy to blend into the background, unlike Gilly Hodges who looked like an explosion in a paint factory. But then if there was one thing all these years of policing had taught her, it was that there's no typical killer.

It was just past eight o'clock. She moved her head from side to side, working out the stiffness from a night of tossing and turning. Thank goodness Gilly had given her some clothes to change into; she'd have caught her death of cold otherwise.

They were recording now.

Mandy Tyson was sitting opposite her, a look of terror on her face, no doubt shaken by a night in the cells at the Clough Road

Custody Suite. The duty solicitor looked like he'd rolled out of bed moments ago. She wasn't sure if he was cutting edge or if his hair was just a mess. She hoped he knew his stuff because if they ended up charging Mandy, the woman was going to need him.

DS Anderson was sitting at her side. He'd already done some preliminaries the night before, but they'd had to sort out her legal counsel before questioning her on the record.

'So, Mandy, why don't you start by telling us how you knew Sister Sophia Brennan?'

From the moment Mandy spoke, Hollie could tell she was a woman who was entirely unaccustomed to dealing with the law. At most, she'd probably stopped a copper for directions or asked for the time as she passed a bobby on the street. She might have had one in the house, perhaps to report details of vandalism or a minor theft. She had none of the baked-in contempt or accomplished guile of a prick like Shane Hardy.

'She was at the home—'

'For the record, which home was this?' DS Anderson interjected.

'The Church of St Mary and the Angels. I was in the mother and baby home. It was 1974. No, I was in the home in 1975, and I fell pregnant in 1974. Sister Brennan was there then. That's when I knew her, though I had met her at my parents' house before then. I'm not even sure she was a proper nun then, but we all called her Sister Brennan.'

'How old were you?' Hollie asked.

'I was fifteen when I fell pregnant, sixteen when I had the baby—'

'Are you still with the father?' Anderson interrupted.

Mandy laughed. Hollie had seen the same reaction from Gilly.

'No, Terry was long gone by the time I had my baby. I've never seen him since.'

Mandy seemed distracted, like she was thinking back to that time and working through some memories.

'What was your relationship with Sister Brennan?' Hollie picked up.

'Have you spoken to anybody else about her?' Mandy replied, looking from DS Anderson to Hollie. When neither of them replied, she continued, 'Well, she was not a nice woman. She was very hostile towards us girls. At times, she would—'

Mandy choked up suddenly. Her eyes moistened as she fought to compose herself.

'She would push and shove us sometimes,' she continued. 'She wouldn't go as far as leaving bruises, but these days, you wouldn't hesitate to call it abuse. I didn't like her, and she didn't like me. She despised us girls for having our babies. I'm not even certain it was because we'd got pregnant out of wedlock. She didn't seem to like the fact we were having babies in the first place. She thought babies were for marriage, I think. She was certainly very angry about something.'

'Were you frightened of her?' Anderson wondered.

'God, yes, of course we were. Sister Brennan was terrifying. She used to prowl that place like an eerie shadow—' Mandy swallowed hard and she looked away, reliving some memory from her past.

Hollie noticed a haunted look in her eyes, as if the hands of the past had reached out to grab her.

Mandy cleared her throat and struggled to compose herself.

'That woman never had a good word to say to us. She never set our minds at rest when we worried about the births. And we were so alone in that place, nobody came to see me or support me—'

Mandy's gaze drifted away again, and Hollie watched as she screwed up her face, reminded no doubt of some painful event from her past.

'Sister Brennan was an evil old cow. She was pure evil.'

Hollie and Anderson exchanged glances momentarily. He'd clocked it, too. *Pure Evil* had been written on the sign hanging around the nun's neck. It was interesting that Gilly had used the same words. Hollie made a mental note to discuss it later; it was a case detail she didn't want to flag up with Mandy just yet.

'That's an interesting phrase to use,' DS Anderson remarked.

Mandy looked at him as if to say *so what?* Gilly had been the same; she'd used the words but showed no signs that she might have given herself away in the process. After a pause, Mandy ventured an explanation.

'Well, it's just what you say, isn't it? If someone is wicked and spiteful, you call it pure evil. That's what Sister Brennan was. She made that place horrible. We'd stay in our rooms and keep out of her way. She's the nastiest woman I've ever met.'

'Is that why you killed her?' Anderson shot his question.

'I—' Mandy corrected herself. 'Yes. She deserved it. As I told you already, she made our lives hell.'

Hollie looked at DS Anderson again. The duty solicitor raised his eyebrows.

'What made you seek revenge now, so many years after the event? This was 1975, you told us. That's a long time to hold a grudge.'

Hollie searched Mandy's face. She could see that the passage of time hadn't lessened the emotions she experienced around the topic of Sister Brennan.

'I just felt like it was time. My old friend, Violet – she was from the home – she's dying... of cancer. I thought she might like to know Sister Brennan's gone. It might give her some peace. It might give all of us some peace.'

This corroborated Gilly's version of events, so it was useful information. Hollie noted the name. They had to prioritise speaking to Violet.

'And was Violet ever reconciled with her son?' DS Anderson asked.

'She had a daughter. Well, the child that was adopted was a daughter. She also had a family with the man who became her husband. But her adopted child was – is – a girl, a daughter. She's called Patricia.'

'What about you, Mandy? Were you reunited with your child?'

'With Clive? Eventually, yes. I hated that name. I wanted to call him Oliver. That's another choice that was taken away from me. We were reunited because Gilly Hodges shared a room with me. Do you know her?'

Hollie retained an expressionless face. This was a well-worn game of cat and mouse. She wouldn't confirm anything useful to Mandy while they were corroborating facts.

'Well, Gilly Hodges was reunited with her son. And when that happened, I looked for my child. And, yes, we're reunited.'

'Was it a happy reunion?'

DS Anderson asked the question. He was an old hand at this, like Hollie. He wasn't dominating either; that was a good sign. It worked best with the to and fro.

'Yes and no. Of course, I was happy to see my baby after more than twenty-five years. Who wouldn't be? But he'd been in trouble with the police. He'd had a difficult life without me. He was estranged from the people who adopted him. I think he became rudderless. Anyway, he's had problems with drink and drugs, and he struggles to hold down jobs. He gets what work he can—'

Mandy's eyes reddened and a single tear ran down each cheek, as if years of sadness and regret refused to go away.

DS Anderson waited a moment, then continued to push her.

'Where might we find your son? Where's he working now?'

Mandy hesitated and looked like she was about to say something, then stopped.

'I don't know where he is. He has casual jobs; I never know where he's working.'

If there was an award for the worst liar ever, Mandy Tyson just picked up a nomination.

'Where has he worked recently?' Hollie encouraged.

'Well, you know. He does a bit here, he does a bit there—'

'Give me an example,' Hollie asked gently.

Mandy wasn't good at this.

'He's working – he worked at the docks—'

'Hull docks?' DS Anderson was straight in there.

'No, sorry, that's wrong. In a pub, he's working in a pub. I can't remember the name of it now.'

Hollie and DS Anderson exchanged a glance, and Hollie made a note. Doctor Ruane told them the rope used to hang Sister Brennan had been exposed to saltwater. It was interesting she had mentioned the docks.

'What sort of trouble has he been in?' Anderson continued.

Mandy's eyes flashed with panic.

'We can check on our records, you know?' Hollie pushed.

'Just a bit of trouble. I'm sure you'll be able to find it on that computer system of yours.'

'Are you angry about what happened to Clive?' Hollie asked.

'Yes, officer, I'm bloody angry about it!'

Mandy Tyson did not strike Hollie as the sort of woman who would swear easily, but she could see the rage still burnt fiercely inside her.

'Angry enough to kill?' Anderson swooped in swiftly with the follow-up.

Mandy paused.

'Yes, angry enough to kill.'

'What was Sister Brennan wearing on the day you killed her?' Hollie asked.

Mandy hesitated.

'Well, you know. Nun clothing. She was dressed like a nun dresses.'

'How did you get to the Humber Bridge?'

'We-I drove there—'

'We? Who were you with, Mandy?'

'I was mistaken, I was thinking about something else—'

'You seem to be very confused about what did and what did not happen—'

'Yes, I'm sorry, your questions are coming so fast—'

'It's almost like you're making it up as you go along—'

'No – no, it's true—'

'Do you even drive, Mandy? It's easy enough to find out, you know.'

Hollie's rapid-fire questioning was flustering Mandy now.

'DI Turner,' the duty solicitor said, a stern tone in his voice. At least he'd done something to justify his fee.

'I'll repeat the question,' Hollie continued, a little more gently. 'Do you drive?'

Mandy looked at the duty solicitor.

'You can answer with a *no comment*,' he reminded her.

'No comment, officer,' she replied quietly.

'How did you move Sister Brennan to the bridge?' DS Anderson interjected.

Mandy looked at her solicitor, who gave her a small nod.

'No comment.'

Hollie could see how this was playing out now.

'I should remind you that if you've handed yourself in here falsely claiming to have killed Sister Brennan, you could be charged with wasting police time or perverting the course of justice. You also know that every minute we spend with you is time wasted when we could be hunting for a killer. I'll ask you again. Did you kill Sister Brennan?'

Mandy waited a while before answering. She swallowed hard.

'No comment.'

'You've come in here saying you murdered the nun, but now you're telling us nothing? Are you protecting somebody, Mandy?'

Hollie could see they were rattling her now.

'Is it your son that you're protecting?' DS Anderson suggested. 'This is all about your son, Mandy. You think he did it, don't you?'

'Steady, detective,' the solicitor warned.

Mandy was straight back with her reply.

'No. No way. Clive would not do something like this. He's had his problems in the past, but he's trying to put things right. Just leave Clive out of this, he's had things hard enough as it is.'

Hollie let that sit a while before replying.

'I'm a mother, too, Mandy. I think if my child had been taken from me and I'd spent my life wondering what happened to him and what had become of him, I think I'd have done the same thing if I was trying to protect him. And if my son had gone off the rails like Clive has, I think I'd be wracked with guilt. I think I'd hate myself for not being able to protect him. I think I might do what you've just done, Mandy. I think I might throw myself under a bus to protect my precious child.'

'Is that what happened?' Anderson added.

Hollie studied Mandy's face. She looked distraught.

'No. That's not what happened. Just leave Clive out of it. I never told him about Sister Brennan and what she did—'

Mandy was barely audible through her sobs.

Anderson was pushing her hard now.

'But he found out somehow, I don't know how. And he was angry with her. He was only trying to get revenge for his

15

mother. He was angry about what happened to you back then. Is that what happened, Mandy?'

Her tears were dripping onto the table now, but she managed to say the words.

'No. There's no way Clive killed Sister Brennan. He's had his problems, but he's not that sort of man. I know he's not that sort of man.'

Hollie and DS Anderson were both looking at Mandy now, trying to figure out what this was all about.

'Every mother thinks their son is incapable of harm,' Hollie began. 'Only, you and I know otherwise, don't we, Mandy? I'm going to send a team over to the docks to pick up your son right now.'

THREE

1974: GILLY'S STORY

Herbie Rides Again was not Gilly's idea of a good film, but the audience seemed to like it well enough. It was packed, but then the evening showings usually were.

Her duties were to collect the tickets as the customers entered the auditorium, make sure nobody was messing around, wait for the lights to dim, and then ensure everything was underway. She usually stuck around until the Pearl & Dean signature tune came on, then waited by the door for ten minutes to escort any late arrivals to their seats with the help of her torch. Once that was done, she was clear for half an hour, until it was time to ready the ice creams for the interval. She'd got a rendezvous set up in the projection room when it was time for her break.

Gilly walked into the Cecil Cinema foyer, the catchy tune from the adverts playing through her head. She knew she and Eric were playing with fire, but she loved him, and he made her laugh. After completing her CSE exams and leaving school, she'd proved her parents wrong by landing the cinema job before the summer holidays were over, and she had no intention of ever going back to that school again.

Gilly gave her stomach a rub as she took her position by the auditorium. She'd been experiencing a strange sensation all day, but she wouldn't say she was ill as such, and she hoped that whatever it was would pass soon enough.

There were one or two late arrivals, but it was mainly an adult audience, so there was none of the bedlam there'd been at the kids' showings over the weekend. The amount of clearing up she'd had to do after that showing was ridiculous; people could behave like animals sometimes.

She checked the time. It was her break. Nobody would be looking for her for the next twenty minutes. That evening's films were all underway. This was her moment, and Eric was waiting.

Gilly checked that none of her work colleagues were around, before slipping into the projection room. She was greeted by the whirring of the films moving through the projectors and the bright, animated beams shining through the windows onto the various screens. And there was Eric, a big grin on his face, his shirt undone so that his chest hair could just be glimpsed by those who cared to look for it.

Eric had awoken feelings in Gilly that she'd not experienced before. The boys at school had been spotty, juvenile idiots, but Eric was cut from a different cloth. Not only was he good-looking and cheeky, but his body was also firm and muscular, and he quite clearly had a thing for her.

Gilly felt her legs weaken and a flutter in her belly. Eric pulled her in close and they began to kiss, deep and passionate. He used his tongue in a way that thrilled her, and she melted into his arms, eager to make the most of their snatched time together.

Eric had arrived at just the right time for Gilly. He was covering the projectors while the usual guy recovered from an operation. He was only there for the summer, but Gilly prayed he'd be able to stay after that. He was a hit with all the girls who worked there, but fortunately, he only had eyes for her.

In the rare moments when she thought in any depth about their relationship, she realised she didn't know that much about him. Eric drove an orange Ford Escort with an engine that growled as he revved it. They'd made out in it a couple of times, but her parents were so controlling, it was difficult to keep coming up with excuses to cover her tracks. Her parents would go spare if they ever met Eric. He was the kind of man her father despised. She could picture him ranting.

Idiots like that need National Service. It never did us any harm. The army life makes a man. It gives you discipline and order.

One of Gilly's uncles had told her once that her father never completed his National Service because he was asthmatic. He'd been posted in Egypt at the time of the Suez Crisis but during one of the world's pivotal, historic moments, he was in a camp hospital under the supervision of a medical orderly. And now, he was a traffic warden. She reckoned he felt like a soldier still, bearing in mind he got to wear a hat and a uniform in civilian life.

Eric unbuttoned Gilly's blouse and placed his masculine, smooth hand under the cup of her bra. She could feel her face flushing, and it was always like this. The moment he touched her, she lost control of her senses.

'Is it safe?' she asked, making a last protest before she was completely swept away.

'It's fine,' he reassured her, that big grin on his face; the cat who was about to get the cream. 'The gaffer's out with his missus this evening. Besides, the only time anyone ever comes in here is when the acetates screw up. We've got ten minutes until my next reel change.'

That was good enough for Gilly. She unbuttoned his shirt and ran her hands across his chest. She loved that hair. The boys at school could barely manage to cultivate a hairy caterpillar across their top lips, whereas Eric was something else.

He released the top button of his flared Wranglers, pulled down the zip, and pushed his jeans down to the top of his knees. His underwear followed. He hoisted Gilly up onto the desk at the back of the projection room and removed her shoes and tights. She knew what was coming, and she couldn't get enough of it. Eric had shown her an aspect of adult life that she'd never even had cause to think about before. He was confident and knowledgeable. He knew exactly what to do, and she felt beautiful and desired in his presence. She'd never experienced feelings like it before. She figured her parents must have been like that once upon a time, but her father barely smiled these days. It was impossible to even imagine there might have ever been a flicker of passion there.

Gilly was still catching her breath when Eric drew away to change one of the reels in the far projector. He pulled up his underwear and jeans, not bothering to fasten them until the job was done. She could feel her cheeks were flushed. She'd need a moment or two before heading back out to prepare the tray of ice creams.

She hopped off the table and pushed her skirt down, attempting to smooth the giveaway creases. She pulled on her knickers, which had been thrown on the floor in the heat of the moment. Eric smiled at her and cupped her head in his hands. He kissed her on the lips and moved to the side, his tongue darting into her ear, caressing its edges. She tingled all over. She couldn't stay, much as she wanted to. His touch set her alight.

Gilly gently pushed him away, picked up her tights, stepped into them, and worked them back up her legs.

'Can I see you this week?' he asked.

'You know what my mum and dad are like,' she replied.

'Can't you sneak out? What about that friend of yours? She'll cover for you, won't she? You can say you're staying at her house overnight, can't you?'

'But our mothers see each other at church. What if my mum finds out?'

'I can't wait until we get our own place.' Eric smiled. 'Then I can enjoy you all day and all night. You're beautiful, Gilly Hodges, you really are.'

Gilly felt the flush in her cheeks again, though this time it was with the embarrassment of him calling her *beautiful*. She still wasn't used to being talked to in that way. You'd have thought the idiots at school hated girls the way they spoke to them. Yet here she was at sixteen years old, with a passionate grown man in his twenties who was unable to keep his hands off her. What girl wouldn't want that?

Gilly stepped into her shoes.

'Do I look all right?' she asked.

'You always look like a million dollars to me.'

'You know what I mean. Can anyone tell what we've been doing?'

'I'm going to be replaying it all night in my head.' He smiled.

She kissed him, pulling herself away sooner than she wanted to, in case she got carried away. Her stomach twinged again, but she dismissed it, focusing instead on how the rest of her body felt. There was an advert on the television for a hot breakfast cereal that they'd illustrate with an orange glow around the kids. That's how she felt; that's how Eric made her feel.

Gilly forced herself out of the projection room. She was busy with her cinema duties for the rest of the evening, and there was a heavy demand for ice creams and sweets during the interval. She had to continue serving at the front of the auditorium while the film resumed, and she worked through the remainder of the queue.

The audience left such a mess after the film that she was late clearing up after them. She'd hoped to catch a last moment with Eric before heading home in the taxi her parents insisted on sending out for her, but she'd missed him. He was able to go as soon as that day's screenings had finished.

She stepped out of the rear doors with her friend Janet, who did the same job as her in the adjacent auditorium and lifted her rubbish bag to throw it into the sturdy metal bin out the back. As she glanced across the staff car park, she spotted Eric in his Ford Escort, reversing out of one of the marked spaces.

Gilly's heart skipped a beat as the car swung round and she got a clearer view. She looked again, thinking it must be a trick of the light. Janet was saying something to her, but she wasn't listening; it was just background noise now.

Even though it was dark, she knew exactly what she'd just seen: a woman was sitting in the passenger seat of Eric's car.

FOUR

'What do you think?' Hollie asked. She reckoned she knew the answer already, but DS Anderson was a new colleague, and she was a long way off being able to read him.

'If she murdered Sister Brennan, I'll buy doughnuts and coffees for the entire investigation team for the next seven days. And I promise not to eat half of the doughnuts.'

They'd left Mandy in the interview room with her solicitor. With some reluctance, she'd finally offered up Clive's surname: Bartram, the name of his adoptive parents. Hollie was mindful of wrapping things up with Mandy, as she wanted to get the team deployed on that day's priorities, locating Clive Bartram being one of them. They were unlikely to move things on with her until they'd got their hands on her son.

'That undecided, eh? I agree, there's no way she would have physically been able to throw Sister Brennan over the side of the bridge. She's protecting her son. But she might be an accomplice.'

'What makes you say that, boss?'

'Something that Doctor Ruane said. Do you remember his theory that there were two different murder methods deployed?

Suffocation and then the very violent disposal of the nun's body. She used the words *Pure Evil*, too. What if Mandy suffocated Sister Brennan and Clive disposed of the body?'

DS Anderson considered that, then nodded in agreement. 'Yes, that's a strong working theory. We need to haul him in for questioning ASAP. I'll get on it, shall I?'

Hollie nodded. Clive had just become prime suspect number one. He was going to get an early morning visit.

'Try the docks first,' Hollie suggested. 'She was bullshitting us about that. See if DS Patel can find a home address for him, and check his previous police record. Pull up his prints, let's see what we can find out about him. I'll finish off with Mandy. We can hold her a bit longer, but we'll need to come up with something more solid if we're going to charge her. Take DC Gordon with you, please. The experience will be good for him.'

'Will do, ma'am.'

Anderson was being unusually compliant. They'd worked well together in the interview room. It was a promising development after a shaky start. He seemed to sense the change in the atmosphere between them.

'I enjoyed the to-and-fro in that interview room,' he said. 'It's good to work with a cop who knows what they're doing. DCI Osmond had a quiet word with me about showing you a bit more support among the troops. I apologise if I came over as unfriendly at first. It's just that you never quite know who you're getting when there's a new kid on the block.'

Was this an apology? They didn't have to be best friends, but it would be good if their working relationship could remain productive.

She gave it a cautious welcome, she'd wait and see.

'Thanks, DS Anderson, I appreciate you saying that.'

Hollie's phone buzzed with a text notification. She picked it up from the arm of her chair and read the screen.

There's industrial action on the trains, we have
to travel down early to get to Hull. Is that okay?

It was Phoebe, with an update on her planned trip for an
interview at the university. More importantly, she'd be seeing
Noah and Lily once again. The one good thing about receiving
the text was that she still had time to prepare for their arrival.
She had no bedding for the kids, let alone beds, and if they
ended up charging Mandy Tyson and her son with murder
tomorrow, all hell was about to break loose.

She sent her reply to Phoebe and re-entered the interview
room.

'Okay, Mandy, we're trying to find Clive so he can answer
some questions directly. You could have made this much easier
on yourself if you'd just told us where he's working.'

'Are we putting this conversation on the record, detective?'
Mandy's solicitor asked.

'We don't have to,' Hollie replied. 'I'd like to know more
about your relationship with your son, Mandy—'

'On the record, please,' the solicitor requested.

Hollie started the recording again, date and time stamped it,
and introduced the people in the room.

'So, Mandy. Can you tell me a little more about Clive?'

Mandy took a long breath.

'He's a gentle man, he wouldn't hurt a fly.'

'You haven't known him that long, have you?'

'Long enough to know—'

'So would you say you know him well?'

'As well as any mother—'

'Even with a gap of – what was it – thirty-five years?'

'Of course. He's my flesh and blood.'

'What was it like when you first met your son after all those
years apart?'

Mandy looked down and she was silent for some time.

'It was difficult, what do you think?'

'How was it difficult?'

'There were a lot of emotions involved. I was – I was nervous, ashamed, excited. He was angrier than I expected—'

'Were you frightened of him?'

'No, no, not that kind of anger. He wanted to know why I'd given him up, he felt abandoned—'

'So the sort of festering anger that's difficult to let go?'

The solicitor shuffled in his chair. Hollie thought he was going to interrupt, but he let it run.

'No, detective, not that sort of anger. He just wanted answers – wouldn't you?'

'Did he get what he came for?'

'Of course he did!'

Mandy was angry now. She realised what she'd done and settled herself once again before speaking.

'There were a lot of tears, on both sides. I think he just wanted to understand why I could have let him go like that. His anger turned away from me and towards the people who'd forced me to give him up—'

'Like Sister Brennan, you mean? He was angry with Sister Brennan.'

'I don't mean like that. Of course he was angry; I'm angry, I still can't forgive them. How do you ever forgive something like that?'

Hollie considered pushing further, but they were going round in circles now.

'We're going to need to hold you in the police cells, you do understand that?'

'Yes,' Mandy said quietly.

'If we need to speak to you about Clive, or if anything you've told me now leads to anything, we'll have to set that on the record. You've opened up a can of worms for yourself confessing to Sister Brennan's murder. This isn't just going to go away now; you've set a train in motion.'

Mandy looked to the duty solicitor for approval. She got a nod and then agreed. From the little Hollie had seen of this woman, she was still seeking the approval of those in authority. She could do with channelling a bit of Gilly's attitude.

'Okay, you're free to speak to your solicitor, but otherwise I'm going to get you returned to your cell. It would help you and your son if you told us everything you know.'

'What will happen to Clive if you find him?'

Mandy's hands were shaking. She looked worn out, as if the questioning had drained her energy.

'Two officers will be over to the docks to chat with him in the next couple of minutes.'

'He's not working at the docks—'

'Come on, Mandy. You're not very good at this, are you?'

'But he'll know it was me who led you to him.'

'That can't be helped. You must see that we need to speak to him. You might want to think about how you'll deal with it when it comes up. I really hope your son is innocent, Mandy, I do. It would be the cruellest blow if he wasn't, I can see that.'

Hollie meant it. This poor woman had lost her son once, and now she was in danger of losing him again. It made her feel all the more guilty about her own children. She mustn't let them slip through her fingers. She'd fight Léon if she had to; he wasn't taking them away from her.

Hollie reached over for the folder which she'd left at the rear of the interview room. She drew out copies of the two photographs: one of the four girls, the other of the netball team.

'Do you see anybody that you recognise, Mandy?'

Mandy looked down and studied them. She became emotional when she spotted her younger self.

'Where did you get this? I haven't seen it in years.'

'Gilly made a copy. What can you tell me about that picture?'

'Just that we had a terrible night immediately after it was taken—'

'Sister Brennan?'

'No, just some mischief which Gilly got us caught up in.'

'Can you confirm the names?'

'Yes. You know Gilly, that's Violet and that's Theresa. I'll bet you know that already though, don't you?'

Mandy looked at the second image.

'That's the girl who took this photo,' she continued.

'Can you remember her name?'

Mandy considered it for a few moments then shook her head.

'I'm sorry. We used to have a nickname for her, I can't remember what it was now. It's so long ago. It was a funny nickname, but I really can't think what it was.'

'Do you know her proper name?'

'None of us did. That's why we used a nickname. I wonder where she is now.'

Hollie pushed a bit more, but it was a dead end. She took her leave, mindful of the morning meeting. Having made sure somebody was on hand to return Mandy to the custody suite at Clough Road, she then headed back into the incident room.

'Briefing in ten!' she called out. There was a scurry from desks as various members of the investigations team readied themselves with toilet visits and replenished hot drinks in the kitchen.

Hollie walked over to her desk and scanned the latest briefing notes. She was still undecided about whether to reveal details of the man with the birthmark and the fact that he'd given her a burner phone. The moment she shared the information, she'd lose him as a contact, and they'd all be hunting for him. As soon as he was in custody, he'd likely clam up. She couldn't risk that; she'd follow her gut instinct and stay quiet about him for now. He was crucial to them solving the case and she couldn't afford to screw it up by spooking him.

A decent contact was like gold dust to a detective, she'd learned that solving cases in Lancaster. But they spooked easily, often fearing exposure or, worse, retribution and violent revenge. Sometimes it was necessary to act on a hunch, and that's what she was doing now. Hollie would keep her contact a secret for the time being, but one whiff of him being up to his neck in it and she'd haul him in before he had a chance to draw breath.

Hollie's mind drifted to her conversation with Gilly the previous night. After all her defensiveness when they'd first met, Gilly had still let her go back to the house to warm up and get a change of clothes. She'd been more useful than Mandy had been in providing some details.

'Where's David Lister School?' Hollie had queried as she attempted to warm herself up on Gilly's radiator, still shivering from her close encounter with the River Hull. The girls in the black and white picture were all sitting behind an old-fashioned lettering board on which the name of the school, the team and the year were all indicated: *David Lister School – U16 Netball*.

'Ha, there's a story in there,' Gilly had laughed. 'The school doesn't exist anymore. I protested against it at the time, but you know how these things pan out. It's now been levelled and turned into a health centre and housing estate. It's nice enough, but it always feels like they're just shuffling the same pack when they bulldoze these old schools. They still have to teach the kids somewhere.'

'It's not a lot of use to us, is it?' Hollie said. 'There's no names on it, just the name of the school. We'll have to check the records, if they still exist.'

'Good luck with that!' Gilly exclaimed.

'Why?'

'Well, the school passed through two council changes in that time. Humberside County Council was formed in 1974, and then they scrapped it all again in 1996. David Lister School closed in, let me think, 2012 it must have been. At least they had computerised records by then.'

'What are you suggesting?'

'Just that this girls' school records are likely to be on paper and, if they still exist, they'll be piled up high in a box right at the back of a storage unit somewhere.'

Hollie turned the photograph over. It was an original print, though it was obviously old because the colour was nowhere near as distinct as a modern image.

'There's a sticker on the back,' she continued, squinting to read the wording. '"Stanley Maddison, photographer. Beverley",' she read. 'What do you think the chances are of him still being alive? Or even being in business, come to that.'

Gilly shrugged.

'I've never heard of him. It sounds like a small outfit. It depends on how old he was when that picture was taken. And even then, everything was paper-based in those days. I still don't fancy your chances of coming up with a name.'

FIVE

They were waiting for her to get started. Hollie looked across the sea of faces. It was the morning briefing and, unusually, she didn't know where to begin. She'd already been hijacked in the ladies' toilets by Jenni Langdon, who seemed to have a sixth sense that she'd been operating off-piste yet wouldn't come out and say it directly.

Start at the beginning, Hollie said to herself. *Just start at the beginning. Nobody knows what happened last night.*

She was wracked with doubt about whether to share what had happened with the man with the birthmark. She'd been involved in cases back in Lancaster where people like him had gone to ground, or in one case been killed, after working in confidence with the police. She'd learned to play her cards close to her chest, until she'd built up complete trust with members of her team. The relationships were still too fresh in Humberside to risk squandering this contact. She'd stick to her guns for now, but it always came with self-doubt and much soul searching.

She picked up the photograph of the girls at David Lister School and pinned it up on the board to her side, next to the photograph of the four girls that she'd copied at Gilly's house.

'These are our girls. Mandy Tyson, Gillian Hodges, Theresa Morgan and Violet Farrow. For simplicity, I'm using the surnames they used back then because that's what will appear on any documentation. These girls were at the care home at the same time as the victim. They knew Sister Brennan and, from what Gilly Hodges says, there was not much love lost between her and the girls. Sister Kay has also expressed some hostility towards her colleague's behaviour and Dr Ruane's examination of the body suggests a woman with an interesting past, what with the small tattoo and the self-harming scars. I'd like to know who – or what – the letters *KT* referred to on her arm.'

Hollie let the gathered detectives take that all in for a moment. She had their full attention.

'I believe this gives us our window of time, and speaking to Mandy Tyson has only confirmed that to me, though she hasn't given anything that's of much use yet. DS Anderson and DC Gordon are at the docks right now, following up on the one small lead that she did give us.'

Hollie filled in the details of the interview with Mandy Tyson. As she moved on to her visit to Gilly Hodges the previous night, she happened to glance at Jenni who seemed less than convinced. It was one thing having a great detective on the team, it was another thing entirely when they could smell your bullshit from across the briefing room. Jenni's crossed arms suggested to Hollie that her colleague was onto her. She moved on quickly, keen to hop to the safety of a different topic.

'Moving on, Father Duffy seems to think there might have been two people in his flat when he was attacked—'

Jenni raised her hand, and Hollie gave her the nod to speak.

'I think he's confused,' she added. 'There's a good chance he's getting mixed up with when we found him out cold on the floor. His version of events is erratic. I think we have to take what he says with a pinch of salt until he starts being more consistent with the things he tells us.'

That was a pretty robust challenge to her superior. Hollie hoped she didn't start hauling her over the coals like that over what she'd been up to last night.

'So, in short, then,' DCI Osmond interrupted her, 'we're no further forward. And you've spent a lot of time with Gilly Hodges, when the DCC specifically steered you away from that course.'

Hollie hadn't noticed him slipping into the briefing room. It was more a case of slithering into the room. She felt her cheeks colouring.

Fuck you! were the words that raced through Hollie's mind.

'Not quite, sir,' were the words that came out of her mouth. 'This photograph of the netball team was procured as a result of my second visit to Gilly Hodges, last night.'

Hollie had no intention of telling them how she'd come across it. It wasn't quite a lie. But she wasn't ready to share what had happened the previous night. She'd got lucky when the man with the birthmark dropped it; it was a vital clue and it had landed straight in her hands.

'This is the girl who took the photograph of Mandy, Violet, Theresa and Gilly,' Hollie continued, confident that she could bat away Osmond's public challenge.

'Why do we care about that?' Osmond followed up.

Fuck you, Crazy Horses went through her head. If she wasn't careful, she'd end up like DS Anderson.

'Well, sir, we have the names of all the girls who were there at the Church of St Mary and the Angels during that crucial period of 1975, when Sister Brennan was there. Even better, we've interviewed two of them and we're going to speak to the others as well. There's just this one girl to identify. I believe if we find her, the pieces will start to fall into place. Besides, why would she be the only name in a long list of girls who stayed at the home to have her name blanked out? There has to be something there.'

Osmond didn't challenge her further, so she assumed she'd satisfied him for now.

'I've also been given the name of the social worker who seemed to be attached to the place at the time. A man called Patrick McCready—'

'That prick!' came a voice.

'Do we know him?' Hollie asked.

'He's the former deputy head of social services, ma'am.'

It was a civilian officer, an older woman. Hollie wished she had a better grasp of everybody's names.

'Go on,' Hollie urged.

'He's always worked in the area. He's been a social worker all his life, too. I think it's fair to say he's not well liked. He always had an eye on the top job but had to retire before he got there. That's all I know.'

'Thank you.'

Hollie ran this through her mind. If McCready was still in the city, he should be easy enough to reach.

'McCready's name has cropped up as many times as an unwelcome ex on Facebook,' DS Patel added.

'Yes, we need to haul him in,' Hollie added. 'Oh, one more thing. There's a sticker on the back of this photograph. It says, *Stanley Maddison, photographer. Beverley.* Is he still in business, does anybody know?'

'Yes, he's old as hell these days, and he doesn't have his shop anymore—'

'DC Philpot, isn't it?' Hollie checked, daring to venture a guess at an unfamiliar name.

'Yes, ma'am. He posts pictures of Beverley in days gone by on the *Beverley Never Forgotten* Facebook page. I follow it. Shall I chase it up?'

'Yes, please. I'd like us to speak to him. I want to know if he can help us identify the girls in this picture. One more thing—'

The assembled officers settled back in their chairs, seemingly receptive to this latest update from their superior.

'I'm expecting an update from DS Anderson and DC Gordon at any time now. Clive Bartram is Mandy Tyson's son, but he still uses his adoptive name. Bartram has past form. I want a full background check on him, please, ASAP, so we have what we need when we question him. If I were a betting woman, I'd say Bartram is our strongest lead at the moment. I want to know if he has any form for violence, too.'

She let that sit for a moment. Bearing in mind she'd withheld details of her encounter with the man with the birthmark, she reckoned the case was starting to take a more positive turn. Some cases took months to piece together, but if Clive Bartram turned out to be their man, it was possible they could move quickly to getting some swift justice for Sister Brennan. With an early arrest, even though it would be a personal blow to Mandy Tyson, it was possible she'd be back to more reasonable hours by the time the kids arrived. For the first time in a couple of days, she was beginning to think they might crack open the case with no further casualties.

Hollie noticed Amber had her hand semi-raised, waiting for her attention.

'Yes, DS Patel.'

'DS Anderson's just been in touch, ma'am. They got to the docks and Bartram was supposed to be working there this morning.'

'Yes, I think we were half-expecting that already—'

'It's not that, ma'am. Anderson said he's done a runner. They chased after him, but they lost him. Bartram got away, ma'am.'

SIX

1974: GILLY'S STORY

Gilly was in danger of falling asleep. She'd done it once before and invoked the wrath of her very religious parents. But Father Duffy's sermons were as dull as ditch water, and she would much rather have been at home listening to Radio 1 in her bedroom. Tony Blackburn knew how to give a Catholic priest a run for his money.

Whenever she became distracted, Gilly would cast her eyes around the church, reminding herself of the fourteen Stations of the Cross, and taking a look at the old, musty paintings that hung around the walls portraying those scenes. It kept her mind active, at least. Only today, it was Eric who was on her mind, despite her battle to remain transfixed on more spiritual matters. Much as she wanted to preoccupy her mind with replays of their passionate encounters, she was unable to shake a feeling of unease. What had Eric been up to that night? And why was that woman in his car?

Her stomach pains hadn't gone away. And she'd not had a period for some time.

She'd sneaked off and booked an appointment with the doctor. Hopefully, it would just be something temporary that a prescription might shift. However, she was getting a nasty feeling that her extracurricular activities in the projection room might have landed her in some trouble.

It was time for Communion. Her backside was sore from the inhospitable pews. She'd never known why churches had to be so uncomfortable. The Catholic Church should take a leaf out of Cecil Cinema's book and provide nice, comfy seats. The *Herbie Rides Again* audiences weren't complaining, that's for sure.

Gilly filed out behind her parents and took Communion. She knew a battle was coming over this. She'd left school now, and she had no plans to return after the summer. And these Sunday church visits felt more and more like her parents' life; this was not what she wanted for herself. It all seemed too grim and self-denying to Gilly. She wanted a life of fun, freedom and frolics, a life preferably with Eric. But who was that she'd seen him with in the cinema car park?

As she accepted the body of Christ, Gilly thought back to their last passionate encounter. There was no doubt in her mind that Eric fancied her. She assumed they were an item.

Gilly went through the motions of concluding the Mass, then headed directly for her friend, Helen, once they'd all been dismissed by Father Duffy. This was the best bit of church for her. She and Helen would tuck themselves away in a corner of the church and gossip while the adults crept up to Father Duffy and exchanged notes about how well their kids were doing in life. She knew she was a disappointment on that score but, as she'd found out since she'd taken up with Eric, she couldn't care less.

'So, tell me about this lad at your work,' Helen began. 'Is it serious?'

'Yes. We're all over each other.'

'You'll have to go to confession. I'm sure Father Duffy will want to know all about it.'

'I'll bet he will, the dirty bugger!' Gilly laughed.

'Really, is it like that?' Helen asked.

'Maybe,' Gilly teased.

A serious look came over Helen's face.

'You are using something, aren't you?'

'What do you mean?'

'Contraception. Rubber johnnies.'

'Oh, we hate those things. We did use them, but Eric says it's not as good for him that way. He says it's like sticking his thingy into a wellington boot.'

Sometimes their conversations at the back of the church made even her blush.

'Still, you should use them,' Helen chided. 'You don't want to get yourself into trouble.'

'Eric says it'll be all right. He reckons he does something at the end that makes it safer. Anyhow, we've been okay so far.'

Even as she said the words, her stomach twinged.

'I need a favour.'

She changed the subject. She didn't want to talk about it anymore.

Her friend looked at her expectantly.

'Can I say I'm staying over at your place again?'

'I told you, if our parents find out, we'll never be able to see each other again.'

'Yes, but you have that flat roof outside your bedroom. There's no way I can sneak out of my house as easily.'

'Are you seeing Eric Gittens?'

'What do you think?'

Helen gave her a playful shove.

'Who am I to stand in the way of true love?' She laughed. 'I take it you still haven't told your parents?'

'That'll be the day. I know his family, though. I've been around for tea, that day my mum and dad drove over to Leeds to do some shopping. I like his family much more than mine. We seem so dull, compared to them.'

'What haven't you told your parents?'

It was Gilly's mother. She'd caught that bit of the conversation. The two girls looked at each other. Gilly felt her face flushing.

'We were just talking about my work—' Gilly began.

'It was just something silly about someone we knew at school—' Helen spoke at the same time.

They shrugged it off and covered their tracks, making up a ridiculous story about someone they knew at school who also worked at the Cecil Cinema. Gilly's mum seemed to buy it.

The church was clearing now, and the girls' parents were making movements to leave. The two great things about Sundays were Sunday lunch and the Top 20 night on the radio. It had been a dreary start to the day, but things generally got much better as they moved into the afternoon.

'Five minutes, girls, then we're heading home.'

Gilly's mother left them to it again. As soon as she was out of earshot, they burst out laughing.

'That was close!' Gilly gasped.

Even Father Duffy had got fed up with his own Mass; he was heading off to the back of the church now, to wherever it was he went to prepare for services. The two girls hurriedly made their plans for the overnight stay, and Gilly promised to phone Helen as soon as she'd agreed on a date with Eric.

Gilly and her family walked home in relative silence, other than the occasional observation about the content of that day's service. To Gilly, it was dry and superficial, but she let them get on with it. They weren't so far from the church when her father stopped dead on the pavement.

'Darn it, I forgot to give Father Duffy our donation for the restoration works. Gilly, run back and give him this cheque, will you?'

Gilly's father held out a small, brown envelope which she assumed contained the cheque.

'Of course,' she said, snatching it from his hand, delighted to conclude the torture of this family activity for the day.

She trotted back to the church, planning her next night out with Eric. Seeing him with that girl had given her a bit of a scare. If she didn't make herself more available, he might lose interest. She was sure there'd be a reasonable explanation, but she knew she'd have to behave more like a regular girlfriend if she was going to hang on to him.

The church was empty when she got there; it was almost hard to imagine it had been so full of activity only fifteen minutes previously.

'Hello!' she called out. It didn't feel right to shout in church. She could hear some voices in the office area at the back, but there didn't appear to be anybody around in the main part of the building.

She walked through the centre of the pews and headed over to the mystery door through which Father Duffy disappeared at the end of services. She placed her hand on the doorknob, uncertain whether to enter.

For a moment she considered leaving the envelope in the collection box at the entrance to the building, but her father would check with her, she knew that much. He'd want to know it had been delivered directly to Father Duffy.

Something wasn't quite right. She could hear voices. They didn't seem to be talking how people usually talked in church. There was a woman's voice.

'Hello,' she called out, but the voices were so caught up in whatever was going on, they didn't respond to her.

She pushed through the door, walking into a small, dark corridor. There were two doors there: a cupboard and what appeared to be Father Duffy's office. She tapped on the solid wooden door. The voices stopped; she heard whispers.

'It's just me, Father Duffy. Gilly Hodges. I've got a cheque for you.'

She pushed open the door. Father Duffy was standing there, trouser-less, his face red and his black shoes abandoned under his desk. She didn't see the source of the female voice at first until a slight movement caught her eye behind the desk. Somebody was crouching down behind it, still and quiet, no doubt praying the hardest they had for a long time that she hadn't spotted them.

SEVEN

The words *for fuck's sake* almost made their way from Hollie's lips, but she opted for the more professional option instead.

'That's a nuisance. Do we need some support down there or are they onto him?'

'He vanished into thin air, ma'am.'

DC Patel had on her don't-shoot-the-messenger face.

'See if Mandy Tyson is still in the building, or if they've taken her back to the Clough Road cells,' she had instructed DC Langdon, who bolted like her life depended on it.

And now, in Anderson's absence, Jenni was sitting at her side, conducting the second interview with Mandy that day.

'Tell me more about Clive, Mandy. Why do you think he ran like that?'

Hollie couldn't believe her luck. She'd thought Mandy would have been on her way back to the Clough Road cells, but she was still sitting with her solicitor, working through administrative matters, after the briefing was interrupted by the news of Clive Bartram's getaway.

'I really don't know,' Mandy replied. 'He probably panicked, thinking it was a stitch up.'

'Has Clive been stitched up before, Mandy? You make it sound like we're on his case all the time.'

She shook her head.

'No, it's not like that. If you've had the kind of life Clive's had, you grow distrustful, that's all.'

'Why's that?' Jenni encouraged her.

'Clive was kicked out of his adopted home when he was still a teenager. Can you imagine how that makes you feel? You're torn away from a mother who loves you when you're a baby and then at sixteen, rejected by the people who promised they'd care for you. I'd say Clive has every reason to be distrustful, wouldn't you?'

Hollie didn't disagree with her, but this wasn't a counselling session.

'Save me some time, Mandy. Why has Clive been in and out of prison?'

Mandy looked at her solicitor.

'No comment.'

'We're not going to find that he's violent, are we, Mandy?'

'No, he's not. My Clive is not a violent man—'

'Yet, you seem to be hiding something from us,' Hollie continued.

Mandy looked at her solicitor who whispered something in her ear.

'Look, he was in and out of prison on short sentences. I'm sure you know the story well enough. He'd lose a job and need to buy drugs, so he'd steal. When he got caught enough times, they'd lock him up for a couple of months. That would make it even harder to get a job again. If they'd never taken him away from me in the first place, I could have cared for him properly. Imagine taking somebody else's child, then throwing him out of the house at sixteen years of age because you can't handle him anymore. Who would do that?'

'What kind of relationship do you have with your son now, Mandy?'

'No comment.'

'It must be difficult, what with Clive being in trouble with the law and you, who must feel so guilty about what happened to him.'

Hollie knew it was below the belt. Jenni shuffled in her seat. Sometimes it was necessary to push a bit harder to get what you wanted.

Mandy began to sob. Hollie took no pleasure from it, but this woman was not making it easy on herself.

'Did I hit a nerve, Mandy?'

'Detective!' the solicitor warned.

'I threw Clive out of my house—' she cried.

'Why?' Jenni asked.

'Because we argued—'

'What, about how you colluded to kill Sister Brennan? Was your joint enterprise tearing you apart, Mandy?'

'Detective!'

Her solicitor was beginning to sound like a broken record.

'You didn't kill Sister Brennan, did you?'

Mandy shook her head, the tears flowing freely now.

'No comment,' she sniffed, wiping her eyes.

'I'm sure you wanted to, once upon a time. I'm certain you have every reason to hate her. But I don't think you killed her, did you, Mandy?'

'No comment.'

'What were you hoping to achieve from this, Mandy?'

'Okay, I didn't kill Sister Brennan!' Mandy shouted. 'All right, officer? I didn't bloody kill her!'

It was completely silent in the interview room. Even the solicitor seemed shocked by the strength of her outburst.

'So, just for the record, Mandy, you're now denying that you killed Sister Brennan, even though you handed yourself in claiming to be the killer?'

Mandy was sobbing now. Hollie had observed that there was usually a point in an interview where it was clear to all parties that the game was up. Mandy had just reached that point.

'I didn't kill that bitch of a woman, of course I didn't—' she sobbed. 'But neither did Clive, there's no way Clive had anything to do with it.'

'Why did he run then, Mandy?'

'I told you, because he was scared. He's just scared of the police, that's all.'

'I'd like a moment alone, to speak to my client,' the solicitor said.

'Of course.'

Hollie timestamped and switched off the tape, and she and Jenni exited the interview room.

'Jeez, I've seen less dramatic episodes of *Eastenders*,' Jenni whispered. 'You were really going for her there, boss.'

'She held out well, but Mandy Tyson is no tough nut. She's just a mother trying to protect her son. She's been covering for him all along.'

The duty solicitor popped his head around the door.

'My client has something she wants to say to you,' the duty solicitor began. 'Off the record, please.'

Hollie and Jenni re-entered the interview room. Hollie liked off the record. It was often where the juiciest morsels came from.

Mandy's eyes were red. It seemed to Hollie like she'd been holding back a lot of anxiety over Clive. The interview had been more of a confessional than an interrogation, and she looked all the better for it.

'I know it's not easy believing your son might be a killer,'

Hollie started. 'Especially when you lost all those years while you weren't in contact. I don't envy you.'

'Are you going to charge me?'

'No, Mandy, not yet. But we're not going to let you walk out of here just yet. I'm sorry about your son. I understand how conflicted you must be. But you've done the right thing by speaking to us. And if he turns out to be innocent, it will be a weight off your mind.'

'I hadn't realised I was so raw still, officer. It still hurts. I feel anger, rage, failure, and frustration. How do you make up for all those lost years? I wish I'd had the guts to stand up to my parents when I was younger. They sold me down the river. Who would do that to their own daughter?'

'It's a complicated matter, I know.'

Hollie knew that however much she became involved with their stories, she had to stay impartial. For all she knew, she might be standing in court condemning either of the women to life in prison in future months; she couldn't get too caught up in the rights and wrongs of what had happened to these women.

'What is it you wanted to say to me?' Hollie asked.

Mandy turned to the duty solicitor, who gave her a small nod.

'Clive did not kill Sister Brennan. My son wouldn't do that, I know he wouldn't. Whatever's gone on, I do think her death is connected with our time at the girls' home.'

'Why do you say that?' Hollie enquired.

'Something was going on there. I was too young and naive to know what it was. But the social worker who used to come around, he was part of it. They used to call him the moral welfare officer, but he was a social worker, that was his job.'

'What's his name?' Hollie picked up a pen and pulled out her notebook.

'He was called Patrick McCready—'

'You're certain?' Hollie checked.

'Definitely.'

'Is he still around?'

Mandy nodded.

'Yes, I'm sure I've spotted his arrogant face in the paper. He must be retired now, though. I'm not connected with him in any way. He was a young man back then, not that much older than we were, now I think back to it. But it was Patrick McCready who sorted the adoption papers with our parents. By the time we were brought in, it was a done deal. I didn't even realise what I was doing, until they took Clive away from me.'

'Why do you think Sister Brennan's murder relates to your time at the girls' home?' Hollie asked.

'There was a strange atmosphere, but I can't put my finger on it. It wasn't just Sister Brennan. It felt so desolate and barren there, like it didn't have a soul. Imagine that in a church home. Have you spoken to Gilly, Theresa or Violet yet? They'll tell you what it was like.'

Hollie made a mental note to send a team member over to chat with Theresa. It was going to be a busy day at this rate. Mandy continued, in the flow now, her tears having subsided.

'Gilly saw something once, but she was too terrified to tell us. And Theresa had a bad run-in with Patrick McCready. We were friends back then, but we were still only girls. We were scared of authority. We didn't question or challenge things. I know it sounds weak, officer, but we were only young, and times were so different in the seventies. I think something bad was going on. It was like there were unspoken secrets in that place.'

EIGHT

'Do you have any idea where Clive might hide?'

Hollie figured now Mandy was feeling more talkative, they might get some useful information out of her before they sent her back to her cell. She still wasn't sure if she was going to charge Mandy with wasting police time or obstructing the investigation; she'd wait to see what happened with Clive Bartram first. They could hold her until the end of the day, but she'd kick the can down the road if it was expedient to get an extension beyond twenty-four hours.

'I asked him to return his house key,' Mandy replied sheepishly. 'I had to be sure. After he stole that money. So he won't be at my place.'

'That must have been hard,' Jenni suggested. At least she wasn't asking questions about Hollie's change of footwear anymore.

'Yes, it was. He's been in and out of a place just off Beverley Road, where they help people like Clive to get back on their feet. You might give that a try.'

Jenni took down the address details, as she figured it out by navigating on her mobile phone and confirming that she'd got the right place with Mandy.

'Okay, we've got everything we need here for now. I could be sending you back to the cells, Mandy, but I'm going to release you on police bail. If you hear from Clive, it's in both of your best interests to tell us immediately. Do you understand?'

Her solicitor looked pleased that it was all over.

'I'll be in touch if we need to speak to you again.'

Hollie ended the recording and left Mandy with her solicitor. DC Langdon checked a PC was available to get her properly discharged, then the two of them returned to the investigation room.

DS Patel updated them with the latest on Clive Bartram.

'DS Anderson said they're scouring the docks for him. Bartram has ID, so he can get in and out, but docks security has been notified.'

'Any thoughts?' Hollie asked as DCI Osmond and DCC Warburton joined them at DS Patel's desk.

'We know he's got a drugs history,' Osmond chimed in. 'It may be worth checking the usual dealing haunts. Perhaps uniform can help with that.'

'Yes,' Hollie replied, a little more enthusiastically than she felt. 'He's likely to seek a fix when the pressure is on.'

She felt a phone vibrate in her pocket. At first, she assumed it was her own phone. Then she remembered; she had the burner phone from last night in her other pocket. It took a force of will to resist glancing at it.

'Are you still pursuing this Gilly Hodges woman?' Warburton snapped at Hollie.

'Yes, ma'am. She's been the best source of leads so far.'

'Focus more on this chap who was adopted. Mandy Tyson's son, Bartram?'

'Yes, ma'am.'

'Put your resources there. That's more likely to yield results.'

'Of course, ma'am.'

DCC Warburton departed as swiftly as she'd arrived.

The burner phone vibrated again. It was nagging her from her pocket. She wished Osmond would finish so she could take a look. But she couldn't risk the questions that would inevitably follow; she wanted to keep her source a secret for now.

Hollie looked about her to see if anybody could hear it; it appeared not. She covered it with her hand in case it went off again.

'We need some resolution with this,' Osmond remarked as soon as Warburton had exited. 'Have you seen the letters page in the *Hull Daily Mail*?'

'No, sir.'

Hollie tended to be more preoccupied with chasing criminals than reading letters about wheelie bins and unsafe play parks.

'We're taking a lot of heat over this. People wonder what they're paying their taxes for if the police can't even protect an innocent nun. They're moaning about how social media outlets were allowed to show such terrible photos of the crime scene. Of course, they don't care about budget cuts and policing priorities. But the Police and Crime Commissioner is breathing down our necks, too. When the Chief gets heat, we all get heat.'

'Understood, sir. I do agree with the DCC that Mandy Tyson's son looks like he might be a strong lead. There's every chance he could be our man.'

Osmond looked around the room. Hollie braced herself. He was making sure they were alone so he could say something in private to her.

'There has been some discussion about taking you off this case—'

'Oh?' was all Hollie could say. That would be a huge kick in the teeth.

'Your lack of familiarity with the area is a problem and turning up late for the press briefing was bad form. The complaint from Shane Hardy is adding insult to injury—'

Hollie didn't like the direction this was heading.

'—but the DCC seems intent that you're the woman for the job. I won't pretend I consider DS Anderson better equipped to deal with this investigation, but at least he's part of the team. Use his local expertise and make the most of it. And if DCC Warburton gives you a steer, listen to what she says. At the moment, she's about the only person who's in your corner.'

Osmond walked off, seemingly unconcerned with how his comments had landed. He could have fooled her. Rose Warburton didn't feel like much of an ally. Why would she stick her neck out over an unknown quantity at Humberside Police?

The burner phone vibrated for a third time. She checked around her to see who was close by, then ducked into a small side office and closed the door behind her. She pulled over one of the plastic chairs and took out the phone, checking once again that she hadn't caught anybody's attention. She'd received one text. She opened it up.

Be careful. I think you're being watched.

It was the man with the birthmark. At last, she had direct access to him.

She felt an overwhelming sensation of nausea. How did he know she was being watched? Why was she being watched?

Hollie located his number in the message data and pressed *Dial*. It rang until the phone system got fed up and ended the call. There was no voicemail. It was most likely another unregistered device.

Hollie walked across the room to an internal phone that was sitting on a table at one side of the briefing room. She dialled the extension of the tech team. Someone picked up promptly at the other end.

'It's DI Turner—'

'Oh, hello, Lance Fairclough here, I'll bet you're up to your ears, aren't you?'

That wasn't quite the formal approach Hollie had been expecting, but she didn't make anything of it.

'You might say that. Look, a hypothetical question for you. What are the chances of tracking an unregistered mobile phone via a mast?'

'Do we know roughly where we're talking about?'

'Hull city centre.'

'Don't hold your breath. If we had a registered phone, we could track the towers it was connecting to. We'd normally do that if some crook reckoned he was in one place, and we needed to prove he was in another. But without knowing who the owner is, it's too much of a stretch.'

'If I give you the number, would you see what you can do?'

'Sure. For your eyes only? Not to sound all James Bond about it, but you get my drift.'

The guy in the tech department sounded like fun. He might just as well have been Q from the Bond films, for all Hollie understood their technical black magic. But she knew from her time in Lancaster, if the tech guys couldn't track the phone, nobody could. She passed on the details, then tried sending a text.

Need to speak to you. Can we meet?

The message was delivered okay, but there was no immediate reply. She'd wait. At least there was some communication between them now, however unreliable.

As Hollie worked her way around the team, checking who was deployed to which task, listening to theories, hunches and gossip, and making notes in the log, the investigation felt suddenly vast and overwhelming. They were still working through the long list of names from the home for girls, and Hollie knew that most of those leads would be dead ends unless linked to the period around 1975. She walked over to DS Patel's desk.

'I want to talk to this social worker. What's his name? McCready. Will you get hold of him for me?'

'Yes, ma'am. We've been working on it, but he's proving elusive. We got his home address from his former employers, but there's nobody at home. It's like he's on holiday or something – there are no signs of life at his house.'

'Okay, keep plugging away, please. And please keep me posted on DS Anderson's progress. Any time, any place, I want to know the moment we get our hands on Clive Bartram.'

DS Patel nodded and added a note to a long list of tasks to be tackled.

'Oh, and—'

Hollie stopped.

'I'm sorry, DS Patel. I feel like I'm loading you up here. And I didn't mean to sound so sharp with you when you relayed Anderson's update during the briefing.'

'It's fine, ma'am, honestly. We're all under pressure. You can't stop to mop everybody's brow every time you hand out a new job. That's what I'm here for.'

Hollie almost expected a *you do you* at the end of the sentence, but it didn't come.

'Good, thank you, DS Patel. I appreciate what you're doing here.'

'What was that last thing?' Patel asked.

'Keep an ear to the ground with Father Duffy. They'll be wanting his hospital bed soon. I want an officer stationed outside his flat when he's discharged, if that's where he goes. If he goes elsewhere to recuperate, I want to know where. He's still vulnerable while our killer is out there. I do not want him left unattended. That's if we can spare the resources.'

Hollie ran through everything in her head and reckoned that was everything sorted for a while. She walked over to the empty briefing room and studied the pictures she'd left pinned up on the board.

The DCC insisted on warning her off Gilly. If it wasn't for Gilly, she wouldn't have the picture of the four girls, neither would she know the significance of the photo taken at David Lister School. The man with the birthmark seemed to think the key lay with the girls. That's what Hollie thought, too, despite Clive Bartram doing a runner and making himself look as guilty as sin.

She keyed a number into her phone and dialled. It was answered after three rings.

'DI Turner?'

'Gilly, yes, it's me. I need your help.'

'Sure, I've given up trying to get rid of you. You're like a bad smell. Speaking of which, I still have your clothes here and a couple of letters and leaflets on the radiator.'

'Great, thanks, can I ask a favour? I want to take a look at the home where you and the girls stayed. I know it's all boarded up. Can you find out who on the council has got the key and get us inside?'

NINE

1974: GILLY'S STORY

'She's just a friend of the family. What did you expect me to do? Leave her on her own in the city centre at night?'

What Eric was saying seemed perfectly reasonable, so why couldn't Gilly shift the feeling that he was telling her lies?

'Look, you're here for the night. Let's not spoil things by having an argument. I promise it was nothing. I was just giving her a lift home.'

He was right. Gilly and Eric were sitting on the drive in his Ford Escort. Her parents thought she was at Helen's house for the night, having gone there immediately after the afternoon shift. They had a whole evening in front of them. Besides, she liked Eric's family and didn't want there to be an atmosphere when they went inside the house.

Eric leant over and kissed Gilly on the lips.

'I'd never hurt you. I promise.'

'Let's go inside. You said tea would be ready at six.'

Gilly loved the boisterousness of Eric's home. His mum and dad joked with each other, and his younger sister loved her big brother and couldn't stop chatting with him. As for the family dog, she was bonkers, but lovely.

Sally, the dog, rushed over to get fussed by both Gilly and Eric. A song by the Mamas and the Papas was playing on the stereo. Gilly might have been tempted to write Eric's parents off as hippies once upon a time, but she'd long since warmed to their carefree attitude. They were completely casual about her staying overnight, and if that's how hippies behaved, it was fine by her.

'Hello, love,' shouted Eric's mum, Sue, from the kitchen.

'Hi, Mrs Gittens. Hi, Mr Gittens!' Gilly called out. They were in the middle of dishing up the food together. In Gilly's house, it was her mother who took care of the catering and her father who appeared from elsewhere in the house to eat it. Mealtimes were not such a fun affair in the Hodges household.

'I've told you before, call us Sue and Ken. We're not all airs and graces in this house, you know.'

'Is that Charlton Heston film still on at your cinema?' Ken asked.

The rapid thudding of feet hastily making their way down the staircase cut off Eric's chance to answer. His sister, Annie, ten years his junior, launched at him as she burst into the living room, wrapping her arms around her big brother, delighted to see him.

'Hiya, Annie.' Gilly smiled. Eric wouldn't cheat on her. He was too good with his little sister to do that, Gilly told herself convincingly.

With Annie now part of the melee and Sally out of her mind with the excitement of it all, the evening meal descended into a cacophony of conversation and laughter.

'So, when will we get to meet your mum and dad?' Sue asked. 'We don't want to have to wait until the big day.'

They'd been teasing her and Eric about marriage ever since she first walked through the door with him. Their families were like chalk and cheese. It was better if a meeting was delayed as long as possible.

'Come on, Mum, it's a bit early for that,' Eric replied.

'Can I be a bridesmaid?' Annie asked.

For a moment, Gilly allowed herself to picture the scene. She could only do it without her parents there. Their presence would have felt like adding the Grim Reaper to the guest list.

'My parents are always very busy,' Gilly lied. 'They'd love to meet you. It's just finding a suitable time.'

Kindly, Ken and Sue didn't push the issue.

'So, where are you going tonight?' Sue asked.

'The cinema,' Eric replied. 'I want to watch the film properly and not through a tiny window for a change.'

'That's a bit of a busman's holiday, isn't it?' Ken teased.

'No, we're going to the ABC, not the Cecil. They'll have me threading up the films if I go there.'

Gilly knew they had no intention of going to the cinema. They'd be heading directly for the usual place, a secluded spot by the River Humber, at Hessle. Eric would blast the car heater, and they'd spend the evening making out. The big movie would have to wait.

The remainder of the evening meal passed in a blur of mayhem, but it was fun, and Gilly loved it. She could picture herself joining this family, even though any talk of marriage seemed way too soon. They'd been seeing each other for nine months. She couldn't contemplate engagements or marriage before she'd even plucked up the courage to tell her parents.

The evening with Eric was spent pretty well as she'd expected. It was cold outside, but that didn't deter them. They headed for Hessle foreshore, the crackly sound of Radio Luxembourg providing the backdrop to a night of passion and playfulness.

As Gilly adjusted her clothing in the back seat, she pulled a pair of tights from under the front seat. She held them up to take a proper look.

'These aren't my tights,' she said, the thoughts in her head coming straight out of her mouth.

'Aren't they?' Eric replied, immediately flustered. 'Oh, I remember. My fan belt is slipping. I asked my mum for a pair of hers in case I needed to fix it.'

'With tights?'

'Yeah, ask your dad. You can bodge up a repair with tights. People do it all the time. What colour are they?'

'Black. They're fishnet.'

'Oh yeah, it's come back to me now. My mum bought them by accident and gave them to me. She told me to keep them in my car in case I needed them. She wouldn't let me use a good pair on the car.'

Gilly had that uneasy feeling in the pit of her stomach again, but she let it go. It seemed a reasonable enough explanation, even though she knew nothing about cars. She finished dressing and they went back to Eric's house.

'How was the film?' Ken asked when they walked into the lounge. Eric's parents were watching the nine o'clock news before bedtime. Richard Baker always looked so serious to Gilly; she didn't know why adults insisted on ruining the end of the day with all that doom and gloom.

'There's a play on afterwards,' Sue said. 'Do you want to stay down and watch it with us?'

'If you don't mind, I'm going up to bed early,' Gilly replied. 'I have to be away early tomorrow. I've got something on.'

Eric seemed put out, but he accompanied her up to his bedroom.

'Are you all right?' he asked. 'It's still a bit early for me to go to bed. I'll stay downstairs a bit and talk to the wrinklies.'

She was pleased he was leaving her. Her stomach was playing up again. Something weird had been going on for a couple of months. She'd put a bit of weight on, too, not that anybody else had noticed. But Gilly saw it when she looked in the mirror. She had a doctor's appointment booked for tomorrow. Staying at Eric's, she could lose the hour or so that it would take her to get to the surgery. Her parents weren't expecting her home until later, and she'd get Eric to drop her off in town. She'd tell him she was shopping for a new bra; he'd be happy enough to leave her to her own devices with that.

When Eric came up to bed, Gilly pretended to be asleep. He wrapped his arm around her, moving in close, but she was having none of it. She remained resolutely still, and he gave up after a few minutes, seemingly resigning himself to a quiet night squeezed tightly into his single bed.

Gilly was distracted at breakfast and keen to get to the surgery. As expected, Eric was deterred by the prospect of a morning traipsing around Hammonds for a new work bra, so he dropped her off at the end of Beverley Road, where he was able to pull up the car easily.

Gilly gave him a tense kiss, then waited until he'd driven well up the road before turning in the direction of the surgery. She'd imagined all sorts of things that might be responsible for the strange sensations she'd been experiencing in her stomach, but she was most scared about the prospect of cancer. She had an aunt who'd died of ovarian cancer, and it was now the thing the women in her family feared most.

The doctor worked through his checks, quietly and methodically.

'This is the first time I've seen you without your mother, isn't it?' he said as he guided her over to the weighing scales.

'Yes,' she replied. 'Now I'm sixteen I thought I'd come on my own.'

The doctor took her blood pressure. She'd never had that done before. She thought it only happened to old people.

'Have you noticed any changes in your body, Gilly?'

'I haven't been getting my period—' she began.

He nodded, like he already had a good idea what he was looking for.

'You said when you came in that your family has some history of ovarian cancer. From a cursory check, there's nothing that would suggest that to me so far, and the symptoms you're describing to me are making me think it's probably something else.'

Gilly exhaled. She hadn't realised how worked up she'd been about that prospect. It was a huge relief to have that burden removed from her.

'Are you in a sexual relationship, Gilly?'

She felt her cheeks flush. She'd only ever discussed colds, measles and chicken pox with the doctor before. This was an unfamiliar world to her, and it made her uneasy.

'No,' she replied. She saw the doctor's expression change. 'Yes. Yes, I am.'

'Have you been using contraception?'

She looked at him blankly.

'Condoms. Spermicidal cream. Anything like that?'

'No, doctor. Why?'

'Well, Gilly, I've got some news which I suspect is going to come as a bit of a surprise to you. You're seven, maybe as late as eight months pregnant. You're barely showing at all, but that's because of your age and how slim you are. But I'm absolutely sure of it. You're going to be having a baby within the next couple of months.'

TEN

'I haven't a clue how you pulled this off so quickly, but I'm very grateful.'

Hollie surveyed the old building. It was nice to be viewing it in daylight. It would have been grand in its day, but now it was weather-beaten and dilapidated. Even the church at its side was for sale.

She didn't confess to Gilly that she'd already visited the building. She'd thought having time to get used to it would help, but even with Gilly accompanying her, Hollie couldn't shake the feeling that this might have been her. She was nineteen when she'd had Isabella, and completely out of her depth when she found out she was pregnant. At first, she'd panicked, then wondered how she'd cope on her own. Then she'd thought about her parents, and how they'd always been there for her. They would be shocked and surprised at first, possibly even annoyed, but they'd stick by her, she knew that even back then. She'd have been even less prepared at fifteen or sixteen, which was the sort of age many of the girls had been when they entered this place.

'The council bought this building from the church when

the girls' home was finally closed, and the church decided they had no further use for it. I think it was supposed to be converted to a young offender's unit or something like that. It turns out the locals were happy to have a building full of immoral girls on their doorsteps, but a bunch of bad lads was a step too far. Maybe they thought the nuns helped to equal it all out. Anyhow, the buildings team said I could look around, as it's the local police and all.'

That sounded about right to Hollie. The not-in-my-back-yard brigade usually found something to fuss about. The council were a bit optimistic if they'd thought they would get away with young offenders in a residential area.

'But how did you get the keys?' Hollie asked again.

'I called in a favour from another council member,' Gilly continued. 'So long as we wear hard hats and keep away from the areas marked as dangerous, we can take a look around. Please don't fall through any floorboards, I don't want any insurance claims.'

Humberside Police wouldn't thank her for any injuries either. She'd decided to come alone. Hollie wanted to get a sense of the girls' home; the other officers already had the advantage of knowing more about the local area than she did. She took out her phone and took several shots from the outside.

'My son's picking me up after. Is that okay?' Gilly checked.

'Of course, I'd love to meet him.'

Hollie wondered if they ought to have questioned him already. They had no reason to suspect him of anything, and his name hadn't come up so far. Still, it didn't stop her from wondering if she'd missed a trick. Gilly's story seemed to have ended happily enough. It was Mandy's son who seemed more likely to be involved in Sister Brennan's death.

'I told him to park outside. We'll meet him when we finish.'

Hollie began to move towards the old building. The inter-locking fencing panels formed a strong barrier, with health and safety signs posted at regular intervals. The lower windows were boarded up, and the glass in the upper windows was smashed, clearly as a result of target practice by the local kids. The building boasted a couple of balconies and heavy pillars at the front door. Even ignoring its current appearance, Hollie thought it a remote and isolated place to be exiled during pregnancy.

'See that balcony on the left?' Gilly pointed.

'Yes.'

'I remember the night Mandy nearly jumped off that balcony. She went crazy. She realised they were taking her baby, and she made a run for it. I swear she sobbed for twenty-four hours straight after they took him. It was horrible.'

Hollie thought about the quiet woman she'd questioned only hours before. She couldn't imagine Mandy Tyson screaming and shouting. She wondered what it must be like for the women still deeply affected by events almost five decades previously. Would she have done what Mandy did if they'd threatened to take Isabella from her? She'd have scratched out their eyes before she let them take her baby.

'So, we have to slip through the fences, apparently,' Gilly continued. 'This is the undignified bit. The guy in the buildings department explained what to do.'

Gilly set about unfastening brackets on the wire fencing panel. After some time, she succeeded in releasing it.

'We've got to squeeze through.' Gilly motioned. 'You go first. Cops are better at this sort of thing, aren't you?'

'You've been watching too many TV shows.' Hollie smiled. She cursed her shoes. An expedition like this was much better executed in a pair of flats.

Hollie squeezed through the gap, retaining as much dignity as possible, considering how narrow it was. Gilly followed, displaying the same lack of physical prowess. She pushed the wire panel back into position without refastening it.

'We don't want anybody following us in, do we?' Gilly warned.

Hollie thought back to the light she thought she'd seen in the building yesterday; surely nobody could have broken through this fencing without knowing how to manoeuvre the panels?

On any other day, she would have laughed it off. It was a weekday, the kids were in school, and they had the place to themselves. Only, the text message she'd received saying someone was following her had unnerved her. Hollie had checked her rear-view mirror on the journey over and was convinced she wasn't being followed. So why had the man with the birthmark told her she was?

The two women made their way along the gravel drive, which was now strewn with weeds and rough grass. Hollie tried to picture the building as it had been in the seventies. It was really quite something. No wonder the church or the council could no longer afford to maintain it. The grounds were so picturesque even with overgrown shrubs and mature trees; she was surprised nobody had bought the land to erect a housing estate.

'You're wondering why it hasn't sold, aren't you?' Gilly remarked.

'Yes. It's a lovely space.'

'It's caught up in a legal wrangle with the church. Something to do with a cock-up over the deeds and some ancient rules about church land. I don't know the details of it, but the council can't sell it off until it's settled. And I think the church wants its pound of flesh. It's a stalemate.'

By instinct, Hollie headed for the front door which had been replaced by long lengths of chipboard, onto which a hefty bolt had been screwed. There were several health and safety notices, most of which were damaged. Somebody had sprayed the words *Fuck off* onto the wood.

'We're around the side,' Gilly advised. 'There's a smaller door. That's what this key opens.'

Gilly led the way to the side of the building. A large section of chipboard had been pulled from the corner of one of the boarded-up windows.

'It looks like somebody already got to the place,' Gilly observed as she moved over to the side door. Once again, it was secured with a large sheet of wood, onto which had been screwed a large bolt. The spray painter had been at work again. It read, *Brofel Entrans*.

'I assume it's supposed to say *Brothel Entrance*?' Gilly wondered aloud. 'Let's hope whoever sprayed that on doesn't get a job as a sign writer.'

'You think they'd teach vandals to spell properly,' Hollie remarked. 'I don't know what the world's coming to.'

Gilly pushed the key deep into the mechanism of the heavy padlock.

'This is rusted. Can you turn it?' she asked Hollie.

Hollie had a go. It took a few tries but, eventually, the lock yielded and they were able to gain access to the building.

'Remember, if it says it's unsafe, it means it,' Gilly warned.

There was just enough light in the building to see where they were going. Some of the smaller windows weren't boarded up, and light flooded through the upstairs windows that had been left smashed but uncovered. Hollie almost jumped out of her skin when a couple of pigeons flew up.

'The squatters have moved in already.' She smiled at Gilly, trying to give off the impression she hadn't been spooked by the sudden movement. 'Can you talk me through it? Wow, what a staircase!'

They'd stepped into the main hallway now, and Hollie had just set eyes on the spectacular central staircase which dominated the entrance.

'It's quite some place, isn't it?' Gilly said. 'It's just a pity we weren't here for a summer camp. It feels as empty and isolated as it did back then.'

She turned and pointed.

'That's the lounge over there, and next to it is the dining area. The kitchen is at the back. They had a couple of rooms downstairs for the posh girls. Those smaller rooms on the right were where the office work was done—'

Gilly stopped, her voice faltering. Hollie squeezed her arm instinctively.

'I'm sorry, I didn't think it would affect me so much. I'm choked up. It feels like yesterday. I can still picture us whispering in our dorm room upstairs. I loved the other girls. Mandy and Theresa... and Violet. We were so naughty while we were waiting for the babies to arrive. But it was so damn sad and lonely here, too. I can still picture Sister Brennan, gliding about this place like a serpent; her eyes and ears were everywhere. We all left this building distraught. Our babies were taken from us. Sometimes I'm not quite sure how I managed to rebuild my life.'

Hollie paused a moment, allowing Gilly to gather her thoughts. She couldn't begin to comprehend what it must have been like. She was so lucky having choices when she'd fallen pregnant with Izzy. She'd never regretted what happened, even if Izzy's father was no longer on the scene.

Hollie tried to picture herself walking to the place for the first time, scared, uncertain what to expect from the birth, and in the threatening presence of Sister Brennan. Even at nineteen she'd have found it gruelling, especially without the support of her family. And then leaving this place without her baby; it was impossible for her to imagine.

'Let's split off and see what's here,' Hollie began, anxious to have a few moments alone to settle her mind.

'What are you looking for?' Gilly said as Hollie took several photographs.

'I don't know, really. I just want to get a sense of the place. I want to understand what happened here. I can't believe all this was going on in my lifetime.'

They separated, each cautiously taking a different side of the staircase. Somebody had spray painted the words *slappers lived here* on the wall. The plaster was beginning to flake and fall. The building wasn't long for this world. Hollie noted that at least this vandal could spell, even if the sentiments were as foul as usual.

'Hollie, over here!' Gilly called.

'Are you okay?'

'Yes, come here, quickly. Take a look at this.'

Hollie moved past the staircase and joined Gilly, who was pointing into a small room that looked like it had been an office at one time. The light was poor in there, so Hollie used the torch on her phone.

On the bare wooden floor behind an old oak desk was a sleeping bag, a gas stove and a couple of tins of food. It looked like somebody had been there recently. Spread across the desk were numerous copies of local papers, with selected articles carefully cut out from their pages. A pair of scissors sat on top.

'It looks like we still have a resident,' Hollie remarked as she moved over to investigate further. 'And they like to keep up to date with the news.'

ELEVEN

'Don't touch anything, please,' Hollie warned Gilly, resisting the impulse to launch at the items on the desk and search through them.

'You think this might be the killer?' Gilly asked.

She moved up to the desk, drew a pen out of her coat pocket, and used it to lift up the newspapers.

'Stay by the door, please, Gilly. I'll have a snoop, then get a team onto this to see if they can find anything.'

She took out her phone and called the office, moving away from Gilly so she could speak privately.

'DS Patel, it's DI Turner. I'm going to give you some dates of editions of the *Hull Daily Mail*. Would you contact their office and see if we can get our hands on some archive copies? If not, try the local library. They usually keep copies in their archive.'

'The archives are kept at Hull History Centre, boss. They've got everything we need in there.'

Hollie read through the dates. They were all within the past two years. It was impossible to know which articles had been cut out as there was no context to work from.

'Any news on Clive Bartram yet?' she checked.

'A couple of potential sightings, but nothing else,' DS Patel updated her.

'Okay, let me know if there are any changes. This man is a murder suspect, we need our hands on him ASAP.'

Hollie felt a pang of guilt as DS Patel hung up. She was loading her up, she knew, but she had officers to deploy to do the grunt work. Perhaps she'd been a bit sharp, but the pressure was on over Bartram.

Hollie took several photographs of the small room from different angles, for personal reference.

'We'll get this all logged properly,' she said aloud, for her benefit as much as Gilly's.

'You know that Mandy's son has some problems in his life?' Gilly said as Hollie exited the room.

'I do. I'm guessing it's not out of the question that he might be dossing down here. Does Mandy give him a room?'

Gilly paused.

'I don't want to gossip about Mandy's home life—' she began.

'It's okay, we've been through this back at the station. I'm aware of what Clive's like.'

'It's a difficult relationship. I feel so sorry for her. What can she do? He has a drug habit. He steals from her sometimes. She'd love him to come and live with her, but for her own sanity, she's had to ask him to leave. The best thing Clive can do is to set himself straight. But I think he's carrying too much life baggage around with him. He just can't seem to let go of his past.'

'What was this room used for?' Hollie asked, changing the subject.

Gilly's expression turned dark.

'What? Have I touched a nerve?'

'You might say that. This is where they signed the paperwork to adopt the babies. This is where it all happened. I can still picture my mum and dad sitting there, with me next to them, and McCready and Father Duffy just there. If only I'd understood what they were doing.'

The two women walked back into the hall and sat on the bottom step of the staircase.

'Do you ever see the ghosts of your past?' Gilly asked.

Hollie saw them every day, all around her. But this was about Gilly, so she left her to speak.

'It's been more emotional than I expected, coming back here. You probably see a ruined property, ready for the bulldozers. Everywhere we walk, I remember it as it was back then. I can see Sister Brennan, prowling the place, casting a threatening shadow wherever she passed. I can hear us girls giggling in our rooms, trying to outwit the nuns, yet always fearing the worst.'

'Were there any happy times here?' Hollie asked.

'Some. Don't forget how young we were at the time. We were just a group of girls thrown together. It was us against them. We didn't stand a chance, though we didn't know that at the time. I had some of the happiest and darkest moments of my life in this building. But more dark moments than anything else, because of that woman.'

Gilly pulled back the sleeve of her top and thrust her wrist in front of Hollie.

'Look. It's not so easy to spot these days.'

Hollie looked down and saw it. It was shocking, unbelievable that a woman like Gilly could have ever contemplated such a thing.

'Yes,' Gilly confirmed. 'I tried to kill myself in the bathroom at the top of those stairs. I was still hormonal after the baby. They'd probably call it post-natal depression these days. But back then, I was just supposed to buck up and get on with it. I was expected to stop my silliness.'

'Did you really mean to kill yourself?' Hollie asked. She thought about Izzy again. She'd had a crash after the day of birth; it had pulled the rug from under her feet at the time. How could she feel so low when such a wonderful thing had just happened? She harboured dark thoughts, too, but never told anyone. What must it have felt like for Gilly to go through all of that and then have her baby forcibly taken from her?

'No, of course I didn't want to die. I just wanted my baby back. I was depressed, too. It was the classic cry for help. I didn't even cut my wrist the correct way. That's why the scar is so faint. You go up the vein if you really want to end your life, not across it. But there was no internet in those days, so we just blundered through everything, suicide attempts included.'

Hollie moved in to give Gilly a hug. It was unprofessional, she knew that. Every part of her hoped Gilly was not her killer. It simply didn't add up. It wouldn't be the first time she'd been wrong. But she took the leap of faith and reached out to her. There was nothing in the police handbook that said she couldn't show a bit of humanity. She might have been driven to such a low point if placed in the same situation. It was difficult enough her being away from home for so long.

'Whose office was that?' Hollie asked.

'That was where the big phone was kept.' Gilly smiled, breaking the tension. 'If any of us got calls, that's where we'd go to take them. It was one telephone for the whole building. It rang so loud you could hear it everywhere. It's in there that I signed my baby away—'

She stopped dead again, choking up.

'What's the name of your son?' Hollie asked.

'Duncan. I didn't name him that, of course. My name for him was Gary. Don't laugh, it was a popular name in the seventies. He maybe dodged a bullet there. You'll meet him shortly, when he comes to pick me up. He's a good kid.'

'What can you tell me about Duncan?'

Doctor Ruane had suggested that two people might have murdered Sister Brennan. They'd already questioned Mandy and were looking for her son, Clive, but why not Gilly and her son, too?

'He works in logistics and has lived in Hull all his life. He's divorced, but it's not acrimonious, they still talk. Oh, and he has no police record, just in case you were wondering.'

Hollie said nothing. She'd see what she thought of Duncan when he came to pick up Gilly. She changed the subject; it wasn't productive to have Gilly so prickly with her.

'What more can you tell me about this social worker, McCready?'

Hollie stood and encouraged Gilly to follow her up the staircase.

'I think he used to be referred to as a moral welfare officer back then?'

Gilly found that hilarious.

'Moral welfare officer – screw that. He was a bastard. Excuse my language, but he was. What a piece of shit. All those girls he separated from their children. I wonder how he feels about that now.'

Hollie felt the churn of impatience in her stomach. McCready was beginning to get under her skin; why was the team having such a hard time locating him? She made a mental note to chase this again. If they didn't find him soon, she'd have to start applying some pressure.

They reached the top of the landing. It was made up of a U-shape of rooms circling the staircase. Many of the doors had been pulled off their hinges. They walked together, peering inside as they chatted.

'He must have been young when you knew him?' Hollie speculated. 'Even if he's retired now, he can't have been that old in the seventies.'

'Yes, he was young. I quite fancied him at first, before I

figured out what his role was.'

'You didn't know he was managing the adoption process?'

'Not until they took Duncan away from me. My parents dealt with all the paperwork. I just signed things I didn't understand. Nobody explained what was going on. They just said it was to assure the wellbeing of my baby. I didn't know I was agreeing to give him up for adoption. I'd never have signed anything if I knew that.'

Hollie thought of all the papers she'd signed when Izzy was born. She just trusted the adults around her. In her case, they had her best interests at heart. But with Gilly, they were deceiving her. That breach of trust must have stung, even if Gilly's parents did think it was for the best.

Gilly had stopped and was taking more time to look inside one of the rooms. They were unable to enter because the floor had been flagged as unsafe by a warning notice. There was a secure barrier across the door.

'This was our room,' she said almost in a whisper, overcome by the emotion of seeing it.

Hollie peered inside. It was empty, just exposed, with rotting floorboards and a ceiling partly collapsed where the rain had made its way through the roof.

'Me, Mandy and Theresa were in here.'

Hollie tried to imagine them all in there. It seemed stark and bare, though it must have changed since the seventies. Lily and Noah had such personalised bedrooms, it was easy to picture how sterile and cold this place must have been. They needed to speak to Theresa, too, and she hoped DS Patel had made progress with that.

'We were so naughty while we were here. It was the only way we could spite Sister Brennan; she was so horrible to us.'

Gilly laughed, but it was reflective and sad. Hollie took more photographs as she spoke.

'It wasn't all bad. I know that sounds crazy, bearing in mind why we were in this building and what happened to our babies. But we had some fun while we were waiting for them to arrive. You know what it's like, you can find light in the darkest of times. It was our way of coping. I put on a brave face for the other girls and tried to cheer them up. But we were all scared of what was going to happen when we gave birth, and Sister Brennan made this place so cold and unwelcoming. It was so lonely here, like nobody really cared about us at all. Thank God we had each other.'

Hollie had seen all she needed to see. The office downstairs was the primary source of interest, but it needed to be handled properly, as a crime scene, in case it led them to their killer. She called DS Patel once again as they were making their way out, keen to get a team sent over as soon as possible to see what they could find.

As she stepped out of the dilapidated building, a man waiting on the other side of the fencing startled her. Her mind immediately recalled the warning on the burner phone.

Be careful. I think you're being watched.

She stopped dead and put out her arm to warn Gilly.

'Oh, he's here already, that was good timing.'

The man's van was parked up next to Hollie's car, with both rear doors open, leaving the contents on display.

'Do you need some help, ladies?' he called over cheekily as they blundered their way through the security barrier, with Gilly leading the way this time.

'This is my son, Duncan,' Gilly announced proudly as they joined him at the van.

'Nice to meet you, officer,' he said, holding out his hand to greet Hollie.

She was about to grasp it when she spotted something at the back of the van. It was a long length of climbing rope. And it looked just like the length of rope that was used to hang Sister Brennan.

TWELVE

1975: GILLY'S STORY

It couldn't be put off any longer. She still didn't understand how she'd been pregnant for so long and not even known it. But Christmas had passed, the doctor had done the tests, and it was all confirmed. The baby was coming in a month or so, and she had to make some plans.

She sat on her bed, running her hand across her stomach. She could see now that her body was changing, but she'd never have put that down to a baby. Stealing too much popcorn from the machine at the cinema, perhaps, but never a pregnancy.

Gilly had sobbed into her pillow for three nights before deciding on a course of action. She couldn't make up her mind who to tell first: Eric or her parents. Finally, she settled on her parents. They still didn't know she was seeing anyone. But whatever happened when she told Eric, she would need the support of her parents. Even if they ended up getting married, there would be no hiding that the baby was conceived out of wedlock.

The time had come. She was dreading it. There would be shouting and anger. She would be called a *disappointment* and a *failure*. But that would pass, and if she could just stare into the eye of the storm, it would be over eventually.

Gilly looked at the small suitcase on her bed. She'd packed what she could carry. If they threw her out of the house – and she had to believe they wouldn't do that – she'd beg to stay with Eric's family. Eric would probably want to get engaged, anyway. But either way, her parents had to know.

Her father was home from work; it would soon be time for the evening meal. Gilly hadn't seen Eric for a couple of days, and she wondered how he would respond to the news that he was going to be a dad.

'Gilly!' came her mother's voice from downstairs. This was it. She pulled her suitcase from under the bed, where it had been hidden away, and placed it by the door. She considered leaving it for another night. She couldn't. If she wasn't so far gone in the pregnancy, it could have waited. But the doctor had warned her about the possibility of the baby coming early and advised her to think through arrangements.

She opened her door and stepped slowly down the stairs. Her mum and dad were already sitting at the dining room table. The conversation was stilted and perfunctory.

'How was your day?'

'Busy. And yours?'

'The same.'

'Hi, Dad,' she said, pulling out her chair.

'Hello, Gilly,' he replied. 'Good day?'

'Yes. Thank you.'

'How are you feeling now?'

'Better. Thank you.'

It didn't help that the conversation around mealtimes was so sparse. She was about to let off a grenade, but with the word count seemingly on tight rationing, it was difficult to just drop it into the conversation.

'There's tomato sauce there if you want it,' her mum said.

'Mum, Dad, I've got something I need to tell you—'

'In a moment, Gilly, let's just have something to eat first,' her mother replied. Could she sense what was coming?

Gilly took a small mouthful, then tried again. She felt so sick at the thought of saying what she had to say that she didn't want to eat anyway.

'It's important. I need to tell you today.'

She couldn't avoid this; she couldn't afford to postpone it any longer. Her heart was pounding so loud, it was a wonder they couldn't hear it.

'What is it, Gilly?' her father grumbled impatiently. 'If it's just a bit of nonsense, it can wait, like your mother said. I'm hungry and I want to eat—'

'Dad, listen, please,' Gilly urged. 'I have to tell you something. Now. It can't wait.'

That had got their attention. She looked nervously between the two of them. Her father put his cutlery down.

'What is it, Gilly?' he said. His eyes were fixed on her now. He was bracing for bad news.

'I'm pregnant,' she whispered. The words were barely audible.

'I beg your pardon?' her dad replied.

'I'm going to have a baby.'

The words were louder this time. Her parents looked across the table at each other but said nothing.

Her pork chop, chips and peas were steaming on the plate. She liked her mum's chips straight out of the pan.

Her father looked down at the table, avoiding her gaze.

Gilly's mum stared, her face white, with a look of sheer terror in her eyes.

'Did you hear me? I'm pregnant,' Gilly repeated, with more courage now. She just wanted them to say something – anything – and get it over with. Her anxiety was racing off the scale.

Her father slammed his fist on the table. Her mother flinched at the force of it. All the cutlery jumped in the air.

'How?' Even in a moment of crisis, her dad managed to keep a tight hold on his words.

Gilly felt the grip of panic seizing her body.

'It's a boy – a man – called Eric Gittens. He's from work. He's the projectionist there.'

Her mum said nothing. It seemed all she could do was stare at Gilly, only now her look was accusing and despising.

'How long?'

'Since I finished school and started working at the Cecil. I think we're in love.'

'You think you're in love?'

'Yes. I like him.'

'Where does he live?'

'He lives on the Gipsyville estate.'

'Gipsyville?' her mother confirmed. It looked like her sole contribution was going to be one of snobbery.

'When is the baby due?' Her father spat out the words.

'The doctor says I'm eight months pregnant.'

'You don't look pregnant. Are you certain?'

'I'm sure. The doctor told me. I've done the tests. I'm not showing due to my age—'

The mention of her age seemed to set off a trigger in her father. For the second time, he thumped the table. He looked like a man on the point of exploding.

'You filthy little whore!' he shouted. Gilly jumped, unaccustomed to shouting in the house. It was the first time she could remember seeing her father express any kind of emotion. Now she wished he'd return to his normal, repressed self.

Her mother cried silently. She looked away from her husband and couldn't meet Gilly's eyes.

'Where does he live?' her father demanded as he stood up and moved towards her. At first, she thought he was going to strike her, and she flinched, moving her arm in front of her face to protect herself.

'Gipsyville, I told you—'

'Which road?'

'River Grove.'

He grabbed her wrist and wrenched her out of her seat. She'd never seen him like this before.

'You're coming with me.'

'Walter,' Gilly's mum pleaded.

'I don't want to hear it,' her father shouted. 'How are we ever going to live this down? She's disgraced this family. What will our friends at church say? This is terrible. You have to end it now—'

'But Dad—' Gilly protested.

'Shut up. Shut your mouth,' he screamed at her.

He pulled her towards the front door, not bothering with coats. Gilly was marched out of the door towards the car.

'Get in!' he shouted.

She did as she was told. She didn't know what he was planning, but she dared not challenge him.

They got in the car. Her father switched on the engine and revved it aggressively. His driving usually frustrated her; it was pedestrian and cautious most of the time.

He roared out of the parking space at the side of the road, spinning the vehicle around in the street and almost hitting one of the neighbour's cars. All the time he was muttering at Gilly.

'I can't believe you'd do this to us. You're a common whore, that's all you are. I thought we'd brought you up better than that. You're nothing but a little slapper. My daughter, the embarrassment of it.'

Gilly was scared now. She'd anticipated tears and shouting. She wasn't expecting this. He was tearing through the city's streets, the anger rising from him like steam off a smouldering volcano.

'Dad, no, please.' He was heading for Eric's house. They'd entered the Gipsyville estate.

'What number?' he shouted.

'I don't... I can't—'

'What number?'

He was so forceful she began to cry in fear.

He slammed the brakes on, and Gilly was thrust forward in her seat. They didn't usually bother with seatbelts as the car seldom went above thirty miles per hour within the city boundary. As the car braked, her head struck the plastic dashboard. For a moment, her father looked like he might apologise. Instead, gripped by fury, he reached over and grasped the neck of her top.

'Which house number?'

She gave him his answer. He released his grip and restarted the engine, which had stalled at the suddenness of his braking.

As they entered River Grove, Gilly spotted Eric's Ford Escort parked up outside the house. Why couldn't he have been working that night? Her father drove along the street, scanning the house numbers, until he reached Eric's. He all but abandoned the car in the middle of the road, swerving it to one side and killing the engine. He was out of his seat before she knew it, storming towards their front door.

'Dad, no, please—' she began. His rage was frightening her.

He wasn't listening. It was like she wasn't even there. He was like a projectile, carried by the momentum of his anger. He was now hammering on the door. Gilly got out, rushing over to the house. What would he do if he got his hands on Eric? Would they have a fight? Surely Eric would be able to beat him; she didn't want to see either of them in conflict.

The front door opened. It was Eric's mum. Gilly's heart jumped. This was out of her control, it was all escalating too fast.

'Hello,' she began, looking at Gilly's father. She then

spotted Gilly approaching the house. Gilly blinked back her tears.

'Dad, please!'

'Where's Eric? Where is he?'

Her dad was inside the house now, shouting.

'What's this about?' Sue asked, completely taken aback by this invasion of her house.

'I'm pregnant,' Gilly cried, out of her mind with fear now.

'I thought you'd split up. Eric told me—'

Eric was coming down the stairs, an unfamiliar girl following after him. It was the same woman Gilly had spotted with him in the staff car park. It only took a moment for Gilly to understand.

'What's going on?' Eric asked, looking dazed at the mayhem before him.

'You've got Gilly pregnant,' Sue replied, her voice shaking.

'What? Gilly?'

'You said it was over with her,' Eric's date screamed at him. She thumped his back on the staircase, trying to get a grip on him while Gilly's father had launched himself at Eric. Gilly never would have believed her dad was capable of it. He smacked Eric in his face before he'd even made it to the second step. All the time, Eric's new girlfriend was screaming at him, accusing him of lying to her and cheating.

Eric's nose was bleeding. He'd been taken by surprise and was trying to recover his footing.

'Leave him alone,' Sue cried, running at Gilly's dad to keep him away from her son.

'How dare you do that to my daughter, you stupid, feckless idiot!' Gilly's father seethed. He punched Eric in the stomach, and he sank to the ground. He finished him off with a knee to the face. Eric knew what was best for him. He sank to the floor and stayed there.

'Don't you ever come near my daughter or my family again,'

Gilly's dad hissed. 'You don't exist anymore. It's over. You keep well away, you piece of shit!'

Gilly was sobbing uncontrollably. Eric's date continued to yell at him, even though he was still and bloodied on the carpet. Sue was crying, too. As Gilly's father grabbed her wrist to drag her back to the car, Sue called out after her.

'Oh, Gilly. I'm so sorry, darling. We thought you'd ended it with him. We thought you'd broken up.'

THIRTEEN

'Can I take a look inside your van?'

Duncan withdrew his hand.

'I thought we'd at least shake hands first.' He smiled, assured and confident.

'Hollie? What's going on?' Gilly asked, her face suddenly confused and alert to trouble.

'I want to take a look at that rope in the back of your van.'

'This is a bit much,' Gilly protested.

'It's fine, Mum. Go ahead, officer. My van is your van.'

Duncan stepped away from the rear of the vehicle. Hollie climbed up into the back so she could take a closer look at the rope. She pulled out her phone and took some photos.

'This is out of order,' Gilly protested. 'You're treating my son like he's some kind of criminal.'

'Mum, it's fine. She won't find anything.'

Hollie looked back at him from inside the van. If he'd been up to no good, he was certainly a cool customer. She examined the other contents. There was a helmet, some boots and crampons.

'You're a climber?' Hollie asked, clambering out.

'Yes, I climb. Sometimes indoors, sometimes outdoors. That's my gear. Is there a problem, officer?'

'Where did you get that rope?' Hollie asked.

'From a climbing store. I can't remember precisely. Somewhere in the Lake District. Why?'

'Is this really necessary?' Gilly remonstrated.

Hollie could tell she was getting riled up, but this was important.

'Mum, it's okay,' Duncan spoke gently, doing his best to calm her.

'I'm going to ask you to come to the station so I can ask some questions.'

'You can't do that,' Gilly interjected. 'He hasn't done anything. This is outrageous.'

'Mum, relax, it's all fine. I haven't done anything. I don't start my shift until later. How about I run you home and then I'll report to the police station?'

'I'm coming with you,' Gilly insisted. 'I take it I can do that... officer?'

She was growing to like Gilly, and she owed her. But she couldn't allow her personal feelings to cloud her judgement.

'I'd like you to come in my car,' Hollie said. 'I don't want you to interfere with that rope in there—'

'You're treating him like you've already decided he's guilty,' Gilly complained.

'I've got a team arriving here at any moment. I'm going to ask them to check your van thoroughly when they get here. I'd like you to step away from it now.'

'I'm not under arrest, am I?'

'This is bloody outrageous!' Gilly was incandescent.

Hollie was annoyed with herself. She knew she might have handled it better, but it was going to be difficult with Gilly however she brought it up.

'You're not under arrest, but I do need to question you. I just need to get that rope looked at.'

'It's just because he's my son, isn't it?' Gilly said.

'Well, you know I'm looking at you and the other girls, Gilly. You know I can't let this pass. You understand that, don't you?'

Gilly relaxed her body. She breathed out slowly, as if doing a yoga exercise.

'I'm sorry, detective. It's just that, well, I lost him once. I can't lose him again.'

Hollie moved to squeeze her hand but Gilly pulled it away.

'Look, Gilly, I'm sure there's a reasonable explanation for all this, but I have to be sure.'

Gilly nodded. Duncan walked over and gave his mother a hug.

'So, what happens now?' he asked.

Hollie waited with them until the scenes of crime team arrived. She alerted them to Duncan's van and made sure they were fully briefed and in possession of the keys to both the building and the vehicle. She then drove Gilly and Duncan back to the station, leaving Gilly in reception with a machine coffee, and depositing Duncan in an interview room.

She checked in at the office. 'How are we doing with that rope? Is it the same pattern?'

DS Patel had the images open on her PC, sent earlier via Hollie's phone.

'We'll have to do the usual checks, but yes, it's exactly the same colour and pattern.'

'A coincidence?' Hollie asked.

'I very much doubt it,' Patel replied. 'I told you that rope is not common. I'd say this is a big find.'

'Do you want to sit in on this one? It must feel a bit quiet, rooted to that desk every day. And you are our rope expert, after all.'

'I don't mind if I do. Oh, I pulled up Clive Bartram's file, too.'

She handed it to Hollie, who scanned the contents. There was a set of prints and details of previous offences. It was all minor stuff, petty theft, soft drugs use, none of it violent and all of it lightweight. It was the photographs which she found most interesting. Clive had a haunted look in his eyes, like he was fearful of something which had never quite caught him. She'd seen countless men like him while she was a beat bobby; drifting, rudderless, lost. She felt for Mandy, it must have been hard to find her son after so many years only to discover he was still searching for something in life.

'Where were the sightings earlier?' Hollie asked. They needed Bartram in custody, she couldn't have him running loose around the city. 'DCI Osmond suggested some of the regular drugs pick up spots, that might be worth a try.'

'Yes, boss, uniform are keeping an eye open there. There's nothing at his hostel address and nothing at Mandy Tyson's place. Until we get a visual or a tip-off, we're stuck, I'm afraid.'

'Okay, let's get Gilly's son interviewed.'

DS Patel stood up and locked the screen on her PC.

'Lead the way, DI Turner.'

'So, Duncan, I need to ask you some questions about the length of climbing rope I spotted in your van.'

'Sure, fire away.'

'Where did you buy it?'

'As I think I told you already, in the Lake District. It was a mountain supplies store in Keswick. I can't remember the name of it, but it's pretty well known in outdoor activity circles. It won't take any trouble to find it.'

'George Fisher?' DS Patel suggested.

'Yes, that's it,' Duncan confirmed. 'Do you know it?'

'I know the Lake District,' she replied. 'I used to go walking there with my ex.'

'When did you buy it?' Hollie interjected. She'd be telling them to get a room if she didn't take charge.

'Oh, sometime in the last two years. Does it matter?'

'Do you have receipts?'

He laughed.

'Do you keep your receipts, officer?'

'That's a no, I take it?'

'Yes, that's a no. I'm sure you'd find it recorded in my bank statements if you went back far enough.'

'Do you have any more rope like this?'

'I do,' he replied.

'Can you tell me where it is?'

'I can't.'

Hollie's phone vibrated in her pocket. She checked the screen.

'Excuse me, I have to get this.'

Hollie exited the interview room and caught the call before it rang off. It was a Lancaster number.

'Hollie?'

'Speaking.'

'Hi, Hollie, it's Phoebe.'

'Hi, Phoebe, is everything okay? How come you're phoning me from a landline?'

'Oh, my phone's dead, but that's not my only issue today; about our travel arrangements...'

Hollie's heart sank. She'd scream if she didn't see the children.

'We need to come down early tomorrow,' Phoebe began.

'How early?'

'There's some rail line maintenance starting. We can get a

train early from Lancaster, and we'll get to Hull just before nine o'clock. Does that work for you? We can avoid bus transfers if that's okay for you.'

'Yes, I can manage that. I'll be at work. I'll pick you up at the railway station. I'll have to drop you off at the flat and leave you to fend for yourselves until I get back. Is that okay?'

'Of course. My interview isn't until Friday, so I'm fine with that. I'll take the kids around the museums. I'd like to get a feel for the city, anyway. It's an early start, though. We leave Lancaster just after five a.m.'

'Rather you than me with the kids at that time of day. I'll clear it with Léon—'

'No need, I've done it already. I thought I'd save you the trouble as I've got his number now.'

'Phoebe, I could kiss you. Thank you so much.'

'No problem. Mum said she'd pick up Noah and Lily and drive us to Lancaster first thing. I'll see you at the station tomorrow morning. I'll email over the train times, too, so you can see the journey.'

They ended the call. Hollie could barely contain her excitement. The children would be with her in no time at all and soon their chattering voices would fill her flat with joy and laughter. She felt like a child on Christmas Eve, having to wait for the big day to come, almost wanting to rush through the afternoon to get to the big event much quicker. But there was still the case to attend to and she knew she had to hold her focus.

Hollie paused for a moment outside the interview room, mentally checking off what preparations had to be made. When she re-entered, DS Patel and Duncan were chatting casually. DS Patel sat up in her chair.

'Sorry to keep you,' Hollie said. 'Now, back to this rope—'

'It's all been cleared up,' DS Patel started.

'I beg your pardon?'

'You were right to check it out, ma'am. Duncan had a length of climbing rope stolen from his van two weeks ago.'

'I didn't see any damage to your van,' Hollie remarked.

'Insurance.' Duncan smiled. 'I got an incident number from your officers. I noticed someone snooping around my house one night a couple of weeks back. I disturbed someone, I reckon. They'd smashed the passenger-side window and grabbed two lengths of climbing rope.'

'Was that all?'

'That was all,' Duncan confirmed.

'Would there be any seawater on those ropes of yours?' Hollie asked.

'I go climbing at Thornwick Bay. They get a good soaking whenever I'm out there with my mates.'

'And can we confirm this version of events?' Hollie challenged.

'We can, ma'am. I rang the office and checked the crime number. It's exactly as Duncan described. I'm guessing that whoever was snooping around Duncan's house is our man. There was no CCTV footage, so he got clean away. There were no fingerprints either. If it's the same rope that was used to kill Sister Brennan, that's a wonderful bit of policing, ma'am. But, as far as Duncan is concerned, I'd say he's free to go.'

FOURTEEN

Hollie churned over in her mind what DS Patel had just told her. If Duncan had got a crime number and could account for the purchase and theft of the rope, it appeared to be the slam dunk that Patel was claiming it to be. They had no reason to hold Gilly's son any longer. Unless he was an exceptionally clever killer, the type who had the foresight to feign a robbery on his van, report it to the police, and then kill a nun, he was not their man.

'I'll leave you to conclude matters then,' Hollie said, after confirming to herself that they were done and dusted.

Hollie walked back into the incident room.

'Have we had anything back yet from the team at the mother and baby home?' she asked, looking at nobody in particular.

'The last I heard, they're still processing everything,' DC Langdon volunteered. 'They're still there to my knowledge.'

Hollie was impatient for progress. She took a beat; she could see everybody was busy, it wasn't as if people were slacking.

'Are you office-bound today?' she checked.

'Yes, I'm dredging through this list of names still.'

'Any joy?'

'Nothing. Just a lot of memories about the girls' home, much anger, and several happy reunions with lost children. Nothing that's made my ears prick up. I've also been chasing adoption agencies used in the seventies, but most people I've spoken to reckon it was mainly handled by social services in those days. A couple of agencies keep coming up, but they either don't exist anymore or they merged with another agency years ago. It would be a lot easier if it was all more recent. You were right about contacting the university by the way; they had an expert there who gave me some background info.'

Hollie was pleased the lead had been useful. Jenni had been pounding the phones, but it didn't seem to be the best use of her talents. She looked over Jenni's notes about the adoption agencies. Things might have seemed simpler when everything was recorded on paper, but it was a damn sight easier when they had computerised records to refer to.

'How about the nuns, were they any more forthcoming when you spoke to them?'

Jenni sighed.

'Sorry, nothing useful to report. If you pushed me, though, I'd say Sister Kay knows more than she's letting on.'

'In what way?'

'I don't know, it's just a feeling. She answered my questions, but I got the feeling she was always omitting the most interesting information.'

Hollie considered that for a couple of seconds.

'Okay, hand all this over to one of the civilian officers. You and I are heading out of the office this afternoon. So long as that ankle of yours is holding up still?'

'Excellent!' Jenni exclaimed, visibly relieved to be let off the leash again. 'Anywhere interesting?'

'Yes, it might be a difficult one, but I want to see Violet

Farrow. I'll need you to find her information while I attend to somebody in reception. Book us a pool car, too, if you would.'

'Will do, boss.'

Jenni seemed delighted at the prospect of escaping the confines of the office.

'Back in a mo.'

Hollie headed out, checking in on colleagues as she did so. It was a hive of industry. Heads were down, and they'd got the bit between their teeth on the case. That's how she liked to see it. She walked down the stairs to find Gilly still waiting. She stood up as soon as she saw Hollie.

'Are you arresting him?'

'No, it's all fine. There's a perfectly reasonable explanation for the rope. In fact, it helps us. Duncan will be downstairs shortly. You said he hasn't got any other family, didn't you?'

Gilly looked prickly at first but then relaxed as she digested the information that her son wasn't in trouble.

'Yes. His first marriage broke up before he and I reconnected. He got a bit obsessed with finding me, I think. Father Duffy helped to reunite us. It's funny how the world turns sometimes.'

'What's your relationship like with Father Duffy?' Hollie asked, thinking them an odd couple.

Gilly thought about that.

'I think we reached an understanding in the end. He put Duncan in touch with me and, despite that place and what happened there, I owe him that. And he was never cruel; he was just so remote in those days and so weak—'

'Why weak?'

Gilly sighed.

'I don't know. It's just that he could have done more. He wasn't mean or nasty, but he was too weak to stand up to Sister Brennan. Nobody ever stood up to her, she was such a bully. If he'd have stepped up, you know, it might have been better for us.'

Hollie couldn't wait to hear from the old man again.

'You described him as remote, too. Can you explain what you mean by that?'

'Have you ever spoken to someone, and words are coming out of their mouth, but you don't know them any better?'

Hollie considered that. She understood it, some people were like a closed book. She nodded.

'Well, we chat away about nothing of any importance, but I never feel like he reveals anything of himself. He's guarded, that's how I'd describe him. He's a man who doesn't give anything away.'

'Does he have anything to hide?' Hollie wondered.

'Ha, that's for you to find out, you're the detective.'

Gilly had relaxed again after being so sensitive about Duncan.

'Just keep your eyes open, Gilly,' Hollie warned. 'Someone has been snooping around Duncan's van, and he may be working through a list of people who are connected with the home. You may be on somebody's radar, so be careful. I'm going to see Violet this afternoon.'

'Oh—' Gilly seemed embarrassed. 'I should get over to see her. I hear she's really poorly. Send her my love. Tell her I'll try to arrange a trip over on the train, me and the other girls.'

'I will,' Hollie promised.

Jenni had just walked into the reception area. She waved a set of car keys at Hollie as she walked over.

'We're all set,' she announced. 'I've got an address and they're expecting us mid-afternoon. I've even got a postcode for the satnav.'

Hollie said her goodbyes to Gilly, asked the officer at reception to make sure DC Patel arranged a ride back to Duncan's van with a uniformed officer, and then walked over to the pool car that Jenni had booked.

'When was the last time you took a lunch break?' Hollie asked.

Jenni's snort gave her an answer.

'Right, you're taking one today. I've got three visitors coming over tomorrow and nowhere to put them. Do you know of any camping shops around here?'

'How about Winfields off Hessle Road?' Jenni suggested. 'There are plenty of places to grab a bite to eat, too.'

Within fifteen minutes, they were walking the aisles of the outdoor supplies store. The lunchtime traffic had obliged, and they'd even found a parking place outside without issue.

'I need three camp beds and three sleeping bags,' Hollie announced. 'They'll have to rough it a bit but needs must. If they don't have camp beds, I'll settle for blow-ups.'

'Look, there are the sleeping bags.' Jenni pointed to a display up ahead.

'They're a lot posher than they were when we were kids,' Hollie observed.

The two women loaded up with equipment, packed it in the boot of Hollie's car, and then stocked up with food supplies at the store opposite.

'Hessle Road is great,' Hollie remarked. 'You can buy what-ever you need along here.'

They resisted a fish and chip shop whose aroma was wafting along the street and opted for sandwiches instead. Hollie checked the time. One of the curses of her job was the guilt that accompanied anything she did for herself. They'd just have enough time to drop off the purchases at her flat, then return to HQ and swap over from her vehicle to the pool car. Having accomplished the task of buying in food, she did not want the frozen provisions thawing out in the back seat while they were visiting Violet.

Hollie and Jenni multitasked as they drove over to Hollie's flat, both eating their sandwiches as they did so. Jenni checked in with DS Anderson, and Hollie made sure there were no new developments in the case.

'They've drawn a blank with Clive Bartram,' came Jenni's update. 'They're coming back with their tails between their legs.'

'Tell them to pick up with the team who were checking out the office at the mother and baby home. I want to know what they found, if there were prints or DNA and I want full details of those newspaper cuttings. We need to find out what news stories were cut out of those old editions. Oh, and ask DS Anderson to keep that watch on Mandy Tyson's house. I reckon he's likely to turn up in one of those locations soon enough.'

Hollie updated Jenni on her activities earlier that day. It helped her to talk over the case, and it allowed her to spot any gaps that she might have missed. She couldn't see any; she was convinced the answer would be found somewhere among the experiences of Gilly's group of girls.

They pulled up outside Hollie's flat.

'This is nice,' Jenni remarked. 'You've got a lovely view of Pearson Park.'

Hollie felt a pang of embarrassment. This looked like a divorcee's pad, not the kind of place where a married, middle-aged woman should be living. Hollie was relieved the drummer wasn't playing. That would have been too much in front of a work colleague.

As Hollie fumbled for her key, the woman who'd suggested going for a night out opened the door from inside.

'Oh, hello.' She smiled. 'I was hoping I'd catch you again. We knocked on your door last night, only you weren't in.'

Hollie felt her face flushing. She'd been shivering on Gilly's armchair the night before, after narrowly avoiding getting swept away by the River Hull.

'Yes, sorry, I was, er, otherwise engaged.'

She could feel Jenni's cop antenna screaming to know what she'd been up to.

'Do you want to join us for that drink tonight? We're heading out on the town. You're welcome to come with us. You can bring along your—'

The woman seemed uncertain of Jenni's status.

'She's my partner—' Hollie explained, then realised what she'd said.

'That's no problem. The more the merrier!'

'No, not that sort of partner. My work partner. A colleague.'

Jenni looked away. Hollie felt stupid.

'It's all fine with us. We prefer the gay-friendly clubs, anyway. You get less man hassle in there. People just go for a good time and a bit of a dance. Shall we say eight o'clock?'

'I'd love to.' Hollie smiled. The woman headed off wherever she was going.

'I don't have to come,' Jenni offered, once the woman was out of earshot.

'What the hell,' Hollie replied. 'We deserve a good night out. I can't stay out late, because the kids arrive early tomorrow. But come along. If that couple proves to be swingers or something terrible like that, you can help to bail me out.'

They entered Hollie's flat and started packing the food into the cupboards and freezer.

A thought struck Hollie as she was cramming a bag of oven chips into the bottom freezer drawer.

'Can you carry on doing this a moment, while I just pop upstairs?'

Jenni obliged while Hollie found a scrap of paper and scrawled out a note. She exited the flat and walked up the stairs, figuring out where the drum sounds were coming from. It didn't take her long. There was a sticker on the door which read: *Drummers Bang Harder*.

Hollie knocked at the door. There was no sound from inside. She tried a couple more times, then re-read her note before posting it under the door.

Please refrain from drumming for the next three days. I have young children staying in the flat below you. Thank you. Hollie, Flat 2.

She took a deep breath. Thank the heavens, she was all ready for the kids now.

FIFTEEN

1975: GILLY'S STORY

It began with a visit by Father Duffy and one of the nuns. Walt and Carmen Hodges – pillars of the community – couldn't wait to get shot of their daughter. After the altercation at Eric's place, Gilly had been under house arrest. Walt had handed in her notice at the Cecil on her behalf, and she was forbidden from getting in contact with her friends. Her parents could barely speak to her. Neither of them looked her directly in the eye. They'd even found a lock for the telephone, to prevent her from contacting her friend Helen from church. The phone was in the living room, anyway, so it wasn't like she could get to it without being spotted.

Father Duffy visited two nights after the events at Eric's house.

Gilly was not supposed to be part of the conversation at first, but she'd sneaked out onto the landing to listen in.

'Everybody thinks she has meningitis.' Walt spoke quietly. 'I've said we've sent her away to a relative to recover. I know it's a white lie, Father Duffy, but it's the best way to stop the neighbours from prying.'

'I've said the same at church,' Father Duffy confirmed. 'I understand the need for discretion. Nobody will find out; you have my assurance.'

'The shame of it,' Walt continued. 'I still can't believe she'd do that to us.'

'Has there been anything from the police after your – er – conversation with the father of the child?'

'The boy's father tracked me down at work today. Gilly must have told them what I do. They're not going to get the police involved. He apologised to me. Can you believe that? He said his son would be getting a good hiding for what he'd done. He said how much they liked Gilly, and that they were disappointed Eric had let the family down. Apparently, he's had two other women on the go, as well as our Gilly.'

Gilly gasped at hearing that, then froze on the landing in case she'd been heard. She hadn't.

'Are the arrangements in place for when the baby comes? Have you got it all sorted, Father Duffy?'

'Everything is in place. The sooner we get Gilly over to the home, the better for you. I think it's for the best.'

'I don't know what we're going to do with the girl when it's all over—'

Gilly stepped back and one of the floorboards creaked.

'Gilly, is that you?' Walt shouted up the stairs.

She retreated to her bedroom, pushing the door closed as gently as she could. That had been the first rational conversation she'd heard from Walt since the big bust up. Every evening, when he got home from work, she'd hear the deep vibration of his voice through the floorboards. She knew they were plotting and planning, but she hadn't got a clue what the future held. She assumed she'd return with the baby, and they'd raise it together. In time, she hoped, they'd love the child, and it would matter less how it had come into the world.

She tensed as she heard footsteps. They were angry and impatient; it had to be her father. He burst through her bedroom door.

'Father Duffy is coming up to have a quiet word with you.'

That was it. He didn't meet her eyes; he didn't ask how she was. It was like he wanted to flick her off the end of his shoe.

Walt's resentful footsteps were followed by more creaking on the stairs.

'Just wait outside a moment if you would, Sister Brennan.'

There was a polite and cautious knock at the door.

'Come in,' Gilly called, nervous about what was happening without her knowledge.

Father Duffy entered her bedroom, and she caught a glimpse of a nun hovering outside.

This felt wrong to her; did her mum and dad know what was going on? Gilly tensed and moved to the furthest end of her bed.

'Ah, Gillian, hello, it's so good to see you—'

She thought about the time she'd caught him in his office. This felt like that time; it was uncomfortable, wrong, unsettling. There was no reason for her to be impolite, but she was on her guard. He was shuffling and struggling to look her directly in the eyes.

'Hello, Father Duffy,' Gilly said quietly. What was he going to do?

'I just wanted to – well, it's good that you and I can have a private chat at last—'

Gilly knew what this was about. She didn't really want to talk about it. Did the nun know he was doing this? Even her parents respected her privacy; or at least did before she told them she was pregnant.

'I need to know what you think you saw that day – not that there was anything to see – it's a very delicate situation, I'm sure you understand—'

Gilly wanted him out of her room. She didn't like this, it made her nervous. It felt dangerous and threatening, even though she could see he wasn't going to harm her.

'I didn't see anything, Father Duffy. I came to give you the cheque, I'm sorry I walked in on you like that.'

Would that be enough to make him go away? She wished she'd never taken that cheque to him, if it was going to cause trouble like this. She still wasn't entirely sure what she'd seen. Whatever it was, it was clearly bothering Father Duffy.

'Just so long as we have a mutual understanding, Gillian. I wouldn't want us to – er – get into difficulties over it.'

She hadn't a clue what that meant, but Gilly knew she was ready for the conversation to end. She didn't know whether to nod or shake her head. What did he want her to do?

'Yes, I understand, Father,' she said. It seemed to do the job.

'Well, it's been lovely catching up with you, Gillian. Your mother and father will explain why we've been visiting. I'll see you again soon.'

He left her room, half coming, half going, as if he still had things on his mind. She began to breathe again; she hadn't realised how tense she'd been. There was some quiet conversation on the landing. Gilly thought he was gone when her bedroom door opened, without the warning of a knock. It was the nun.

'Who are you?' Gilly asked. She'd seen this nun in church, but never spoken to her directly.

The nun closed the door behind her but said nothing. She lurched at Gilly and pushed her, so she landed on her bed. Gilly was so taken by surprise, she was unable to speak.

The nun moved her face up close so Gilly could feel her breath against her face.

'Whatever you think you saw, you're wrong. Nobody will believe you and nobody cares what you think. You've already shown what kind of girl you are by getting pregnant. So just keep your mouth shut and you'll be okay. Besides, you're coming to stay with me soon. Nobody can help you in the mother and baby home, you'll be all on your own.'

Gilly's whole body was trembling; her legs felt like they might crumple at any moment. She felt so alone. Even when her parents were angry with her, her bedroom remained her sanctuary. But now this woman – this hateful woman – was threatening her in her own home.

There was a knock at the door; it was her mother. Had she sensed something was up? Gilly got off the bed before calling her in, as if ashamed to acknowledge what had just happened. She didn't know how to process it, she was still in shock. Sister Brennan's body relaxed, her wicked aggression now well concealed behind a welcoming demeanour. Gilly's mother entered.

'I thought I'd better check on you and make sure everything is okay, Sister Brennan—'

'Oh yes, no need to worry, Carmen,' Sister Brennan answered before Gilly could speak. Like a chameleon, she'd changed her guise to one of charm and reassurance. 'I've just been explaining to Gillian what good care we'll take of her when she stays with us.'

Carmen seemed uncertain still, like she sensed something was wrong, but Sister Brennan just looked at her, and guided her back out of the room, pulling the bedroom door tightly shut behind her. Gilly sobbed into her pillow, fearful that they'd hear her downstairs.

The gates at the head of the drive to the mother and baby home were wrought iron, heavy, ornate and painted black. Gilly had been to the adjacent church many a time, but she'd never stepped beyond these gates or even wondered what went on here.

It was already dark; Walt had insisted she leave in a taxi, under the cover of night. Carmen had wanted to come with her, but that idea was shot down immediately.

'She was stupid enough to get herself into this fix, she can figure out how to get through it on her own. Maybe it will make her think about what she's done.'

Gilly picked up her case and her footsteps crunched on the gravel as she made her way up the long drive. She was surrounded by trees and shrubs which loomed up as dark silhouettes all around her, and she felt small and insignificant as she made her way slowly towards the front door.

Her lower back ached as she struggled with the case, and she had to fight back her tears, wishing somebody had come with her to offer some reassurance. As she got closer to the building, it was much bigger than she'd imagined, and it felt unwelcoming to her, like it didn't want her there.

She struggled up to the solid, heavy door, pulling her case up one step at a time, stopping after each one to rub her back.

It had been so bleak in her house; she'd thought there was no way things could get any worse. She was wrong. Knowing that the nun was there, waiting for her, watching for a wrong move, made her feel sick.

Gilly wiped the tears from her eyes and struck the door's knocker. It was loud and abrasive in the quietness of the night. She heard movement from inside. A hand grasped the handle on the other side and slowly, arduously, it swung open.

'Welcome to the mother and baby home, I'm Sister Kay,' said one of the nuns. She was gentle and had a soft Scottish accent. Her tone sounded familiar, but she could not place the voice. At least it was a warm welcome; she'd been terrified that the first face she might see would be Sister Brennan's. The greeting from the nun was the first kindness she'd experienced since revealing to her parents what was going on.

The entrance hall was huge. Gilly had never seen

anything so grand; it was like checking into a hotel, not that she'd ever had that experience, but this place was cold and eerie. It felt like it was swallowing her up as soon as she stepped inside, and her voice was lost in the emptiness when she spoke. It was bleak and bare, with very little decoration, and only austere artwork and crucifixes on the walls, if anything.

'I'll show you to your room. You're sharing with a girl called Theresa. There are three beds in that room, so you might end up getting a companion. Theresa is a lovely girl. I'm sure you'll get on like a house on fire.'

The nun picked up Gilly's suitcase.

'Let the girl carry her own suitcase,' came a sharp voice. Another nun emerged from the shadows, her face scowling and angry. Sister Kay jumped at the sight of her, as did Gilly. Had she been lying in wait, a predator ready to attack?

Sister Kay released the handle of the suitcase and Gilly moved over to pick it up. Her back twinged again as she lifted it, but she put a brave face on it, not wanting to anger Sister Brennan further.

They made their way silently up the stairs as if a shroud of darkness had descended upon the place. Gilly pulled the case with her, one step at a time, her body tiring with each movement.

By the time she reached the top, fatigue had set in, and she was desperate to rest.

Sister Brennan stood at the bottom of the staircase, watching them.

'See you later, Gillian.' She scowled. 'I'm looking forward to getting to know you.'

'Ignore her,' Sister Kay advised. 'Stay out of her way if you can.'

Gilly waited until she was out of sight, then whispered to Sister Kay, 'Will my mum and dad be able to visit?' Tears formed in her eyes as it dawned upon her just how isolated she would be in this place.

'Of course they will. They can come any time they want. My first name is Ursula, by the way. You're welcome to call me Sister Ursula when it's just us. I don't mind at all. Don't let Sister Brennan hear. Here's your room.'

Sister Kay knocked on the door and opened it when a girl's voice called for her to come in.

'Theresa, this is Gilly. Gilly, this is Theresa. I'll leave you two girls to get to know each other.'

Sister Kay watched Gilly in with the suitcase and made her exit, closing the door behind her.

Gilly smiled nervously at Theresa. She seemed a lot younger. She was sitting quietly in the room, on her own. It was a much bigger room than her bedroom and it struck Gilly how solitary it must have been in there, all alone.

'Hello,' Gilly began. 'This room seems okay.'

'It is, it's the best place to stay if you want to avoid some of the grumpier nuns.'

Theresa was speaking softly, as Gilly might have done at school, hoping the teacher wouldn't hear her gossiping in class. It was as if she didn't want to draw attention to herself.

'How old are you?' Gilly asked. She wasn't sure whether she should have pried, but she had to know.

'Sixteen,' Theresa replied.

'How did you get pregnant?' Gilly asked.

'My boyfriend from school. We're in love.'

'Is he sticking by you?'

'Yes. We want to get married.'

'What do your parents say?'

Theresa's face gave her answer.

'I need their permission first,' Theresa continued. 'We'll just wait. I'll look after the baby, and we'll get married as soon as I'm old enough. What about you?'

Gilly set about telling her story. It'd be the first time she'd said it aloud.

'My boyfriend was cheating on me. I've been played for a fool.'

'Did you consider an abortion?'

It was the first time Gilly had thought about that.

'No, actually, I didn't. The Church is against it, anyway. But no, I'd rather have the baby. Just think, I'll still be young and beautiful by the time it's grown up. I rather like the idea of that.'

Theresa put down the book she'd been reading and got off the bed.

'I'm so pleased you're here,' she began. 'It's been so quiet. There are a couple of other girls here, but only one who chats. She's called Violet. You'll like her. She's nice.'

'Can you give me a tour?' Gilly asked. 'Is it allowed?'

'Yes, but only because Sister Kay is on duty. She's nice. Keep a look out for Sister Brennan though. Come on, I'll show you!'

Theresa led the way. As they chatted quietly, Gilly saw that her new friend was more mature than her age. She seemed to have a good head on her shoulders; she was no silly young girl.

'We don't have a television here,' Theresa explained, 'and it's best to take a bath before bedtime as all the nuns get up early and run off the hot water from the water tank.'

Gilly's house didn't have radiators, so the fact the building wasn't warmed by a single coal fire seemed the height of luxury to her.

'What happens when we have the babies?' Gilly wondered aloud as Theresa whisked her past various rooms, explaining what was what.

'There are two large rooms across the landing. They're nice, and they have balconies. We move in there when the babies come. There's more space and we can nurse them at night without disturbing everybody else. We'd better get a move on. They're changing to the overnight staff soon. They like us in our bedrooms in the evening.'

Gilly could hear voices in the hallway.

'I'm just going to pop to the loo,' Theresa continued. 'The baby sits on my bladder. I can't hold my wee in when that happens.'

She giggled like she'd said something naughty.

'I'll wait here for you,' Gilly replied. This was promising, at least. Theresa seemed nice and the room was okay, too.

The moment Theresa left, Gilly felt alone and vulnerable, like someone had just snuffed out a candle. She sensed a movement in her direction. It was one of the nuns. She expected it to be Sister Kay, but it was not. It was Sister Brennan.

'Why aren't you in your bedroom?' the nun asked sharply.

'I'm just waiting for Theresa. She's in the toilet.'

Sister Brennan grabbed her arm and pulled it.

'Get upstairs. You're supposed to be in your rooms at this time of night. Follow me. I want to make sure you stay there.'

'But—' Gilly began.

The nun ignored Gilly and tugged at her arm roughly, pushing her along the hallway, not releasing Gilly along the staircase, until they reached the girls' room.

'Please stop, you're hurting me,' Gilly pleaded.

Gilly turned around, stunned by the forcefulness used to compel her to her room.

'I know what you are,' the nun seethed at her. 'And I know what you think you saw that day in church. Well, you're wrong. You're just a silly, misguided harlot who nobody will listen to. So, you listen to me. You keep your mouth shut. Do you hear me? Nobody wants to hear any nonsense from a little slut like you.'

The nun jabbed her finger into Gilly's chest and her eyes flared with hatred. She turned around and left the room. Gilly buried her face in her pillow and began to cry. She'd never felt more scared or alone in her life.

SIXTEEN

'I've never been to Goole before. What do I need to know?'

'Don't get your hopes up,' Jenni advised. 'In fact, lower your expectations, then lower them a bit more, just for good measure.'

'Really?' Hollie asked, watching the road as they spoke.

Jenni laughed.

'No, I'm winding you up, boss. People joke about Goole being a dump, but it's like everywhere else. It has its good bits, and it has its bad bits. It's weathered some hard times, too. It has a port, so that's in its favour.'

'I've never been,' Hollie continued. 'This is all a good education for me. The sooner I get to grips with my new patch, the better.'

For the first time in several days, Hollie was feeling slightly more in control. She was ready for the kids, which was the main thing. They'd dropped her car off at HQ and exchanged it for a pool car, catching up briefly in the office before heading out once again. And if DS Anderson got his arse in gear, they'd soon have Clive Bartram in for questioning. She was certain Clive was their man. She'd secured Anderson more resources to track down their fugitive. Once he'd been hauled in, she was optimistic they'd have the case done and dusted. The only item outstanding was the man with the birthmark. He seemed to have other ideas. With all that said, Hollie supposed she ought to be approaching a state of mind verging on calm, but something wasn't sitting right with her, and she couldn't put her finger on it.

The satnav announced that it was time to leave the M62, so Hollie took the slip lane and allowed the device to guide her into the Oakhill Hospice. She pulled up in the car park and readied herself for what was coming.

'Okay, this is going to be a tough one,' Hollie said, turning to look at Jenni.

'Yes, I know from personal experience. I had a friend from school come to one of these places. It's all a bit grim.'

'We probably have one chance with Violet. We can go gently, but we have to leave with the information we came for.'

The two women made their way to the hospice entrance. It was beautifully planted, with seating areas all around and numerous plaques acknowledging financial contributions in memory of people who'd been cared for there.

'DI Turner and DC Langdon to see Violet. You're expecting us, I believe? My colleague rang ahead to set up the appointment.'

A hospice nurse was summoned to take them to Violet's room. She stopped at the end of a tastefully decorated corridor.

'Violet's quite ill now, and we're letting her take care of her own pain relief. Her daughter is with her. Please don't tire her out.'

'Does she know about the death of Sister Brennan?' Hollie checked. She wanted to know if they were going to have to break the bad news.

'I'm not sure,' the nurse replied. 'Her daughter is certainly aware of it, but I'm not sure if she has told Violet yet. It's maybe not the best time to be sharing news like that.'

She led the way and announced them at the door. Hollie stepped in first. It wasn't what she'd expected. There was no doubt this was a building devoted to medical care, but it was much more colourful than a hospital. The room had a patio door, too, so it looked out onto a beautiful garden. The usual medical paraphernalia was there but, somehow, it all seemed to be less clinical than usual.

Violet was propped up by pillows on the bed. She was attached to monitoring equipment, and Hollie observed the device in her hand to administer morphine when she needed it. Her daughter was reading a magazine in a high-backed chair. She stood up as they entered the room.

'Officers, thank you for coming,' she began. 'Mum is very tired, but she's keen to speak to you.'

'Hello, Violet,' Jenni said. Hollie greeted her, too.

'I'll pull up a chair for you,' Violet's daughter said. 'My name is Patricia, by the way. I'm Violet's daughter. I was adopted. Though you probably know that.'

Hollie shook her hand. She'd been crying. She must have known that Violet was entering her final days.

Hollie pulled up the chair, and Jenni found a place to perch on the bedside table.

'I'm very sorry to see that you're unwell, Violet. I know you're in excellent hands here. We won't keep you long. We just have a few questions about the home.'

Hollie reckoned she must be in her mid-sixties. What an age to confront death. She wondered how she would fare if faced with the same illness as this poor woman. She looked weak and drained.

'I want to help, officers.'

Her voice was reedy. Patricia leant over and held a glass of water to her lips. Violet took a small sip.

'I know I'll be gone soon, but I'm at peace with that now. I have Patricia with me. She's all I ever wanted. She's so special, my beautiful little girl.'

Patricia began to cry.

'I'm sorry,' she said, wiping her eyes.

'Cry as much as you need to,' Jenni reassured her, walking over to offer her a hug. She accepted it and seemed desperate for someone to cling to.

'If she only knew how happy I am to have her back in my life,' Violet continued. 'All the years she was away from me, I was dead inside. But having her close to me now, it's all I wanted, officer. She's all I ever needed.'

Hollie steadied herself. She'd known this would be difficult, but she was shocked by how little life was left in Violet's frail body. It made her appreciate how precious her own children were to her. Even though she had to work and was often caught up with cases, she loved them deeply and whatever accusations Léon threw at her, he could never deny that she cared passionately about the kids.

'May I ask you some questions about the mother and baby home?' Hollie asked gently. She held up the photograph of the four girls.

Violet tried to speak, but her voice didn't come. She gave a small nod instead.

'What do you remember about the girls you were with?'

Violet let out a small laugh.

'I remember Gilly Hodges best. She was such a minx, that one. We stay in touch, you know—'

'Gilly's planning to come over and see you. I saw her earlier today.'

'That'd be lovely,' Violet said, her voice trailing off. She didn't sound at all convinced that she'd still be around by then.

'Theresa and Mandy were such lovely girls. We had some fun, you know, despite what happened to us. Gilly was the ringleader, though. My goodness, that girl led those nuns on a merry dance.'

It didn't sound like Gilly had changed much.

'Would you pass me the photograph please, DC Langdon?'

Jenni stepped forward and handed over the two photographs of the girls: one taken at the home, the other of the sports team at David Lister School.

Violet smiled as much as she could through her dry lips. She held up the photo of the four girls. Hollie noticed how bruised her hand was from the needles.

'Just look at us. Don't we all look so young—'

'We want to know what you can remember about the girl who took that photograph,' Hollie continued. 'Nobody seems to remember her name.'

Violet studied the second photograph, from David Lister School.

'It's not a very good photograph,' she remarked, 'but that's her there. That poor girl.'

Hollie leant over and checked which of the pictured girls Violet was referring to. They were just teenage girls. To Hollie, they seemed less worldly-wise than girls now. They could have been anybody, though. She'd picked out the same girl as Gilly.

'I felt so sorry for that girl. She was only fifteen years old. Can you believe that? And her father was something posh. He wanted to brush it all under the carpet.'

'Why was she there?' Jenni asked. 'Why did they keep her away from the other girls?'

'Oh, there was a good reason for that,' Violet began. 'She was in a much bigger mess than the rest of us. Yet she was so brave about it. She'd been attacked. The girl in that photograph had been raped.'

SEVENTEEN

'Raped?'

'I know, it's horrific, isn't it? A girl of that age.'

Hollie was taken aback by the revelation. She'd thought this was all about young women and unplanned pregnancies. She'd never expected it to take this dark turn.

'How did you find out?'

'It was not general knowledge. I happened to overhear the social worker discussing it in the hallway one day. I wasn't supposed to be there. None of the other girls knew.'

'Did you tell them, Violet?'

Hollie watched as Violet administered a shot of morphine, attempting to move her hand under the covers so that her daughter wouldn't see. She paused a moment while the drug took effect.

'No, I never told them. Even back then, when I was still so young, it felt like her story to tell. I didn't really understand it fully, either. I knew what rape was, I just didn't grasp the enormity of it.'

'Do you know what happened?' Jenni asked.

Violet shook her head.

'No, I just caught half a whisper.'

She picked up the photograph that was still lying on top of her sheets.

'Look at her. She's just a girl in that picture. Life does horrible things to us.'

Hollie could see Violet was tired. The nurse came back into the room, perfectly timed, and checked her over, a reminder not to outstay their welcome.

'Can you remember her name?' Hollie pushed. This was the one piece of information she needed. If they found the girl, it would enable them to close that particular loop in the investigation.

Violet took the sip of water offered to her by the nurse.

'No more than five minutes now, officer,' she warned.

Hollie nodded.

'We never knew her name. Whoever she was, she was the child of someone important in the area. They did not want any details getting out. Most parents were ashamed of their daughters in that place, and that's why they hid us away. It's why they could do something as barbaric as tearing our babies from our arms.'

Violet stopped and took in a slow and difficult breath.

'I still vividly remember them taking Patricia and that terrible, numbing knowledge that I'd just heard her last cry. But there was something different about this girl. Maybe they didn't want anybody to know she'd been raped. Perhaps they thought that brought extra shame on the poor thing. It still upsets me thinking about her.'

Violet was rambling. Hollie knew they were on borrowed time now; the nurse was impatiently busying herself with unnecessary tasks around the room. Hollie felt like they were being swatted away.

'Can you think of her name, Violet?'

'Yes, I remember now. We didn't know her name, but we had a nickname for her. We called her Twiggy.'

'Twiggy?' Jenni asked.

'She was a famous model in the sixties,' Hollie explained. 'She was iconic. She still pops up here and there.'

'She was even skinnier than Gilly,' Violet continued. 'None of us could believe how slender Gilly was. I had a round baby bump, but Gilly didn't, and neither did Twiggy. We called her that because she was so slight. We didn't know her name, so we had to call her something. We weren't being mean. It was a compliment, more than anything.'

'When did she take that photo?' Jenni asked. 'How come you got to spend some time with her?'

'She sneaked into the other girls' room once. I just happened to be there. She was checking in on Gilly and Theresa. She'd seen something unpleasant happen to them, and she wanted to make sure they were okay. She took all her meals in her room, and we only ever caught glimpses of her. She used to have this Polaroid camera. They were expensive in those days, so her parents must've had money. She was so excited to see us, she wanted to take a photograph so she could remember us. She took two if I remember. One for us – that's this one here – and one for her to keep. I still worry about her, even now. I wonder if she ever managed to set her life straight, after that.'

'That's enough now, officers,' the nurse announced. 'Violet needs her rest.'

Hollie stood up. The meeting had been useful for context and corroboration – it had also revealed a new and unexpected element – but it didn't move the case on. She retrieved the photos from the top of the bed cover.

'Remember, Gilly hopes to pay a visit. She's going to try to get all the girls together—' She was about to say *one more time* but stopped short of that.

'I'll show you out while the nurse attends to Mum,' Patricia said.

The three of them stepped out of the room after thanking Violet and wishing her well.

'How did you find her?' Patricia asked, her eyes red.

'Lucid and helpful,' Hollie replied. 'Thank you for letting us do that. We appreciate it.'

'I don't think she's got long left. The staff are always so positive about it, but I think we're close to the end now.'

'I'm so sorry,' Hollie answered. 'I can't imagine what it's like to find your mother, then lose her again. Do you have stepbrothers or sisters?'

'Yes, but we're estranged. When I reunited with Violet, they thought I was some kind of gold-digger, after my share of any inheritance. But believe me, officer, I got all the riches I ever needed when I finally found my birth mother again. It took me thirty-two years to find her. Can you believe that?'

'Is there anything else you would add to what Violet told us?' Jenni checked. 'Anything you can think of, please let us know. The same for Violet, too. If she remembers anything else, please get in touch.'

'I will,' Patricia promised. 'I don't know any of the people involved, really. I've heard about Mandy, Gilly and Theresa, of course, but I've never met them. I don't know anybody who was connected with the home, either.'

'Do you stay in touch with your adoptive parents?' Hollie asked.

'Yes, I love them, just like I love Violet. They were great parents. Only, I should never have been taken from my birth mum. I'm angry about it, even though it happened a long time ago. The children were victims, too. It wasn't just the girls.'

Hollie wondered if that might spur them on to seek revenge. Jenni clearly agreed with her.

'In your opinion, might one of the adopted children be

moved to kill?' Jenni asked gently.

Patricia thought about that for a while.

'I feel so angry about what happened, but I don't know who to be angry with. I'm angry on behalf of the younger version of my mum, whose life was messed up by bullying adults who thought they knew better. I'm furious she was told to be ashamed, and her own family shunned her for a simple, youthful mistake. I'm also frustrated that it was so damn difficult to trace her, and that nobody helped me with that process until I was an adult and could do it for myself. And I'm even angrier that my mum is being taken from me before we've been able to make up for all that lost time. So, yes, there's a huge rage in me.'

She swallowed. Hollie could see this was all still so raw.

'I can't speak for all the other people whose lives were ruined, but it takes a special kind of damaged person to kill. The rest of us just smoulder for the rest of our lives and push it deep down inside. I do wonder if that's what's killing Mum. Perhaps that's why cancer got her.'

Hollie reached out her hand and took Patricia's, giving it a gentle squeeze.

'I know the next few days are going to be difficult, but I hope you get to spend lots more time with your mum,' Hollie said gently. Jenni gave Patricia a hug, pulling her in close. They watched as she went back into Violet's room, and then they began the walk up the corridor to the reception area.

'That was tough,' Jenni whispered. 'What must it be like having to watch someone you love die in slow motion?'

'There are so many emotions tied up in this case,' Hollie responded, noting how the bright decoration along the corridor helped to make the hospice a happier place, despite what was happening behind each of those doors.

'What do you think about what she told us?' Jenni asked.

'It's interesting, but does it move things forward? We said

from the outset that any number of people might have good reason to harm Sister Brennan. And we still don't know for certain that it's anything to do with this group of girls—'

'It is though, isn't it, boss? It has to be.'

Hollie thought about the man with the birthmark. She wished he'd get in touch. He was at an advantage: he had her mobile number, but he wouldn't respond to her when she reached out.

'I think it is. If you asked me to place a bet right now, I'd guess that Clive Bartram is our man, and that the theft of the rope was opportunistic. Maybe he was trying to frame Gilly and her son. I know that's how it looks, but it just doesn't feel right. It seems too neat. We need to lay our hands on Clive Bartram, I know that much—'

'And we could really use a name for this Twiggy girl,' Jenni reminded her.

As the two women walked out into the reception area, ready to hand over their visitor passes, Hollie became aware of someone running up the corridor behind them. She glanced back.

'Hang on a mo. I think we must have left something.'

Patricia caught up with them but was a little out of breath.

'I'm so pleased I caught you. Mum remembered something else. She reckons it's the morphine. She's got a surname for you. The surname of the girl they called Twiggy.'

'How? Where did she see it?'

'She told me she spotted it on a file once—'

'She's quite the detective, is Violet,' Jenni remarked.

'What was the surname, Patricia? This could be really important.'

'Watson. It was Watson.'

'She's certain about that?'

'The name on the file was Watson. That's who you're looking for.'

EIGHTEEN

1975: GILLY'S STORY

Gilly kept quiet about Sister Brennan. She didn't know what to do with the information. Nobody would listen to her, anyway. Who would believe a pregnant teenage girl over the word of a nun? Instead, she kept it to herself.

The following day, she walked directly into Father Duffy who'd been in the main office for some reason; she'd been watching out for Sister Brennan at the time.

'Oh, er, Gillian, it's you—' was all he could say.

Apart from the awkward conversation in her bedroom, Gilly only had a transactional relationship with the priest through church, but he'd been there at her confirmation, and she took Communion from him every week. He seemed uncertain what to say and hesitated for a while as he stumbled for his words. His awkwardness gave her the creeps.

'I – er – I wonder if I might have a quiet word with you, Gillian?'

'Yes, Father, of course.' She wished he'd just leave her alone.

He walked across the hallway to the office, peering inside first to make sure it was vacant.

'Come in, come in.' He motioned to her, closing the door behind them. 'Please, take a seat.'

He shuffled about at the desk, moving items around, straightening them, although they didn't really need it.

'I just... er, wanted to discuss a little matter with you, now we can speak in... er, in private—'

'I don't know what was going on that day,' Gilly volunteered. She knew what this was about. She'd long ago decided to keep her mouth shut about it. Nothing good would come of making accusations about the priest.

'I don't know what you think you saw that day—'

'I didn't see anything, Father. I just wanted to give you my dad's cheque—'

She wished this could all be over, it had already caused her enough trouble.

'I was changing after the service, you just happened to catch me at – er – an awkward moment.'

Gilly felt hot and sick. The baby picked up on her tension and began to stir in her belly.

'I won't say anything, Father, I promise.'

She meant it, why couldn't he grasp that? Why did Father Duffy keep pushing this issue? She just wanted to forget it ever happened.

'Have you spoken about it to anyone?'

He was sweating, beads dripping off his forehead and onto the desk.

Her hands were clammy now. She held his stare as best she could, hoping it would give him the reassurance he seemed to crave.

'No, Father, and I swear I won't say anything.'

He studied her face; he seemed scared, but like a cornered animal which might lash out if it felt threatened. There was a darkness to him that scared her.

'That's good, Gillian, you're a good girl.'

Quietly, Gilly released a long breath at the relief of it. He seemed reassured by her promise. She meant it, too; it could only land her in deep trouble if she blabbed about it.

'Your parents can be very proud of you, Gillian, you're a very sensible girl.'

He sent her on her way.

It only took her two days to learn the ropes of the place: avoid Sister Brennan at all costs. She was a nasty, spiteful woman. Gilly had first-hand experience with that. Father Duffy seemed to be in and out of the place, mainly on pastoral and administrative duties, as far as she could tell. The other nuns weren't like Sister Brennan, but it was very clear which side of the fence they sat on when it came to the moral aspect of being pregnant out of wedlock. They'd make little digs and chide the girls. Only Sister Kay was nice. She didn't seem to care very much about the girls' pasts; she just took good care of them and was concerned about their welfare. Sister Kay had told her she could call her by her first name, but Gilly didn't want to risk the wrath of Sister Brennan. She didn't want to do anything which might make that woman come anywhere near her.

The morning Sister Kay came to collect Gilly with an ashen look on her face, it immediately put her on her guard.

'Your parents are here, Gilly. Can you put your book down and come downstairs?'

One of the few things Gilly liked about the home was the cupboard packed with second-hand baby clothes and equipment. It was also packed with books which had been donated, but which were unsorted. It was a bookworm's dream. There were titles in there that she'd never have been able to get her hands on at home. She'd learnt the trick of leaving age-appropriate books on her bedside table and hiding the unsuitable titles under the mattress. Her books were just another little secret which she kept to herself.

Gilly placed her book on her pillow and jumped off the bed. Theresa looked worried.

'What's up?' Gilly asked. 'Is something going on?'

'Mr McCready, the moral welfare officer, is here,' Sister Kay explained.

'Who's he?'

'I don't like him,' Theresa chimed in. 'They're going to do some paperwork with you. I didn't understand it. He gives me the creeps.'

'Try to put a brave face on it, Gilly, dear,' Sister Kay reassured her. 'If nothing else, it'll be nice to see your mum and dad again.'

Sister Kay led the way. Gilly gave Theresa a wave and followed her. She had an uneasy feeling deep in the pit of her stomach.

'By the way, girls, you're getting a new roommate later today. She's a young girl called Mandy. She'll be here later.'

The girls were excited at the prospect, but Sister Kay ended the chatter and urged Gilly not to hold up her parents.

They walked down the long staircase, into the hallway, and over to the office. As they made their way through the building, it seemed emptier than usual, the sound of their footsteps lost in the hollowness.

'Ah, Gilly, good morning.'

A young man stood up, a wisp of a beard struggling to sustain life on his chin. He was handsome in a plain way, his hair dark and his style of dress informal, where she might have expected a jacket and tie. He was confident, too, so grabbed Gilly's hand and shook it.

'I'm Patrick McCready. I'm a social worker and your moral welfare officer. Take a seat, Gilly.'

His voice was calm and authoritative, it sounded warm

enough, but she could see he wasn't asking her to sit down, he was telling her.

Her parents were there. Walt didn't even look up to greet her. He was tense, staring at the papers that were spread out on the table. Carmen turned to face her as she entered, began a smile, then ended it before it had the chance to blossom. Father Duffy was there, too. Gilly and her family were separated from Patrick McCready and Father Duffy by a solid, dark-wood desk. There was a dominating black phone on the corner of the desk and a filing cabinet at the back of the room. A cross hung on the wall, just behind Patrick McCready's head.

'So, welcome everybody,' McCready began as he settled into his chair. Gilly and her family were seated on the uncomfortable plastic chairs that the girls sat on in the small dining room. They'd been moved through for this meeting.

'How are you settling in, Gilly?' McCready asked.

'Fine, thanks,' she said quietly.

Gilly was still trying to figure out what was going on here. It felt like the time she'd been cornered in the girls' toilet block at school and pounced on by a group of older girls. She couldn't put her finger on it, but that's what this meeting reminded her of: a set-up.

'Good, good. So, I've invited your mum and dad over – and Father Duffy – because there are just a couple of things we need to take care of before you have your baby. There's nothing to worry about. We've done all the hard work already.'

This was news to Gilly. She thought she'd have the baby and spend a few weeks recovering at the home. She hadn't figured out what would happen after that. She assumed she'd go back with her parents and look after the baby there. She waited for the social worker to explain.

'As the social worker assigned to your case, I'm here to take care of your wellbeing. Do you understand what that means, Gilly?'

She said nothing.

'Answer Mr McCready, Gilly. Don't be rude.'

It was the first thing her father said.

'Yes.'

'Because you're having this baby, and there's no father—'

'There is a father!' Gilly interjected.

'Shh, Gilly,' her father snapped. 'Just listen. We don't need to know what you think. You've caused enough trouble as it is.'

For a moment Gilly thought Carmen was going to move her hand over slightly to touch her, but she stopped short.

'Because the baby will be born out of wedlock, I'm also in charge of overseeing your moral welfare—'

'We're very disappointed in you,' Father Duffy chimed in. 'You've let us all down, Gilly. Do you understand how hard this is for your parents? You've caused a lot of shame, and this is going to cause great financial hardship for them. It's a very difficult situation.'

Father Duffy was delivering a script, but Gilly could tell he was doing his best to soften it; perhaps he was scared she'd reveal his secret.

It didn't feel so difficult for Gilly. She was angry with Eric, of course she was. She'd thought what they had was real. But it wasn't so bad. She could have the baby; she'd figure it out somehow. She had a bed of her own, and the church had a cupboard stuffed with charitable donations, so she was struggling to understand what the problem was. And, despite everything everybody told her, she felt no shame. What she'd done with Eric was fun. She'd got pregnant, and that wouldn't have been her first choice of outcomes, yet it didn't feel like the end of the world to her. She liked the idea of looking after a baby.

'You've made things very tricky, Gilly,' Walt added. 'This has been such an embarrassment for your mother and me. We're having to lie to people at church and to Helen's mum, who telephoned today. And we found out you haven't been staying at her house, either. Can you imagine how we feel about all that deception? You've brought so much shame on our family.'

Gilly had never realised it before, but the anger that'd burst out when her father drove around to Eric's house and punched him on the stairs was always just below the surface. She'd always thought he was tense and withdrawn, but she saw now that it was all suppressed anger. Walt went through life holding in his rage. She wondered what was fuelling it. He had a decent life, and it seemed simple enough to her.

'So, you see, Gilly,' McCready continued, 'we have to take certain measures to ensure the ongoing physical and moral welfare of you and the baby. We've just got some paperwork you need to sign, and that will all be taken care of for you. You can have your child safe in the knowledge that there's nothing to worry about.'

'What will happen after the baby is born?' Gilly asked. 'Will I go back home?'

'There's a lot to think about,' Father Duffy picked up. 'Let's just take it one step at a time. There's plenty of time to discuss that. For now, we have to take care of the paperwork.'

McCready pushed a document forward on the table. It was stapled in the corner and folded back so only the signature area was visible. Her parents had already signed and dated the document.

'What is this?' she asked.

'This is just a document confirming that the baby will be taken care of in a suitable, moral manner—' Father Duffy answered.

'There's a lot of legal language in it,' McCready added. 'It's very difficult to understand. But as Father Duffy says, it means the best for you and your baby.'

'Just sign the bloody thing, Gilly,' Walt seethed. 'I apologise for swearing, Father.'

Carmen's hand moved up to her face, and she wiped something away from her eye.

'Compose yourself, Carmen, for God's sake,' Walt whispered.

McCready offered Gilly a pen.

'This will help both you and your family,' Father Duffy said. 'This is the right thing for you to do, Gilly.'

She held the pen over the typed line that required her signature. She moved her spare hand to turn over the document, but Walt stopped her.

'Don't cause even more fuss, Gilly. Mr McCready and Father Duffy are busy and important men. They don't have time for all your childish nonsense. Get on with it, then me and your mother can be on our way.'

Gilly placed the pen on the paper and then removed it once again. She'd left a dot of ink where she was expected to sign. She experienced a sudden pang of anxiety, not entirely certain what they thought was best for her child but reassured that they appeared to have her interests at heart. She placed her hand on her belly, thinking of the baby inside her waiting to come out, and wanting what was best for her child.

She decided at that moment to trust the adults in her life. Although it felt like they were ganging up on her, these people were supposed to have her best interests at heart. She'd known Father Duffy since she was a toddler; he'd known her since she was born. She could see that Walt and Carmen were angry, but they were her mum and dad; they'd taken care of her all her life. She didn't really understand what Mr McCready did, but he used words like *welfare* for both her and her baby. Gilly placed the pen back on the paper and signed. And when Mr McCready passed over two more documents, both of which had already been signed by everybody else in the room, she added her signature to both of them, too.

NINETEEN

'Maccy D's?' Jenni suggested.

'I think I need it,' Hollie replied. 'I feel completely drained after that.'

They got back into the car. Jenni found the nearest drive-through, and they sat in the car park working their way through their hot drinks and burgers as they discussed the visit.

'How long do you think she'll live?' Jenni asked.

'Not long now. It's horrible, isn't it? What must it be like to have to go into a hospice? You know you're never coming out. Maybe you've resigned yourself to it by then.'

'When I die, I want to go fast. And I don't want to have time to think about it. Oh, and preferably when I'm over one hundred years old.'

'You can say that again!' Hollie agreed. 'Here's to a long life.'

They clinked their cardboard coffee containers like they were made from the finest crystal glass.

'Where does this surname leave us, ma'am? It's little use, isn't it?'

'If she married, then it's not much help at the moment. At least it's a start.'

Hollie finished her mouthful of food and dialled the office. DS Patel was at her desk and picked up.

'I'm pleased you called, boss. I've got an update for you—'

'Please tell me we have Clive Bartram in custody, and he's confessed to everything.'

'Sorry, boss, still no sign of Bartram—'

'Is DS Anderson on the case?'

'We've thrown everything we've got at it, boss. It's like whack-a-mole; until he shows his face, we can't clobber him.'

'Okay, let me know the moment we have him. Would you speak to DCI Osmond and the press team about releasing a photo of him to the press and via our social channels. It's time we flushed him out.'

Hollie waited while DS Patel added that to her list. She thought about Mandy and considered how horrified she might be to see pictures of her son plastered across the media channels. It couldn't be helped, Clive had brought this upon himself, and Mandy had been obstructive and unhelpful to say the least.

'What news did you want to share with me?'

'It's the photographer from Beverley, the guy whose name was on the photo sticker.'

'Go on. This is excellent timing. I was just calling for a progress check on that,' Hollie said.

'It's good news and bad news. The good news is he doesn't have the shop anymore, but he does still work locally as a photographer.'

'That's a start,' Hollie replied, encouraging her to continue.

'The bad news is he's on holiday in Spain and won't be back for two days.'

'Can we reach him?'

'That's the final bit of bad news. He's photographing wild

birds in some remote spot in Andalusia. There's no phone signal.'

'Okay, diary it and let's get over there ASAP when he's back. We've got a surname for the girl in the David Lister photo. Watson. But that will be her maiden name, of course. I want the photographer to cross-reference it if he has a first name for us. Maybe there's someone who can access his records. Keep trying his mobile number. You never know, he might come in range. It could save us waiting two days for him.'

'Will do, ma'am.'

'What about the home? Did we get anything there?'

'DC Philpot is picking up copies of the full newspaper pages from the *Hull Daily Mail* as I speak. There were finger-prints in the room, but nothing we have on file. So, whoever was in there doesn't have a Humberside Police record, or they were cautious enough to be wearing gloves. We're casting the net further afield to see if they have form elsewhere.'

'Anything DNA related?'

'Yes, they've got samples, and they're off to the lab. But if the fingerprints don't come up—'

'Yes, yes, I know, it's unlikely that the DNA will match anything on file. But it might be useful later, so let's go belt and braces on this one. Anything else I need to know, DS Patel?'

'Just that Father Duffy is getting discharged today. They're going to care for him at the convent rather than at his flat. I hope this level of service will be on offer by the police when I'm his age.'

Hollie laughed.

'I will not be cooking your dinners and running your baths when you're in your nineties, DS Patel, so banish that thought from your head right now.'

They ended the call, and Hollie brought Jenni up to date with the latest updates. They finished their food and drove back to Hull. Hollie dropped off the pool car keys and checked in with the team once again, but they were in a holding position. Clive Bartram was next on her list. Uniform was on the lookout for him. They'd placed a watch on the derelict girls' home and Mandy's house, so it was a case of wait-and-see. If they were lucky, Bartram would come in overnight, and she'd land a big, juicy catch in time for the morning briefing. If not, she had to brace herself for the brass on her back again.

It was half past six by the time she left the office, and the logbook was fully up to date. It could be so hard dragging herself away, but she knew she had to fight this. Police cases didn't operate on a convenient nine-to-five rotation. They were 24/7 by their very nature. It could be a wrench to go home, even though home was where she wanted to be. She informed DS Anderson that she'd be picking her kids up from the station the next day and asked that he should lead the briefing if she was delayed. It was all sorted now; she was seeing the children very soon. She couldn't wait. She could almost hear their laughter and jokes already, an echo which made her long for their presence. She craved the simple day-to-day stuff, meals, companionship, chatter, and fun activities. They nourished her life and made her live her days in technicolour; she'd missed them terribly.

Hollie's stomach was still full after the fast food in Goole, so she decided she needed to grab only a snack while she was in town. She'd arranged to meet Jenni in the Banks Harbour, along with her new friends from the flats. As she locked up her car, she was relieved to hear that the drummer was giving it a break. She hoped her note had done the job. Only a prick would carry on making a racket like that if it was disturbing children.

For the first time in weeks, her mind shut off from the job, and she allowed herself to get excited about the children's impending visit. She might even take Friday off if Clive

Bartram got charged. She hoped they would locate him, even if that would be sad news for Mandy Tyson.

It felt good to roll out the red carpet and dig out a nice dress from her stacked boxes. It took her a while to find one that hadn't creased, but she eventually succeeded, putting on some tights, the tiniest touch of make-up, and the shoes she'd been wearing all day at work due to soaking her more comfortable pair. She looked at herself in the bathroom mirror. Was this to be her new life? Would she now be thrust back into the world of singles, relying on others for an excuse to get out of the house? She felt too old to be out boozing in town and too young to have given up all hope, spending the remainder of her evenings propped up in front of the TV. She hoped Léon would eventually see sense. But could she forgive him or trust him again after his affair with Veronique? There had been no particular catalyst to their marital problems, it was just life getting in the way, draining the romance and excitement out of everything. They could have fixed that if they'd spoken more and been honest with each other. Instead, his answer was a younger woman, that tired old cliché.

She would send herself crazy if she kept thinking like that. Hollie resolved to shut out all thoughts of marital breakdown for the night. She had a night ahead with a nice couple who seemed friendly and fun. Jenni was coming, too, so if the couple turned out to be Fred and Rosemary West, she had a get-out-of-jail-free card. The kids were arriving first thing, and although there were a-million-and-one things she might have been doing to progress the case, Jenni had sensed her guilt and reluctance and persuaded her to give herself a night off. She deserved this night out and she'd be all the better a detective for a short break.

Hollie made one more check in the mirror then wandered around the living room, awaiting a knock at the door from the couple upstairs. She heard a shuffle in the corridor outside and walked over to the entrance, not wanting to appear too desperate by opening it before they knocked. She heard the main door to the hallway slamming and wondered for a moment if she'd got the arrangements wrong. Looking down, she saw she'd missed a piece of paper that had been stuck under the door; there was only a corner to indicate that anything was there at all. She stooped and teased it out from underneath the door. It was a single sheet of notepaper, folded into quarters. She unfolded it, recognising it as the piece of paper she'd slipped under the drummer's flat door when she and Jenni had come to drop off her food shopping.

There were her own words:

Please refrain from drumming for the next three days. I have young children staying in the flat below you. Thank you. Hollie, Flat 2.

Written in red pen directly below was the drummer's reply:

Screw you! Lenny, Flat 5.

TWENTY

'Well, screw you, too, Lenny!' Hollie cursed under her breath. If she hadn't already heard the guy leaving the flats, she'd have given him a piece of her mind. Before she could get too worked up, there was a tap at the door. Still holding the note, she went to check who was there.

'Hi, are you ready to sample the heady delights of Beverley Road?'

Hollie smiled. 'You know we haven't introduced ourselves yet. I'm Hollie. Hollie Turner.'

'Hey, Hollie. I'm Maxine and this is Jed. Pleased to meet you.'

'I'm entirely in your hands. My work colleague, Jenni, is waiting for us at the Banks Harbour, so I'll need to text her if we're diverting our course.'

'No, the Banks Harbour is fine. It's karaoke night tonight, that's always fun.'

It was a reasonable walking distance to the pub, so it gave Hollie time to get to know her neighbours as they took a turn away from Pearson Park and out onto Beverley Road, one of the main arterial routes through the city centre. It was lined on either side by shops and houses that were too big for single families, so had consequently been converted into flats. The municipal baths was still there, which Hollie recalled from her time in the city during the nineties, but in the main, it could have been any inner-city road to her, with shops coming and going and graffiti gradually spreading like a slow incubating rash.

The Banks Harbour was just ahead of them, and Hollie could see Jenni sitting in a window seat. She gave her a wave to catch her attention.

Jenni stood up to greet them as they walked in. They made their introductions, and Hollie got the first round in. As she waited for the drinks to arrive, she glanced around the pub. It was a pleasant place and seemed like it attracted a more mature clientele. They served food, too, which was always useful. As Maxine had suggested, there was evidence of a karaoke night about to begin.

'So, how's the case going?' Maxine asked as Hollie placed the drinks on the table. Everyone was on pints.

'We can't discuss the specific details,' Hollie reminded her, 'but we're always receptive to any information which might be useful.'

'Funny you should say that.' Maxine smiled. 'There's a lady who comes into our Co-op. She was talking about it the other day in the cafe. She reckoned she once knew a girl who'd been to that church home they're talking about on the news, the one for the pregnant girls. She was at her school. The kids made her life hell after they knew she'd been there. She was only fourteen at the time, too. She ended up committing suicide.'

'Oh no, really?' Jenni asked. 'I can't believe we're living in a world where something that's no big deal was made such a fuss of. It's like an alien world to my generation. At my school, a girl had her baby at fifteen, and she was able to leave during an exam to nurse it. There was no shame there at all.'

Jenni took a sip of her pint. 'We were all having sex at that age, anyway. She was just unlucky enough to get caught out. She didn't want to have an abortion, so she kept the baby. The kid's at secondary school now, and she's studying for a degree. It didn't mess up her life at all. It simply changed the order of events.'

Hollie kept quiet. She wasn't ready to tell the story about Isabella just yet.

There were several taps on a microphone and a voice came over a loudspeaker.

'Ladies and gentlemen, the karaoke evening is open. If you'd like to sign up for a song, we'd love to hear you giving it your all. To get things underway, here's Mavis with a firm favourite. Please give Mavis a round of applause for her rendition of Celine Dion's "My Heart Will Go On".'

'Have you ever done karaoke?' Jenni asked nobody in particular.

'Why do you think we're here?' Maxine answered. 'Jed and I specialise in couples' songs. We like classic stuff. Sonny and Cher, Dollar, Dolly Parton and Kenny Rogers. If it's sung by a couple, we do it.'

'Brilliant!' Jenni exclaimed, clapping her hands with joy. 'What about you, ma'am – boss?'

'Call me Hollie at social events, please. I've never done it before. I can't even sing.'

'The night is still young,' Jed teased her.

It was an easy evening, and just what Hollie needed. Maxine and Jed were closer to Jenni's age than her own, but it was refreshing to be involved in a young person's conversation rather than bogged down by talk of mortgage rates, career progression and kids. So much so that when it came time for the next round, she decided to let Jenni buy her a second pint, despite having promised herself the next drink would be a Coke. Besides, it coincided with Maxine and Jed's first performance of the evening, and she could not possibly miss their rendition of 'Islands in the Stream' as she had a soft spot for country music. She helped Jenni over from the bar with the drinks, while Jed and Maxine gave the signal to start the backing track for their song.

'Those two are good fun,' Jenni shouted over the music. 'Look at them go.'

They looked like they'd worked on cruise ships, they played to the audience so well. Their song went down a storm. There was a huge round of applause as the backing track faded out and they both gave a bow. Maxine and Jed rejoined them at the table.

When she'd left her flat that night, Hollie had no intention of drinking more than a pint. She wasn't a drinker as a rule, but she'd made an exception and now, three pints later, she didn't particularly care. Jed and Maxine were amazing company, and she hadn't laughed as much in a long time. Jenni, too, was hilarious away from the formality of the office environment and all thoughts of rank, responsibility and respectability were soon forgotten.

Egged on by Jed and Maxine, and fuelled by drink, the two detectives stepped up to the front and delivered their karaoke version of 'It Takes Two', which Hollie vaguely recollected had been performed by Rod Stewart and Tina Turner.

What followed was not a pretty sight, but it amused the crowd well enough and energized Hollie sufficiently to agree to move on to The Welly nightclub, which was just across the street.

After a dance, the group of four revellers found a seat and supped their drinks, which Jed had kindly ordered at the bar.

'Hey, aren't you that copper from the TV?' came a voice from their side. It was an older woman, possibly in her sixties, done up for a night on the town.

Hollie squirmed in her seat for a moment.

'Hey, you're famous!' Jed exclaimed.

'Yes, that's me,' Hollie answered, reluctant. Here was her work intruding on a good night out.

'I thought so. I saw you in the *Hull Daily Mail*. You look a lot less stern in your glad rags.'

Hollie didn't know how to take that, but the woman seemed like she was getting in the flow.

'Mind if I join you?' she asked, pulling up a seat.

Hollie and Jenni shuffled to one side to make some space.

'I'm really pleased to see you actually, as I wouldn't know who to say this to,' she began, settling herself in.

Hollie glanced at Jenni, who returned it with a small smile.

'I was one of the girls who went to that church home—'

The small smile on Jenni's face immediately disappeared and her brow furrowed. Maxine clapped her hands in glee.

'You should see the look on your faces.' She laughed. 'I've never seen two people sober up faster.'

'Go on,' Hollie said, taking two attempts at the words because she was struggling to make her mouth operate properly.

'What year?' Jenni asked.

'In 1976,' the woman replied. 'I was seventeen. I remember that nun, the one who got killed. She was a bitch to the girls. I don't know what her problem was. The three of them had it stitched up between them. The priest, the nun and that social worker.'

Hollie and Jenni exchanged a glance. They weren't so drunk that they couldn't spot an interesting contact when they saw one.

'Stitched up? What do you mean by that?'

'They were colluding, if you ask me. They were like a pack, the three of them. Us girls were their prey—'

'Was anything inappropriate going on?' Jenni interrupted.

'You mean sexually?'

Jenni nodded.

'Other than the fact we'd all got pregnant out of wedlock,

no, nothing weird in the home. There was no sexual abuse or anything like that, if that's what you're suggesting. Though that social worker always gave me the creeps. But he never did anything as far as I know.'

She paused for a moment, then seemed to make the decision to add something extra.

'It dawned on me when I was older that he could have been getting the babies adopted out on demand. You know, for wealthy clients. But I don't have any evidence of that, it's just from what I observed. A girl I knew there said something to me once.'

'Was your child adopted?' Hollie asked.

'No. She was supposed to be, but I managed to keep her. It split up my mum and dad, mind you. My dad was so ashamed of me. He wouldn't hear of me keeping the baby. But my mum fought for me to keep it. She told me not to sign the papers and she stood up to my dad. He left her in the end; he couldn't bear the embarrassment of it. He moved out of the family house, and I moved back in, with my mum and the baby, and we loved it. I carried on at school, my mum looked after my daughter, and we cherished every minute of it. I'd even go as far as to say that it was the best thing that ever happened to me. I'm out with my girl tonight. It's lovely later in life; there's not much difference in our ages.' She pointed to her left where a woman in her forties was standing, conspiratorially viewing something on a smartphone.

'Joy, come over here,' the woman shouted.

Her daughter walked up to the small group and greeted them.

'What were you looking at on that phone?' her mother asked.

'Oh, nothing much,' Joy replied. 'It's just that the police officer here is famous already. There's a video doing the rounds of the city.'

'Let me look,' Hollie demanded, more assertive than she would have liked.

'Okay, but don't shoot the messenger,' Joy warned.

Hollie knew it was going to be bad news the moment the tinny sound of 'It Takes Two' started playing from the speakers. Joy turned the phone around so that she could see the video, but Hollie knew what it was already. Somebody had recognised her from her media appearance and decided to film her and Jenni's performance at the Banks Harbour. It had gone viral via Hull's nightlife. But it was the caption that concerned her the most.

So this is what Hull cops do when they're supposed to be investigating murders!!!

She took a slow breath and sat up straighter. The repercussions of the video could wait. For now, she needed more information about the social worker.

TWENTY-ONE

1975: GILLY'S STORY

Gilly couldn't shake the feeling that there'd been something else going on in that room that she couldn't put her finger on, but with the paperwork signed, everybody seemed a lot happier. Walt relaxed in his chair and Carmen let him take her hand and give it a squeeze with more visible affection than Gilly had seen in months. Father Duffy even managed a smile, which was a very rare event. Gilly picked up on the mood and, in turn, felt more at ease. It had got tense in there for a while, but now the atmosphere had completely changed.

'What are your plans for after the baby's birth?' McCready asked. Gilly wasn't sure who that was aimed at, so ventured an answer.

'I'll come home, look after the baby, and—'

'Sorry, Gilly, I was asking your parents,' McCready interrupted.

'Oh. Sorry.'

'Gilly can stay with Carmen's sister for a short while—'

It was Gilly's turn to cut off Walt this time. 'I'm not coming home?'

'You'll need a period of recovery,' Father Duffy said. 'It's an exhausting experience having a baby.'

Gilly's impulse was to ask him why she couldn't go home to recover, but she kept her mouth shut. She preferred it when everybody was getting along, and they probably knew better than she did about these things anyway.

'She lives in York, so we'll drive Gilly up there and she can have some time to... get used to her new situation.'

'When will I come home?' Gilly asked.

'When the time is right,' McCready answered, looking at Walt and Carmen and giving a small nod in search of their agreement.

'Yes,' Carmen added. 'You can come back when the time is right. Your body will need time to adjust after the birth.'

'So, that's all sorted then,' McCready announced, pulling the papers together and pushing them into a file. 'Thank you, Gilly.'

She was being dismissed, and she recalled that technique from school. Carmen and Walt began to move, too, but McCready stopped them.

'Just a couple of I's to dot and T's to cross,' he said, motioning that they should sit down. They returned to their seated positions.

Gilly searched the faces in the room and concluded that the last instruction didn't apply to her. She walked over to the door.

'Not long now, Gilly, eh?' McCready said to her as her hand touched the door handle.

'No, Mr McCready. I'm quite looking forward to it. I can't wait to see my baby.'

He didn't meet her eyes, so she exited the room, closing the door behind her. Sister Kay had been lurking in readiness and rushed over to her. She wrapped her arms around Gilly and gave her a hug.

'Was everything all right?' she asked.

'I think so,' Gilly replied, grateful for the concern. 'I don't like that McCready guy. He's weird. I'm going to call him Mr McCreepy from now on.'

Sister Kay giggled, as if laughter was forbidden and she'd be scolded for even venturing to make such a joyful sound.

'You're so naughty, Gilly. Don't let Sister Brennan hear you say that, please.'

Gilly accepted a second hug and returned to her room.

Theresa was awaiting her return, eager to hear what had happened. She, too, liked the re-christening of McCready and they vowed to refer to him with his new name from that point onward.

'I'm going down to the donations cupboard to sort out some things for the baby,' Theresa said. 'Are you coming?'

Gilly was mindful that she needed to start putting bits aside, so agreed. The two girls headed downstairs. There was no sign of Sister Brennan, so they continued to the hallway. It was more of a storeroom than a cupboard and even had a dedicated light inside, which was operated by a switch on the hall side of the door. Gilly turned it on and called over to Sister Kay to let her know what they were doing. The two girls entered the cupboard.

'Where are you staying after your baby is born?' Gilly asked. It seemed strange to banish her to York with a newborn baby. She'd assumed her mother would want to get involved with the new arrival.

'I'm going home, but we live on a farm, so my dad and mum aren't worried about the neighbours.'

'You think they'd be used to births by now,' Gilly said. 'What's a human baby among all those lambs, calves and foals? You'd think the more the merrier.'

'Well,' Theresa began earnestly, 'Dad's a tenant farmer, and the landowner is a bit religious. He's worried it might cause problems, I think. If he lost the farm, I'm not sure what he'd do.'

The girls started pulling out boxes and rifling through the clothes.

'Are you scared?' Theresa asked.

'What of? Having the baby?'

'Yes. Does it frighten you?'

Gilly paused and thought about it.

'I wish we had someone to talk to about it. I don't really know what happens. I'm worried that it will hurt. What about you?'

'The same. Nobody tells us anything. If you weren't here, I think I'd be crying myself to sleep every night.'

Gilly gave her a hug and returned to the boxes.

'Look at all this stuff,' Gilly remarked. 'Everybody might call us whores, but the people of Hull don't seem to care too much. A lot of this equipment is new. Look at that carrycot.'

It was like Christmas Day; the cupboard had just been replenished with new donations, and Gilly felt like she'd found buried treasure. Through the door, she heard the voices of her parents as they left the office.

'Are you going to say goodbye?' Theresa asked, holding up a yellow Babygro with a teddy bear logo across the chest.

'I don't think so,' Gilly said after a while. 'They can come and find me if they want to speak to me. I don't think they very much care. They came to see Mr McCreepy and Father Fluffy. I was just there to sign the paperwork. I think it reminds them of the shame I've brought on the family every time they see me. That's a lovely Babygro, by the way.'

They worked in silence, excavating the boxes like they were gold-diggers who'd just struck a new seam. Eventually, Gilly came across a box of books.

'Oh look, new supplies!'

'It says they're headed to the tip.' Theresa pointed to a scribble on the side of the box made in black marker pen.

'Who cares?' Gilly scoffed. 'If there's anything decent in here to read, I'm putting it aside.'

She raked through the assortment and then held up a book.

'Look, they've got Mills and Boon in here. My mum reads these at home, but I can never get my hands on them. She hides them around the house. I think they're quite naughty in places. She probably uses them as a substitute for my dad.'

Without warning, they were plunged into darkness. The girls called out to alert whoever it was who'd switched off the light that they were in there. The door opened slowly, and the silhouette of a nun appeared. It was Sister Brennan.

'What are you both doing in here?' she shouted at them. 'Put that box back. You can read what it says, can't you?'

Gilly placed the box back where she'd found it. She was frightened now. Sister Brennan had got them cornered in there.

'We're just sorting out some bits for the babies—' Theresa began.

Sister Brennan looked over her shoulder, switched the light back on, then entered the cupboard, letting the door close behind her.

'These clothes would be better going to married mothers, not a couple of harlots who couldn't keep their legs together.'

Theresa tensed; Gilly knew how much she hated this behaviour. Sister Brennan's face was right up close to Theresa's.

'The people who donated them seemed happy enough to let us have them,' Gilly said bravely, knowing she was playing with fire, but she wanted to divert Sister Brennan from her friend.

'You shut your slutty little mouth!' Sister Brennan scolded her.

Sister Brennan grabbed at Theresa's arm, spinning her around and pulling her towards the door.

'Hey, don't do that. You leave her alone,' Gilly retorted through her tears.

'Get out of here and go to your room, both of you,' Sister Brennan continued, undeterred.

'Just remember, I know things about Father Duffy—'

Gilly had never seen the nun move so fast. Sister Brennan released Theresa's arm and marched directly over to her, slapping her across the face. She froze on the spot; she'd never been struck like that in her life. The baby was doing acrobatics in her stomach. She was on the verge of tears but did not want this woman to see her in a moment of weakness.

Sister Brennan pushed her hand against Gilly's neck, forcing her against the shelves. Gilly was crying now, she'd never seen anything like this, and Theresa was trying to pull the nun away.

'You keep your filthy mouth shut, you whore,' Sister Brennan whispered to her, up close. 'Come on, you,' she continued, grasping Theresa once again. Theresa looked terrified. She was crying and scared. It took Gilly a moment to recover herself; she still couldn't believe what had just happened. Sister Brennan opened the cupboard door and pushed Theresa through it, shoving her in her stomach to force her along.

'You can't do that!' Gilly shouted, running towards the door to come to her friend's defence. She spotted a girl she hadn't seen before hovering by the staircase. She was carrying a hot-water bottle. She'd seen something was going on and seemed undecided about whether to loiter or continue on her way.

As Gilly neared the door, Sister Brennan slammed it shut on her. She tugged at the door handle, but it would not move. Sister Brennan must have been holding onto it.

'You can stay in there until you learn some manners,' came the nun's voice, lowered, she assumed, so it wouldn't draw attention to what had been going on. Seconds later, she heard a key in the door. The store cupboard was always open during the day, and now she was being punished there. The light went off and Gilly was plunged into darkness. She was still breathing fast, adrenaline pumping furiously at the altercation. The baby had picked up on it and was going crazy in her belly.

Gilly pulled out a box and sat on it. She saw a pair of feet draw up outside, their outline visible through the crack under the door. Whoever it was hesitated for a moment, and then the light went on. The feet scurried away. The person on the other side seemed nervous about getting caught. But at that moment, wretched and alone, Gilly saw she had another friend in that place, an ally who knew what was going on, along with Theresa. They'd seen what had happened and, like her, it would be difficult to forget.

TWENTY-TWO

It took Hollie a few minutes to figure out where she was. For a moment, she reckoned she'd woken up in the family home in Lancaster. But as her eyes traced the edges of the ornate coving, she realised this was her flat in Hull. Her mouth was dry, and her head was pounding. The curtains hadn't been drawn, but being winter, it was still half-dark outside. She moved her leg and felt something – or someone – in the bed beside her. She pushed gently against the object. It was a someone. They stirred in the bed at her side.

Hollie did her best to recall the last moments of the previous night. She remembered the karaoke and The Welly. The music was great.

After that, she had vague memories of stumbling along Beverley Road with Jenni, Jed and Maxine. So who was in the bed sleeping next to her? She took in a deep breath and slowly turned over, not wanting to disturb whoever it was. Slowly, the figure came into view. It was Jenni and she was awake.

The two women shuffled in the bed, so they were able to face each other. Jenni was fully clothed, like she'd rolled into bed as she'd come in from the street. Hollie realised she was still dressed, too; they must have come in and passed out on the bed.

'I feel terrible,' Jenni said. 'We really should have known better.'

'I'm getting far too old for this,' Hollie agreed. Her head was throbbing.

'What's the time?' Jenni asked urgently. She was right. They were chatting as if it was a lazy Sunday morning. It definitely was not; it was a workday.

Hollie leant over to her bedside table to search for her phone.

'Thanks for letting me stay last night,' Jenni said as Hollie fumbled around. 'Even in your inebriated state, you insisted I didn't walk home on my own. I appreciate it.'

Hollie found her phone next to her discarded shoes.

'Oh, shit!'

'What?' Jenni asked, sitting up in bed at the urgency of Hollie's voice.

'The kids. I've got to pick the kids up at the station.'

'Are you late?'

'By ten minutes. Shit, shit, shit!'

Hollie leapt out of bed and hunted for a change of clothing she could put on quickly. She pulled the previous day's work trousers out of the linen basket and grabbed a top from the wardrobe.

'I'm going to have to dash,' Hollie said, throwing her spare house key onto the bed. 'Help yourself to anything in the kitchen and feel free to take a shower. I'll see you at work!'

'No problem. Good luck!'

'Oh, and if you can make the bedroom look like a whirlwind didn't just hit it, I'd be grateful. The kids won't notice, but my adult house guest will!'

Hollie found her car keys, picked up her work bag, and left the flat.

. . .

Within ten minutes, she was parked up at the rear of the railway station and dashing toward the platform entrance, checking her phone messages along the way.

> The train departed fine, the kids were sleepy, but we left Lancaster on time! Phoebe x

That was a start. If she was lucky, the train would hit a minor hold-up and be delayed by a short time. That way, it would give the appearance of everything being normal, just the way it would need to be as far as Léon was concerned.

> Made our train changes okay. The kids had a Maccy D's breakfast, so v. happy. We'll be there on time. Phoebe x

For once, Hollie wished that the British rail service had done what it usually did and screwed up the journey, just a bit. Instead, it had decided to display exceptional customer service on the very day she didn't want it to. A sense of panic began to overwhelm her, and Hollie felt her chest tighten. She scanned the concourse, praying that she'd see Phoebe and the children waiting there. It didn't help that her head was still pounding, and her mouth felt like she'd been gargling on sand all night. She was starving, too, and in desperate need of something to steady her stomach. What the hell was she thinking, going for a drink at the pub like that? And damn Jed and Maxine for being so much fun and leading her astray. Jenni was to blame as well; they'd had such a laugh together.

Hollie spotted a member of the station staff from their uniform and rushed up to them.

'Is the Manchester train in yet?' she checked.

'A quarter of an hour ago,' the man replied.

'Which platform?'

He pointed, and she followed his lead.

'Is there an official meeting point at this station?' It'd been so long since Hollie had been in this station that she couldn't remember.

'Most people meet in the covered area outside,' he continued.

'Thank you.'

Hollie rushed off towards the platform, looking around her all the time as she walked. There was no train waiting there and just a couple of passengers lurking for whatever was due on the opposite platform. She checked her phone again. Why wouldn't Phoebe leave a message if she was waiting somewhere? She cursed that she'd not thought far enough ahead to come up with a backup plan.

She walked back onto the concourse, all the time glancing around her, willing Phoebe to be there with the children. She followed the flow of travellers and found the outside area that the station attendant had mentioned. There was a woman there with two youngsters, but it wasn't Phoebe. Hollie felt her legs weaken. She needed food.

She checked her phone one more time, ensuring there was a signal. Nothing. What the hell was Phoebe up to? Surely, she'd call if Hollie wasn't there to meet them. She rang Phoebe's phone, but it went to voicemail.

'Please call me when you get this, Phoebe. Where are you all?'

Then she had an idea. She texted Phoebe's mum, Caitlen.

> Hi, sorry to bother you. Have you heard from Phoebe? They've arrived but I can't find them. Don't tell Léon!!! Thanks, Hollie

There was a coffee outlet across the road. Hollie had to eat and drink; she'd be useless if she didn't find food. She ordered a fresh orange juice, a large black coffee and a breakfast roll, then walked back over to the covered area and tucked in. As she swigged her orange juice, she checked her phone again. Caitlen had got back to her already.

> Sorry, nothing from Phoebe. I dropped them off at Lancaster and they set off on time. PS Mum's the word with Léon :-) PPS Unfit mother :-) :-)

Hollie now understood how flowers feel when they get a drop of rain after a drought. The sensation of cold orange juice flowing through her mouth was bliss. The feeling of food filling her belly was just as good, and her energy was coming back fast as she sat on the bench. She checked her phone for the umpteenth time. She had a decision to make: hang around in search of the kids, or make it back to the station in time to host the morning briefing? All she wanted to do was go back to bed for an hour.

Hollie considered the crisis management training she'd received as she moved up the policing ranks. This seemed like a good time to apply some of its principles. She worked through the situation. Phoebe was a responsible adult and in charge of her kids. They were safe, even though they were lost, and she couldn't contact them. She had to assume there was a reason why Phoebe wasn't messaging her. She knew where Hollie worked. She knew Caitlen could get in touch if Phoebe could not. It would work itself out. She just had to pray Phoebe didn't check in with Léon.

Hollie opted for the morning briefing. She wanted to know where they were up to with Clive Bartram. She rushed back to her car, made sure all alerts were activated on her phone, and drove back to the office. She called DS Patel on her way over, to let them know she'd be ten minutes late. The traffic played ball, and she rushed into the briefing room, fifteen minutes after the meeting should have started. Everybody was gathered there, waiting for her. But as she entered the room, a familiar sound greeted her as it was played on a smartphone. Whoever it was switched it off the moment they'd seen her enter the room. It was Rod Stewart and Tina Turner singing 'It Takes Two'.

TWENTY-THREE

There was something vaguely familiar about that song, but the fog in Hollie's mind wouldn't clear enough for her to recall what it was. Several of the officers in the briefing room had their heads together; it looked like something funny was doing the rounds on mobile phones.

'You might want to sit this one out,' DS Anderson suggested, lowering his voice to speak.

'I don't think so. I'll take the briefing,' Hollie replied huffily.

'No, I mean I've been asked to take the briefing. Osmond wants to see you and I don't think it's "Puppy Love".'

'What's up?'

'You really don't know?'

Hollie was at a loss. Something was going on though, she could feel it in the air. She wished her head would clear; her mind felt like a car engine that wouldn't fire on a cold morning.

DS Anderson held up his phone and started playing the video from her performance at the Banks Harbour.

Hollie screwed up her face in a wince. Now she remembered. She reached out to snatch the phone from his hands to make it stop, but he was too fast for her.

'Turn it off, DS Anderson. That's an order, by the way.'

It was all coming back to her: the video, that bloody video. She'd gone completely against type by ordering another pint of lager when the enormity of it had sunk in. It could be a career-ender.

'What are we going to do about it?' she'd drunkenly asked Jenni, as if their ranks were reversed.

She'd never gone viral before. From the commotion at The Welly, it seemed like everybody there had got their hands on it.

'Deal with it when you come to it,' Jenni had slurred, as if she were some wise sage dispensing wisdom. 'If you're lucky, it'll pass by everybody in the office. Coppers aren't known for being the greatest clubbers in the city.'

'I hope you're right,' Hollie replied. She suspected Jenni was being overoptimistic. Those fatal words were now coming back to torment her.

'Has Osmond seen it?'

'Who hasn't?' Anderson grimaced. 'Which one were you, by the way? Rod or Tina?'

'Is DC Langdon in the doghouse?'

'I think you're in line for the questions first. May the force be with you. You're going to need it.'

'Okay, thanks, DS Anderson. Hopefully, this will be brief, if painful. I hope to join you before the end, but if I don't, get Jenni to talk you through what we learnt from Violet Farrow and a woman we met at The Welly last night—'

'That was filmed at The Welly?'

'And why not?'

'I didn't know you had it in you, that's all. The Welly, though, that's almost cool.'

'It was filmed at the Banks Harbour, but we went to The Welly, so I'm still cool.'

Hollie nodded at Jenni, whose eye she'd managed to catch across the room. At least Jenni had made it to work from the flat on time, and hopefully, she'd had time to tidy things up a bit before leaving. Her colleague looked as rough as Hollie felt.

'I'll leave it with you, DS Anderson. Thanks for taking care of the briefing.'

Hollie motioned for Jenni to join her at the front of the room. She hadn't even taken her coat off yet, and something made her put her hand in her pockets as Jenni was approaching. She took out a beer mat on which were scrawled a name, phone number and address.

'We're not going to get an encore, are we?' some joker commented. There was restrained laughter from the gathered team, uncertain as to how Hollie might take the ribbing.

'Leave your song requests with DS Anderson, and I'll see what we can do at the end of the briefing.' She smiled.

Brazen it out, that was her only option. She hadn't broken any laws, but she was bracing for a brass-sized bollocking.

'Just pop outside with me a moment,' Hollie said to Jenni.

They exited the briefing room and closed the door behind them.

'How bad is it?' Hollie asked.

'Well, you've just increased your popularity in the office by about five hundred per cent,' Jenni replied. 'They all think it's hilarious.'

'What about the comments on the video?'

'Not so good, but if you take a look this morning, people are divided. The old moaners seem to think policing is a 24/7 job and you shouldn't even sleep or eat during an investigation. The more moderate majority have come to your defence. The gist of it is we're all entitled to let our hair down.'

'How are you?' Hollie checked. 'Hungover? Tired? Embarrassed?'

'I'm expecting a telling-off, but the guys have all been asking me what you're like out of the office.'

'What did you tell them?'

'I said you're great fun. I also said you'd give Rod Stewart a run for his money.'

Hollie burst out laughing.

'I'm a bit hungover, to be honest with you, but I'm only admitting that to you because you'll know I'm lying if I say anything else. It was a good night out, though, wasn't it?'

'I had a great time, and I really needed it. I can tell you that for certain.'

Hollie paused a moment, checking her recollection of the previous night's events. She showed the beer mat to Jenni.

'Can I just check with you, did that woman really say what I remember her saying last night? Or is that the drink making me imagine it?'

'She said it,' Jenni replied. 'Look, that beer mat is a great example of brilliant policing. Even when we were drunk, we were on fire.'

'I've a feeling I'm going to need it to save my life with DCI Osmond.'

'Oh, I forgot to ask,' Jenni said, 'did the kids arrive okay?'

'I'll tell you later,' Hollie answered, seeing that DS Anderson was about to start the briefing. 'You'd best get in there, and I'd better get DCI Osmond over and done with. If I don't make it out alive, I want to be buried, not cremated, and I don't want a religious service.'

'Good luck in there, boss. We'll play "It Takes Two" at your funeral.'

Hollie made her way to DCI Osmond's office and tapped at the door. He beckoned her in; he looked like a troubled man.

'Don't bother sitting, DI Turner. You know why you're in here, I assume?'

'Yes, sir.'

'I'll cut to the chase. There are several of us who want you taken off the case, as I've conveyed to you already. For some unfathomable reason, DCC Warburton has insisted you stay on it. So, you know who your allies are. But let me be very plain. That sort of behaviour brings the entire force into disrepute. I mean, in the middle of a high-profile investigation, what were you thinking? And with a junior colleague, too. Do I have to remind you of the standards of appropriate behaviour expected of senior officers, particularly when it comes to their junior colleagues? You should set an example at all times.'

'Yes, sir. I'm very sorry, sir. I really didn't think about somebody recognising me and sharing a video on social media. We were just letting off steam with the pressure of the case—'

Osmond held his hand up. 'I don't want to hear your excuses, DI Turner. I just don't want it to happen again. Have you heard what the talking point is on BBC Radio Humberside this morning?'

'No, sir.'

'Should serving officers investigating high-profile cases be allowed to party or do we expect them to behave with dignity and respect at all times?'

Hollie wished the fire alarms would go off. This was excruciating. She'd received dressing-downs in the past, but this one was fully justified. She had this coming.

'I'd like to speak in defence of DC Langdon, sir. She was encouraged by me, and I take full responsibility for her being there.'

'DC Langdon is a junior officer, and she does not share the public profile that accompanies your senior role in this case.'

'Point taken, sir. I apologise once again. It won't happen again, sir.'

Osmond seemed particularly relieved that Hollie had just taken this reprimand on the chin.

'There is one more thing, sir.'

Osmond looked at her, waiting for her to continue.

'We met a woman last night who recognised me from the TV. She came over to us to share her story. We think she may have given us a lead that we might not have come across any other way, sir.'

Hollie could tell she'd piqued Osmond's interest. All cops were the same. They feasted on scraps of information connected with live cases.

'One name keeps coming up again and again, sir. A man called Patrick McCready—'

'He's been mentioned before, hasn't he? Have we pulled him in for questioning yet?'

'I know the team are on it, sir. I'll need to check on progress after this morning's briefing. I think we're having trouble finding him. We've called at his home address several times, but he's out and the neighbours are unable to shed any light on his whereabouts. He may be on holiday, of course, but as he's retired now it's proving difficult to get a grasp on his social network to find out where he might be. The moment we get anything we can work with, we'll be straight onto it, sir. It's what this woman told us that puts a slant on the case, though.'

'Okay, DI Turner, you've got me. Tell me what it is that will get you off the hook for that video on social media. It had better be good.'

'It is, sir. The woman claimed—' Hollie consulted the beer mat in her hand. DCI Osmond shook his head. 'She's called Sue Wilcox. She suspects McCready had a sideline in getting babies adopted out for private clients. They were supposed to pass through the proper procedures and processes. Sue Wilcox reckons one of the girls in the mother and baby home was coerced to give up her child and that it was kept off the books.'

'How does she know?'

'She signed on different paperwork. This girl was in the

fostering system, so it was McCready's own social services department that was responsible for her *in loco parentis*.'

'Were the priest and the nun involved?'

'It would make sense, sir. How could Father Duffy not be involved if he was in charge of the home through his role at the church?'

'This is dynamite, DI Turner.'

'It is if we can stand it up, sir.'

'You'd best get on with it,' Osmond said, his tone completely changed now. She'd come in for a dressing-down and had left with his grudging respect.

'Thank you, sir.'

Hollie exited and searched the corridor for a spare room. She had another off-the-record investigation of her own to chase up.

She dialled a familiar number.

'Hi, it's DI Turner. Hollie Summers.'

'Oh, hello, Hollie. How's it going down there? We're all missing you in sunny Lancaster.'

'It's going well, thanks,' she lied. 'Is Acting DI Burns on shift?'

He was, and Hollie was put through to his phone.

Burns owed her one. He'd made a bad decision before she'd left Lancaster, but she'd lobbied on his behalf to get a look-in on her old job when it was advertised. He'd got it, too, albeit in a trial capacity.

'Hollie, great to hear from you. I take it this isn't a social call?'

'Chance would be a fine thing,' she replied. 'Can you do me a favour?'

'Of course, so long as it's legal.'

'It is, I just want it done away from this office. I'd like you to find out what you can about DCC Rose Warburton. Have a scratch around and let me know what you can find out, will you? Oh, and keep it discreet, please.'

'Will do. What's all this about? Is she causing problems for you?'

'On the contrary. She appears to be my guardian angel. And I want to know why.'

TWENTY-FOUR

1975: GILLY'S STORY

Gilly was burning with resentment, but with nobody to talk to or confide in, she saw that she had nowhere to turn. She'd never felt so alone or defenceless. So she resolved to get one up on Sister Brennan.

Mandy had been with them for a couple of days, and they had gelled well as a group. If it wasn't for the sense that their babies might arrive at any moment, the home would have felt to Gilly like a boarding school, or what she imagined it would be like at university. If they could only get rid of Sister Brennan, things might not be so bad. She couldn't figure out why the nun would be so hateful; she must have had some seriously bad stuff going on in her life.

Being a Saturday morning, things were more relaxed. The girls got to lie in a little longer, and breakfast would be served until nine o'clock. Gilly woke first and couldn't wait for Theresa and Mandy to join her. She'd been saving a surprise.

Mandy woke first, then Theresa.

'I've got something to show you,' Gilly erupted with enthusiasm. 'I've been saving it for a special occasion.'

'What's the occasion?' Mandy asked, confused.

'It's Saturday!' Gilly smiled. 'You know when I was locked in the cupboard the other day?'

Gilly wanted to cry again when she thought about it, but she was determined to press on with this.

The girls nodded. Mandy had already been brought up to speed in great detail. She'd also been warned about Sister Brennan and how to steer clear of her.

'I smuggled some books out. Not just those Mills and Boon stories. I put one behind the plant pot in the hall. I'm going to bring it up after breakfast. You're going to love it!'

For the past two days, Gilly had been secretly transporting Mills and Boon books that she'd removed from the throw-outs box and had carefully hidden them under piles of baby clothes, where they wouldn't be detected. She'd also found a gold nugget in there which she knew they'd have some fun with.

As the girls headed down the hallway, they were aware of something going on just outside the front door. Gilly went to investigate, still in her nightie and dressing gown.

'What was it?' Theresa asked as she rejoined her friends in the small dining room.

'Just a guy painting over some vandalism on the signage outside. It looks like we had some unwanted visitors last night.'

'What did it say?' Mandy asked.

'You're sure you want to know?'

It had shaken Gilly. It felt like they were hidden away in the home, but this message suggested some people were bothered by their presence. Is this what people thought of her?

'Of course.'

'*Home For Whores*. It's being painted over, so it'll be gone soon.'

They finished their breakfast then Gilly called in her fellow conspirators for a briefing.

'Mandy, you watch this end of the hall. You take the far

end, Theresa. Let me know when it's all-clear and I'll grab the book. You're going to love it.'

They left the dining room, and the girls took their posts. Gilly was tense and she knew her friends were. She was terrified of having another run-in with Sister Brennan. That woman was poison.

When it was safe, Gilly rushed toward the potted plant and pulled out the wooden table on which it was placed. The book was still there; she was relieved to see that. She picked it up, concealed it under her dressing gown, and then hurried over to the stairs. She looked around, making sure Sister Brennan wasn't lurking somewhere in the shadows. The three girls rushed up to their room, made sure the door was securely closed, and then huddled around Gilly on her bed.

'Close your eyes,' she instructed her friends. Theresa and Mandy did as they were told.

'Ta-da!'

Gilly held the book in front of her and the two girls opened their eyes.

'*The Joy of Sex*?' Mandy said. 'What's that?'

'It's a naughty book that I found in the throw-outs box. It's all about sex and stuff. I've heard of it before, but I daren't buy it or look at it in the library. I'd be too embarrassed.'

'What's it all about?' Theresa asked.

Gilly laughed.

'What do you think it's about?'

'They look like they're blowing into each other's mouths,' Mandy observed, looking at the cover.

Gilly opened the book and selected a page.

'He's got a lot of hair,' Theresa said. 'I can't tell who's the woman and who's the man.'

'What are they doing?' Mandy asked.

'That's called a Viennese oyster,' Gilly replied, reading from the text in the book. 'It sounds like something you'd eat in a restaurant.'

'It all looks a bit uncomfortable to me,' Theresa remarked, a look of distaste on her face. 'I'm not sure my legs would even bend into that position.'

'I can't believe you two are both about to give birth to babies and you're not aware of any of this.'

Theresa's face reddened.

'We just did it... normally. I don't know about any of this stuff. What did you do with Eric?'

'Well, it was nothing weird like this—'

Gilly flicked through the pages.

'Look, here's one I know. Doggy-fashion. We tried that once.'

'What was it like?' Theresa asked.

'I kept banging my head against Eric's headboard. His parents were in the room next door, so we had to stop. In the morning, we told them the lamp had fallen off his bedside table. After that, we just did it the normal way.'

'You're very quiet,' Theresa remarked, looking up at Mandy.

'I don't really know much about any of this stuff,' she sighed. 'I thought it was just kissing and hugging. I didn't know all this was involved. I can't imagine my mum and dad doing things like this.'

Gilly continued flicking through the pages. The girls would laugh out loud as Gilly moved the book around in her hands, pretending to figure out which way around the drawings should be. They'd been laughing and chatting for some time when the door burst open.

'What on earth are you girls doing?'

It was Sister Brennan. Her face was like thunder. They'd forgotten themselves and made too much noise.

'What is this?'

She snatched the book from Gilly's hands.

'Where did you get this?'

'From the throw-outs box in the cupboard downstairs. You can borrow it, if you want—' Before she could finish, Sister Brennan's spare hand shot out and struck her across the face.

'You old cow!' Gilly shouted, before collapsing on the bed in tears.

'This book is the devil's work!' Sister Brennan screamed at them. 'Do you not understand that you're already sinners? You should keep well away from filth like this. You'd be better working on your moral compass, you dirty whores.'

'I'm going to tell on you!' Mandy cried, in terrified frustration.

'And who will listen to a group of daft girls like you?' Sister Brennan sneered. 'Unless you haven't realised it yet, you're all alone here. Nobody wants you; nobody cares much what happens to you. You're an embarrassment and everybody would rather just forget you.'

Sister Brennan stormed out of the room and slammed the door. The girls heard the key in the lock. Gilly continued sobbing. Theresa moved over to Mandy, and they hugged in silence.

'At least we're not locked in the cupboard,' Mandy said after some time.

Gilly laughed through her snuffling.

'There was something good to read in there, to help pass the time,' she said, sitting up and facing her roommate. Her eyes were red, as was her cheek where she'd been struck.

'Are you going to tell your mum and dad?' Mandy asked.

'What will I tell them?' Gilly replied. 'They won't talk to me as it is. They think I deserve to be here. They'd never believe me, anyway. They don't trust me after I hid my relationship with Eric for so long. I don't think they'll ever trust me again.'

'What about one of the other nuns? Or Father Duffy?' Theresa suggested.

'The other nuns are scared of her, too. And she and Father Fluffy... well, that's never going to happen.'

For a moment she considered sharing what she knew with her friends. Gilly decided against it; she still wasn't entirely sure what she'd seen that day, though she had a pretty good idea. It would only cause more trouble with that horrible woman.

'What about that social worker? What do you call him? Mr McCreepy?'

Mandy burst out laughing as she said the name. She stifled the laugh, not wanting to attract Sister Brennan again.

'He's in with them. They don't care about us,' Gilly answered. 'They all just want us to hide out of sight until we have our babies. They're ashamed of us—'

Gilly stopped dead, wiped her face, and then grinned at her friends.

'I've got an idea.'

'I hope it works out better than the last one,' Theresa said.

'Well, we won't get caught this time, will we?'

'I don't like the sound of this,' Mandy added.

'When are you due, Mandy?' Gilly asked.

'Thursday next week.'

'And you, Theresa?'

'Next weekend, if my dates are right. They don't come on time though, remember?'

'I know, I know. I'm due at about the same time as Mandy. Look, who thinks we should have some fun before the babies arrive? We're all young. We shouldn't be locked up in a room like this, being told off for reading a book that we're all old enough to be reading.'

Theresa and Mandy exchanged a glance, which suggested to Gilly they weren't so sure about what was coming next.

'We're going to escape from here—'

'What, forever?' Mandy asked.

'No, just for one night. I know how we can do it, too. We can sneak out without anybody knowing.'

'What have you got planned?' Theresa's words dripped with uncertainty.

'We're going to Tiffany's—'

'What's that?' her friends asked at the same time.

'It's a nightclub, in the city centre. I'm going to call on Eric, too, before we go. It'll be great fun, I promise you.'

'And when are we doing this?'

'Tonight, of course, Theresa. We're going to sneak out after our evening meal.'

TWENTY-FIVE

As soon as she left Osmond's office, Hollie began to fret about the children. The distractions of the video and the DCI's ticking off had taken her mind off it, but she was desperate to know their whereabouts. She kept reassuring herself that they were with Phoebe and that they were in safe hands, but it didn't stop her anxiety racing. Léon's voice sounded in her head.

You see, this is why they can't live with you. Your work is all-consuming. You can't be there for them when they need you.

'Piss off, Léon,' she muttered.

She entered the briefing room with DS Anderson still in full flow. She reckoned she was better facing the fallout head-on, rather than avoiding it. Anderson paused to acknowledge her when she came in.

'Sorry to join you so late,' Hollie addressed the room. She checked for any members of the top brass. They were still nursing their early morning coffees in their offices. 'I was just sharing some of my dance moves with DCI Osmond.'

There was relieved laughter throughout the room and even an attempt at a round of applause in the far corner. Hollie didn't require the applause, but experience had taught her she was best not taking herself too seriously in front of her colleagues.

'May I check in on some key issues and throw in some new intel?' she asked.

'Be my guest,' DS Anderson replied, moving towards a spare chair.

'No, please, DS Anderson. This is your meeting. I just need to play catch-up. Number one on my list is Clive Bartram. Please retrieve my morning by telling me we've got him locked up in the cells somewhere—'

She looked at DS Anderson, then around the room.

'I have some positive news on that, boss. A member of the public reported that somebody has been sleeping near one of the drains along Victoria Dock. There's a path that runs from the docks along the Humber, so it's very possible it's our man. A switched-on member of the community team rang it in first thing. They're checking it out now.'

'Excellent, that sounds promising. You can't beat a phone call from a concerned resident. Clive Bartram cuts through everything today. If you get a whiff of him, then let me know, whatever I'm doing.'

Hollie scanned the room to make sure that had sunk in. She could see from the nods that it had.

'Okay, to other matters. Where are we with the newspaper cuttings and the squatter at the old girls' home?'

'I'm just about to come to that,' DS Anderson resumed. He reached out for a folder at his side and pinned a series of photocopies to the display board.

'DI Turner and DS Patel played a blinder with this—'

Hollie couldn't help but clock that he'd just paid her a big compliment in front of the team.

'The *Hull Daily Mail* sent over copies of the editions that DI Turner found at the old mother and baby home. DS Patel also followed an amazing hunch and checked with the city's

History Centre. These newspapers were stolen from their archives just over one month ago. The stories relate to key public figures in the case. 'That's Gilly Hodges' – he pointed to the first image – 'and this is that Patrick McCready fellow, the social worker.' He gestured to the second photocopy. 'And, interestingly, here' – he waved – 'is a small article and photograph that includes Theresa Morgan. Ms Morgan is not a public figure, like the others, but the photograph pictures her with a patchwork group. The caption uses her married name, so we were a bit slower making the connection with that one. We think whoever cut out these newspaper articles was looking for faces and background info. They've also taken a feature item about the nuns who live in the convent, but there's not a lot in there of much use. There's also someone else in there, but I'd like to discuss that with you in confidence, ma'am.'

'What about our Beverley photographer?' Hollie checked. 'Has he returned from sunny Spain yet?'

DS Patel shuffled some papers and checked a scribbled note.

'He's coming back tomorrow now – he responded to our voicemails the moment he got a signal. We got his number from a family member who we traced through the Facebook page where he posts his images. He'll call in first thing so we can speak to him. He also said he'd check his records beforehand.'

'Great. We need to speak to Theresa Morgan and Patrick McCready as a matter of urgency,' Hollie continued.

'I've had an initial phone conversation with Theresa Morgan,' DC Gordon said, 'and we just got word while you were in with the DCI that McCready got picked up outside his house by uniform about twenty minutes ago. He's been away from home visiting a friend, apparently, so he's been out of town. Theresa Morgan is coming in this morning, just after the briefing. She should be here any time now.'

'Good, thank you. We need to eliminate both of these people as potential suspects during the course of our interviews with them. I also want to hear what they have to say about their experiences in the home during the window of time that we're investigating.'

Hollie pointed at the Polaroid of the four girls and the photograph of the sports team at David Lister School.

'These women may be accomplices. It's possible they were involved in a murder plot, but I do not think any of them threw the body over.'

Hollie thought about the man with the birthmark. Who was he, and why did he care about the case? If she'd had to place a bet, she'd have put her money on this man being able to fill in some of the background. She intended to retain him as a confidential source for the time being. She thought neither he nor the women who'd been in the home would be capable of such violent crimes. It was high time he contacted her though.

'Still no prints from the office in the old mother and baby home?' Hollie asked, for the benefit of the room.

'Nothing on record,' DS Anderson informed her. 'Plenty of prints, but nothing in the police database.'

Hollie wondered if Mandy's son would have been finger-printed or not. He was a small-time thief, stealing for drugs. He might have slipped through the net.

'Have we checked against Clive Bartram's prints? I need to know if it was him sleeping rough in that old building.'

DS Patel tapped her arm for attention.

'No, he wasn't in the old building, boss. We cross-refer-enced his file.'

'Thank you, DS Patel. Is that everything from you, DS Anderson?' Hollie enquired. He nodded.

'This is good work, everyone. We're getting there now. It won't be long. Let's step up the search for Bartram and see what Patrick McCready, Theresa Morgan, and our photographer, Stanley Maddison, have to say.'

Hollie brought the team up to date on her own enquiries, sharing the theory about McCready's potentially shady dealings and Violet's nickname for the mystery girl in the photograph. The meeting concluded and DS Anderson hovered to the side as Hollie checked in with various team members before they headed back to their desks.

'I think we got away with it,' she whispered to Jenni as she passed by.

'Phew, I thought I might be looking for a job in retail,' she replied. 'The rest of the team think it's hilarious.'

She headed back to her desk, and DS Anderson approached.

'What's so important that we need to keep it on the QT?' Hollie asked.

DS Anderson took three sheets of paper from his folder and handed them to Hollie. She examined them.

'Jeez. Who knows about this?'

'You, me and DS Patel. Nobody else.'

'What about the brass?'

'Not the brass. That's why I wanted to run it by you first.'

'Fuck. Excuse my language.'

'There were three articles in the collection, all of them relating to public appearances by DCC Warburton.'

'Fuck,' Hollie said again.

'That was my reaction,' said DS Anderson.

This was a new development. It made sense that the killer would have cut out articles about people who were connected with the mother and baby home, so why include the DCC in that collection?

'Any idea why?'

'I haven't a clue. Maybe because she was at the press conference like you, so she's connected with the case?'

'But these newspapers were stolen a month ago, before

Sister Brennan was murdered. So she hadn't appeared at the press conference then.'

'True, but perhaps whoever cut them out found them after they'd done their research. It's not as if the DCC isn't in the newspapers all the time. She's always spouting off about some initiative or other. You know what it's like. She's rent-a-gob for the force. If you picked up ten random editions of the *Hull Daily Mail* since she's been in post, I'll bet she's in at least one of them.'

'She's not a patron of some related charity or something like that, is she? Why would the killer include her in his background research?' Hollie wondered aloud.

'Not that I'm aware of.' Anderson shook his head, a look of confusion on his face.

'Can we keep this to ourselves for now? Can we trust DS Patel to be discreet?'

'Patel is the very essence of discretion,' Anderson reassured her. It appeared to Hollie that he might have some personal experience of that. He seemed so certain.

'Okay, let's keep this between ourselves. If you get a chance to probe the DCC, do so, and let me know if you find anything. Does she have a family?'

'Why? Yes, a husband and two kids.'

'I just wondered.'

'Happily married for years, as far as I know.'

'Okay, good. That was the answer I was hoping for. It makes life simpler for us,' Hollie responded, as much for her own benefit as Anderson's. 'I'd like you to question Theresa Morgan when she comes in, please. And can I assign you to keep on top of developments with Mandy Tyson's son? I need to know everybody's onto this, including uniform. If we've not got him by tomorrow morning, we should consider issuing a photograph to the press. I've asked for them to get one ready, just in case.'

'Good call, ma'am.'

Anderson exited the briefing room, leaving Hollie on her own.

She checked her phone and was surprised to see a missed call, a voicemail notification and two text messages. Damn it! She'd somehow managed to turn the volume down on her phone while it was in her pocket. Hollie scrolled through the menu, deciding to check the texts first for speed. They were from Caitlen. She opened up the first one and read it.

What do you want first, the good news or the bad news?

TWENTY-SIX

Hollie could barely bring herself to open up the second text. What did Caitlen mean by bad news? And why wasn't Phoebe sending the message? She bit the bullet and moved on to the second text.

> Bad news – Phoebe left her phone on the train.
> Good news – everything is fine. I left a voice
> message on your phone to save my fingers. Cx

Hollie hadn't realised how tense she was until she read the good news. She relaxed her body and accessed the voicemail. As Caitlen updated her on what was going on, she felt the pain of missing her friend.

'Hi, Hollie. Don't panic, everything is okay. Phoebe's phone is getting a free ride back to Manchester as I speak. She left it on the train and was unable to contact you. They arrived on time, but couldn't find you, so headed into the city to try to find a phone box. That's easier said than done these days. Anyway, she took the kids for their second McDonald's meal of the day. The kids are now in love with her. She found a phone box after asking the staff at McDonald's, called me, and they're waiting for you in the city library. I hope you have a lovely time. Please text me as soon as you get this message. Byeee.'

Hollie wanted to meet Theresa Morgan, but she'd already lined Anderson up to speak to her; she'd have to trust her colleagues to handle it the way she would. Since taking a more senior position, Hollie constantly had to remind herself that she wasn't there to do all the grunt work. Other officers were available to do that, and she had to allow them to get on with their jobs. Much as she wanted to, she couldn't be everywhere at once. She had to pick her priorities carefully. Perhaps if she'd been a little better at doing that, her marriage might not have gone off the rails.

She sent a text back to Caitlen.

> Hurrah! You're a lifesaver. Thanks so much, will pick them up now. Hx

Hollie checked in with DS Patel before heading out and made sure she'd hear her phone if it sounded.

'Great work on those *Hull Daily Mail* cuttings,' she said. 'I'm just going to the library now. Is there anything I can do while I'm there? Call in at the History Centre, perhaps?'

'Thanks, boss, but I think it's covered. Their CCTV doesn't go that far back so there's no chance of a visual ID. Whoever it was didn't use an ID card either, so we can't go via that route. DS Anderson has warned me off sharing the info about the DCC. I'll keep my mouth shut until you say otherwise.'

'Thanks, I appreciate it. Let's just see if it means anything first. I'm hoping it doesn't, and that it's just a coincidence. It would be easier if I'd been around a bit longer. If our phantom cuttings collector had cut out some articles mentioning me, his motive might be more obvious. Unfortunately, I was packing up boxes at home in Lancaster at that time.'

'Oh, you've just reminded me, Jenni was chasing after you,

but she's had to head out to check on Father Duffy. She says she has a spare house key of yours.'

'Yes, I could do with that now you mention it, as I have guests. If you see her before I do, tell her I'll do my best to catch her later. Thank you.'

Hollie was about to head out when DS Patel lowered her voice.

'By the way, boss, I'm sorry if it caused problems for you with DCI Osmond, but you're a bit of a hero after your performance last night. I think that's just the kind of reassurance everybody needed.'

'What do you mean by reassurance?'

'May I speak freely, ma'am?'

'Always. Always speak freely, please.'

'It confirms you're not a wanker. There's a lot to live up to after DI MacKenzie's death. Even though the boss – our former boss – had his faults, it tends to glorify a man when he's killed in the line of duty. He could be a difficult man, but everybody had forgotten that by the time you arrived. The troops just like to know if you're on their side or the side of the higher-ups. I guess they know now.'

'I appreciate you saying so, DS Patel. I'll get that added to my CV. *Not a wanker.* That should help secure my next promotion.'

As Hollie headed out to her car, she reckoned it was as good a start to the day as she might have hoped for. It could have been a lot worse. And it was official: she wasn't a wanker. As career pinnacles go, that wasn't so bad an accolade to receive as a cop.

She entered the central library as a destination on her satnav and followed the route to the nearest car park. As she neared the library, her sense of excitement increased, and thoughts of the case subsided. Her kids were just up the road; she couldn't wait to see them. She parked up and withdrew some cash on the way over. She reckoned that Phoebe would have them somewhere near the children's section. She was right. She spotted Phoebe first, looking much more adult than she remembered her. And sitting on the floor, completely absorbed in their books, were Lily and Noah. Her heart jumped when she saw them.

Noah had had his hair cut in the style he'd been nagging her about when she left for Hull. She'd been against it at the time, but she liked it like that; it was still long on top, and he hadn't quite eliminated his curls. His trainers were grass-stained, and he was wearing a Fortnite sweatshirt, a sign that he hadn't grown up that much since she'd been away.

Lily's hair was longer than she remembered it and it made her seem older than her thirteen years. The giveaways were still there though, and Hollie smiled to see that her daughter was still accessorising at Claire's.

Phoebe spotted her and gave a wave. Hollie rushed over, Phoebe alerted the kids, and in a moment, they were up on their feet, charging over to her and giving her a hug.

'Mum, we missed you so much,' said Lily.

'We don't like Dad's new girlfriend,' Noah continued. 'We want him to live with you again.'

Trust the kids to get directly to the nub of the matter. Her heart went from a state of elation to a moment of despondency, then back to elation, within a minute. There was plenty of time to talk. For now, she had her kids.

'What are you reading at the moment, kids?' she asked, mindful of how much she must have missed. They showed her their books – *The Owl Service* for Noah and *Looking for Alaska* for Lily.

'Phoebe has let us have two McDonald's meals today, Mum.'

Hollie hoped that her son would continue to view such

tame pursuits as the height of recklessness for many years to come.

'I know it's naughty' – Phoebe shrugged – 'but whenever you're in need of a quick bite to eat or a clean toilet, there's never one far away.'

'You're learning lots of secret parent tricks,' Hollie laughed. 'There's no problem so great for children that it can't be solved by a Maccy D's.'

Their news was superficial and mostly related to school, but she lapped it up, enjoying the nourishment of their youthful enthusiasm.

'We're doing a project on lizards at school, Mum.'

Noah had a unique habit of being able to bring something completely left of field into any conversation.

'I've joined the drama group, Mum,' Lily added. 'We're doing *Les Misérables* for the end of year performance.'

This was what made policing possible for her. Without the normality of her family, the world seemed too brutal. With the children back in her life, it allowed her to enjoy the world differently and see it as a more innocent and joyful place.

It didn't take the kids long to return to their books, only this time, they sat on either side of Hollie, resting against her.

'I'm sorry I messed things up,' Phoebe apologised. 'I was so concerned about the kids gathering up their stuff, I left my phone on the table on the train. What an idiot!'

'It's not a problem, honestly. I'm just so grateful that you're here. How was Léon?'

'Between you and me, I think he was grateful to get a bit of time to himself. I didn't know you'd split up. I'm so sorry to hear that.'

'Does your mum know yet? Has she figured it out?'

'I think so, but she doesn't want to say. What happened?'

'You know we got caught up in that case in Lancaster? The

one where I sent Léon and the kids over to his parents in France to be on the safe side?'

'Yes, I remember my mum telling me about that—'

'Well, he met somebody then. But if you want a broad explanation, it's because of my job. Anyway, let's not dwell on the negative stuff. Congratulations on getting your interview. Are you really going to study in Hull?'

'Yes, they have exactly the course I was looking for. It's all a bit last minute, but I'm so excited.'

There was something about Phoebe that had changed. When she'd first met Caitlen, Phoebe was a bit of a handful and caused her friend no end of worry. But now she seemed calmer and more mature. She was wearing more colour, too, and a lot less black.

Hollie took some money out of her pocket and handed it to Phoebe.

'I'm paying for everything while you're here. I'll pay your rail fare, too. Just send me a PayPal bill for everything you've spent today. There's two hundred pounds there, the fridge is full, and if you don't spend it, keep what's left.'

'Wow, thanks, Hollie! Are you sure? That seems like a lot of money.'

'I'll probably bung you some extra for childminding fees. I really appreciate it, Phoebe. Thank you.'

Hollie's phone sounded; it was DS Patel on the line.

'Sorry to disturb you, boss. I know you're doing family stuff.'

'It's no problem, DS Patel. How can I help you?'

It always came to this. The job had to come first.

'Patrick McCready has kicked off big time and he's making an almighty fuss. He's insisting he speaks to you. He won't talk to anybody else.'

TWENTY-SEVEN

1975: GILLY'S STORY

'If we're going to do it, we've got to do it now.'

Gilly still wasn't certain they were going ahead with the plan. They'd chatted to Violet over their evening meal, and she was there in the room, but Gilly could see her heart wasn't in it.

All four of them were terrified of getting caught in the act by Sister Brennan, but Gilly was determined to push on.

'I'll keep watch if that's all right?' Violet apologised. 'I don't have the nerve for it, but I'll help you get out.'

'Are you still coming?' Gilly checked with Theresa and Mandy. The two girls looked at each other. She needed them to agree to this. She wasn't even sure she had the nerve for it, but with her friends at her side, they could do this. They'd been so shaken by Sister Brennan's hostility towards them that they were paralysed by the thought of her discovering their plan.

'This is our last chance for freedom before our babies come,' Gilly urged. 'It's now or never.'

'Oh, okay,' Theresa said. Mandy followed but seemed to be more in agreement with Violet's line of thinking.

There was a gentle tap at the door.

The girls looked at each other, wondering who it could be at that time of night, fearful that it might be Sister Brennan coming in to scold them. Nobody came in, so they all breathed again. The nun didn't usually bother to knock anyway.

Mandy opened the door. It was the girl from downstairs, the one they'd decided between themselves to call Twiggy. She was holding a Polaroid camera in her hand.

'Can I come in?' she whispered.

'Of course,' Mandy replied. 'What's going on? We never see you.'

'I'm not supposed to talk to the other girls,' she replied. 'I've sneaked out because I wanted to make sure you're okay. That nasty nun isn't about this evening, so I chanced it.'

The girl was looking at Gilly.

'Was it you who switched the light on when she locked me in the cupboard?' Gilly asked.

The girl nodded.

'Thank you so much. I thought it was you. Did you see what happened?'

'Yes. I tried to tell my dad about it today when he came to visit, but he told me to stop talking nonsense. He said I was making things up. But I saw what that nun did. I just wanted to help you.'

'Well, thank you once again. It would have been a lot worse if I was on my own in the dark. What's that in your hand?'

The girl held up her camera.

'It's a Polaroid camera,' she replied. 'You can take a photo and it prints out immediately. I'm interested in photography. Other than reading books, it's about all I have to do around here. I just sit on my own in that room all day. At least I had my dog at home.'

Gilly felt a pang of sadness for this girl. She was so grateful for the company of the other girls, she reckoned she'd go crazy if they weren't able to laugh and chat together.

'Here, shall I take a picture?' Twiggy asked.

'Yes, please!' they replied, almost in unison. They arranged themselves along the bed. The girl took their picture and a small square of paper slid out of the bottom of the device.

'I'm going to take another,' she said, handing it over to the girls. 'Stay in your positions. I caught one of you looking the wrong way. I want to get a good one.'

The girls held their poses. There was a click and a flash, and a second piece of paper glided out at the bottom of the camera.

'That'll be better,' she said. 'I'd like to keep one, so I remember you all. You can keep that one.'

Twiggy seemed on edge, no doubt nervous that she might be caught mingling with the girls.

'I've got to go now. It's been nice meeting you. I'm sorry I can't stay and chat. I hope everything goes well with your babies.'

She was gone as fast as she came.

'She seems really nice,' Mandy said.

'I wish she didn't have to stay away from us,' Theresa added. 'It must be horrible for her. How lonely to be stuck in a room all your own.'

Gilly picked up the Polaroid and checked out the picture.

'It looks like we're all ghosts. It doesn't even take a proper picture.'

'I think you have to leave it for a couple of minutes,' Violet informed her. 'They take a while to develop. It's very clever.'

Gilly placed the picture back on her bedside table.

'Right, let's go. If we don't do this now, we'll lose our nerve. Besides, you heard what Twiggy said: Sister Brennan isn't on the prowl. Put your coats on. It'll be cold outside.'

Gilly was not prepared to let the interruption interfere with her big plan. She led the way. It was about the only time of day an escape would be possible. The girls were supposed to be in their rooms for the night, and the nuns were at prayer in their rooms. One nun would remain on duty, but if she could be distracted, Gilly's plan would be easily executed.

The four girls left the room, creeping along the landing, with Violet at the rear.

Gilly looked all around, searching in the shadows, making sure they were safe to continue their secret venture.

'Go to the far side of the hall and say you think your waters have broken,' Gilly whispered. 'We'll sneak around the back and out through the office. Are you sure you're not coming?'

'I'm sure,' Violet confirmed.

The four girls made their way down the staircase, creeping in silence, checking all the time that they hadn't been spotted. Gilly laughed to herself at how ridiculous they looked, what with two of them manoeuvring huge bellies through coats they'd worn before they became pregnant. Even she didn't fit into her coat. She knew they were doing a crazy thing, but she was sure they could make their escape undetected.

Violet went ahead and took her position at the far side of the hall. Gilly and the other two girls moved around the back of the staircase. Gilly gave a wave.

'Sister, help. I think my baby is coming!' Violet called out.

There was movement in the office. Gilly was relieved to see it wasn't Sister Brennan on duty; she'd have called it off immediately if that had been the case. She felt a pang of guilt at deceiving one of the nicer nuns.

As she'd predicted, the nun – Sister Payne – ran some checks on Violet and then accompanied her back to her room. Violet had been briefed to keep her talking.

'Right, now!' Gilly instructed. She led the way to the office. It was illuminated only by a desk lamp and seemed much more welcoming than it had been when she'd signed papers in there. She scanned the room. All the time she expected Sister Brennan to come in and catch them red-handed, so pervasive was the fear she'd struck into them.

'Hey look, the dirty things, they've kept our book!'

Gilly held up the confiscated copy of *The Joy of Sex* like it was a trophy. 'I'll bet that's made them all reconsider their life choices.'

She rolled it up and forced it into her coat pocket.

'Oh look, that'll be useful, too.'

Tucked away in one corner of the window ledge was a can of spray-paint.

'This is what that guy was using to fix up the sign earlier. I can make use of that.'

'What have you got planned?' Mandy said. 'I thought we were going to the nightclub.'

'We are,' Gilly reassured her, 'but this is my neighbourhood, and I want to make a couple of visits first.'

Mandy and Theresa looked at each other again, but they were in too deep now and Gilly wasn't going to give up.

'We'd better be quick, before Sister Payne comes back.'

Gilly shot out her hand and opened the top drawer to the side of the desk. She examined the contents, then just as quickly slid it shut.

'Theresa, open the blinds and pull up that window, will you?'

Theresa did as she was told, and Gilly checked the other drawers. Her hands were shaking.

'Bingo!' she said when she opened the bottom one.

She pulled out a metal box and gave it a shake.

'Money, money, money!' she exclaimed.

'We can't steal money,' Mandy protested.

'Yes, we can. It's not like you haven't stolen before.'

She knew that was mean, but Mandy had told her she'd stolen a record from Woolworths, and she didn't want her chickening out with lame excuses. If the other girls showed too much doubt, Gilly might lose her courage as well.

The key was in the lock, so she opened the box and took out a five-pound note.

'What do you reckon, girls? Two taxi fares, three entrance fees and our drinks for the night. That should just about cover it, shouldn't it?'

She took two pound notes, just in case.

'You first, Mandy,' she urged. 'Sister Payne will be back soon.'

Even as she was saying it, Gilly knew Theresa and Mandy would never have gone through with this if it wasn't for her cajoling. But they needed this. They were young girls locked up like they were in prison. It was worth the risk. Everything would change when the babies arrived.

The office window was now fully open. It took some shuffling and pushing to get each of the girls through, but it was the ground floor and not high, so they managed the undignified process between them. Gilly was last through as she was the most agile. She'd taken two pencils from inside one of the drawers. She pulled the blinds behind her, then gently lowered the window frame back into place, resting it on the pencils so that it wasn't fully closed.

'That's so we can sneak back in later.' She smiled at her friends.

'What now?' Mandy asked, shivering. 'And why did you bring that book and the paint with you?'

'All will be revealed shortly.' Gilly grinned. 'First, we're heading next door to the church. I've got a little surprise planned for the people at Mass on Sunday. This is one of Father Duffy's sermons that they won't forget in a hurry.'

TWENTY-EIGHT

'I'm going to have to head straight back to the office. And we need to fix you up with a new phone.'

Hollie had driven them around to the flat and had given Phoebe a quick tour. She was thankful Jenni had tidied the bedroom before leaving.

'Mum called the rail company,' Phoebe said, 'and my phone's been handed in. The guard said he'd leave it with the transport police in Manchester. It's a pain, but I can pick it up on the way back. We're just lucky that route wasn't caught up in the industrial action.'

'You can say that again. Did you notice the supermarket along Beverley Road as we were driving in? It's about a ten-minute walk away. Use the money I gave you to buy a cheap phone. We may as well get a pay-as-you-go SIM to keep you going. It won't have all your apps on it, but at least it means I can call you. Is that okay?'

Phoebe smiled. 'It'll be like going old-school with a cronky phone. Will you write your numbers down so I can put them in?'

Hollie nodded but didn't want to move away from the children. Both were nestled against her, quietly reading their books on the sofa, and it was glorious. She shuffled her phone so that she could take a swift photo of the three of them.

'Smile for the camera,' she said as they looked up and posed for the picture.

'There's a pen over there and I'll scribble my numbers down on that flyer that came through the letterbox. You wouldn't get it for me, would you? I can't bring myself to leave these two just yet.'

Phoebe walked over to the table, retrieved the items, and handed them to Hollie, who jotted down her contact information.

'I've given you the office number, too. Just ask for DS Patel. She manages things in the office and will be able to tell you where I am at any given time. There's food in the fridge and there's that great big park outside. It's well worth a wander. The kids will love the play area, or they're big enough for the outdoor gym. There's a pond there, a conservatory and a band-stand, if you're feeling really keen.' Hollie noticed Phoebe was looking in the direction of the window. 'And on the far side is Princes Avenue. They call that area The Avenues. The shops are great over there. That should keep you all busy. I only have one key at the moment. I lent one to a friend at work, so here's mine. I'll try and catch my colleague and retrieve the spare. I think that's everything?'

Phoebe nodded. 'Oh, my interview is at eleven o'clock tomorrow morning. Will that be all right?'

'I hope so,' Hollie answered. 'We may have to look up activity centres or somewhere where I can safely leave the kids. If we get a breakthrough in the case today, I might even be able to venture a day off.'

Hollie moved and the kids stirred. Just a few more minutes.

'Shall we finish that Connect 4 game before I go?' she asked.

'Do you have to go, Mum?' Lily asked.

'We want to stay with you, Mum,' Noah picked up.

Hollie's stomach tightened; it always came back to this impossible conflict. She picked up a yellow counter and slid it into the pocket version of the game that was sitting on the coffee table in front of them.

'Put it there—' Noah pointed to Lily, who snatched a red counter and swiftly dropped it into one of the slots.

'You little devils' – Hollie smiled – 'you were setting me up for that all along.'

She dropped in her counter, seeing that she couldn't retrieve the situation, and Noah darted over to make the victory move.

'Winners!' he declared, waving his arms above his head.

Hollie tousled his hair and gave Lily a kiss on her head. She wouldn't be allowed to do that for much longer.

'We prefer it with you. Even if you have to go to work,' Lily said, allowing the kiss.

'Dad and Veronique always speak in French,' Noah added. 'I don't like it when they do that. It doesn't feel like home.'

Hollie felt the pang of failure again and she pulled both children in tight, giving them a long hug. It was useful that all was not sweetness and light at Léon's end. That might give her some leverage, after all. If she shipped in a nanny, it might work. The money would be hellish tight, but it was worth it to keep the children close and in the UK. There was also the possibility of getting a promotion, too. A bit more time in the office would help with life at home.

For a moment, she felt a glimmer of optimism. Perhaps she might be able to fight Léon. What the kids wanted was the most important thing and, despite his affair, she still believed Léon wanted that, too.

'Have a great time with Phoebe. I'll get back as soon as I can for tea. Perhaps we can go bowling while you're all here?'

'Yes!' both children shouted. Hollie stood up, kissed them, and headed for the door purposefully, in case she caved again and rejoined them on the sofa.

'See you later, and thanks once again, Phoebe!'

Her only thought on the drive back to the station was the children. She was still pondering childcare possibilities when she checked in with DS Patel. There were twelve red roses on her desk, sitting in plastic wrapping.

'I'm assuming DS Anderson wasn't thanking you for a job well done?' Hollie smiled.

'No, you know who sent these, don't you?'

'Duncan's a fast worker – he must have liked your interview technique. I hope he's not our bad guy, I really do. Just stay patient a while longer, and then you have my blessing to go on a date. Listen to me, I sound like your mum!'

'I'll keep him keen a bit longer, don't worry. I'm not screwing up my career over a guy. I know how this works. But I won't deny a bit of flattery can bring a flush to a girl's face in the middle of a working day.'

'You know what I'm going to ask you, don't you?'

'Yes, boss, and the answer is no. Still. The man at Victoria Dock had bolted by the time the community team got there. People on the estate who saw anything reckon he's keeping to the quiet paths and heading over towards The Deep and possibly the Old Town. We've got uniform patrols looking out for him. Honestly, boss, when we finally catch up with this guy, you'll see the fireworks.'

Hollie smiled.

'I appreciate what you're doing here, but don't expect any red roses. Which room is McCready in?' Hollie asked, thinking she'd better get her head back in the game.

'Interview Room 3. Theresa Morgan is still in Room 1 with DS Anderson and DC Gordon—'

'She's still here?'

'Yes, apparently.'

'Will you offer McCready a top-up of coffee? I'll be with him shortly. I'd like to see Theresa Morgan, just to get a sense of the fourth girl in our little gang. I want DS Anderson in with me for McCready, too. I'll need a confident pair of hands with me on that interview, I reckon.'

DS Patel nodded, and Hollie headed for the interview rooms. She knocked on the door of Room 1. It appeared that she was in the nick of time. The conversation was relaxed and chatty. Everybody was standing up, so it seemed the formal part of the interview was over.

'Sorry to interrupt. I was keen to meet Theresa before she left,' Hollie began. She raised her eyebrows at DS Anderson who understood her silent question. He gave a small shake of his head. Theresa hadn't been able to offer anything useful.

Hollie shook Theresa's hand. She was slight and skinny and seemed quite shy.

'I'd just like five minutes with Theresa, if that's all right, DS Anderson? If you grab yourself a coffee, we've got Patrick McCready in Interview Room 3—'

'Patrick McCready?' Theresa asked.

'Yes. He's just helping with our enquiries.'

'He's here?'

'Yes, just across the corridor,' Hollie replied. 'I'm so sorry. I should have thought. I'm sorry if that's distressing to you—'

'It's not distressing. It's just that you might have a second murder on your hands if you leave me in the same room as that man—'

She looked at the faces of the three officers who were all staring at her. Hollie wouldn't have thought a quiet woman could sound quite so assertive.

'I'm sorry. You know I don't really mean that. I shouldn't be spouting off in a police station, of all places.'

'It's no problem,' DS Anderson replied. 'I'll head off now. Thank you for your time – I'll make sure you've exited the building before Mr McCready leaves his interview room.'

DS Anderson and DC Gordon left the room.

'Take a seat for a minute,' Hollie suggested. Theresa sat back on the chair she'd been using. Hollie pulled up a chair next to her, choosing not to speak across the desk.

'I went to see your old friend Violet Farrow yesterday,' Hollie said. 'She's in a bad way.'

'It's so sad. We're hoping to be able to go and see her, but her daughter thinks it's almost the end. It feels like a lot of things are coming to an end right now.'

'What do you mean by that, Theresa?'

'Well, you know, this murder. With Sister Brennan's death, it feels like the past is demanding some answers. The chickens are coming home to roost. It's high time if you ask me.'

'Gilly told me you reckon Sister Brennan got what she deserved when you met up for a coffee on Monday. Did you mean that?'

Theresa looked at her, like she'd just been hijacked.

'You must know I didn't mean that, detective? That woman frightened me out of my wits when I was a teenager. She hurt me, too. I wouldn't have wished a death like that on her, but she did have it coming. I won't be the only person she bullied and intimidated in that mother and baby home. We all wanted her dead when we were young girls in that place. I guess someone finally followed through on it.'

Hollie studied Theresa. All four women were just regular members of the public, yet any one of them had given her a strong motive for killing the nun. There must have been hundreds of others who felt the same way. It wasn't much of a legacy to leave behind.

'You were reunited with your son, weren't you, Theresa?'

'Yes, I'm one of the lucky ones. In fact, I was the first of our little trio to find my boy. He's called Colin, by the way. I wanted him to be named David, but I didn't get a choice in that. It was so funny how all of us from our dorm had boys. You'd have thought one of us would've had a girl. At least Violet had a daughter.' Theresa paused for a moment. 'My son lives in London, but I Skype him regularly, and he's a part of my life now.'

'Did he find you or did you go in search of him?'

'He found me. It came out of the blue. He was eighteen years old, and his adoptive parents had both died in a car accident. He found some documentation when he was clearing out their stuff, did a bit of detective work, and eventually found me in Hull. It was the best day of my life when he turned up at my door.'

Hollie was suddenly alert to a new possibility.

'You can't recall any details, can you? Was an adoption agency used, for instance? We're struggling to find details of which organisations worked with the home in order to place the children.'

'I can't remember any of the details, but I can certainly check for you.'

This was good; at last, a paperwork trail. This was exactly what they needed.

'Theresa, I know you've spoken to DS Anderson and DC Gordon already, but I just want to check with you. There was a girl that you all called Twiggy in the mother and baby home. Can you remember anything about her? I'm particularly after a name.'

'It's so many years ago, and she was just a fleeting acquaintance, we barely even knew her. That's why we gave her a nickname. I told your colleagues this. I did once catch her parents speaking to one of the nuns in the hallway. It was a common name, which made me laugh because we all reckoned she was quite posh. She had her own room and this nice camera which must have cost a pretty penny.'

'Is it her first name or surname you think you can remember?'

'Just her surname. The nun referred to them as Mr and Mrs whatever-it-was. It was something really ordinary. Smith, Brown, Taylor or Jones, something like that. I wish I could help you more, officer, but I just can't remember it clearly. I hope that helps.'

'Watson?' Hollie pushed. 'Might it have been Watson?'

'That's it,' Theresa confirmed. 'Watson. That's definitely the name. It's been so many years, but I can remember clear as day now you've said it.'

TWENTY-NINE

Hollie was still wondering if Theresa's partial intel was of any help when she walked back up the stairs to join DS Anderson for the interview with McCready. She'd seen Theresa off in a taxi.

'So did your son keep the paperwork connected with the adoption process?' Hollie had asked as she was dropping Theresa off at reception.

'Yes, I think so. Why?'

'Do you think he'd send it over to us? Maybe he could scan it and email it to you? If not, perhaps he could photocopy it and pop it in the post?'

'I'll ask him, DI Turner. Is there any reason why?'

'No particular reason other than that it will help me get a feel for how these things were done back in the seventies. There may also be some clues in there. Names, addresses, agencies – I don't know what. I'm just grasping at straws, really. I'm particularly keen to get some names of agencies so we can go ringing round and check their records. It was so long ago, and the records were all on paper. I think this might be a fast track to getting my hands on some official paperwork. We're struggling to track down anything at our end.'

Theresa agreed that she'd do her best to sort it out, and Hollie put it to the back of her mind, not expecting it to yield very much.

She took a dislike to Patrick McCready the moment she entered the interview room. DS Anderson was there already. It was unusual to see him so uncomfortable.

'Ah, the DI is here at last,' McCready began, without standing up. 'Nice of you to show your face. I've been here almost two hours already. No wonder your clear-up rate is so piss poor if you can't even get around to interviewing people.'

DS Anderson shot Hollie a glance that told her everything she needed to know.

'This is not a formal interview, Mr McCready, and I should stress that you are not a suspect in this case—'

'I know that already, DI Tierney—'

'Turner,' Hollie corrected.

'Whatever,' McCready continued. 'I came here of my own free will because your officers were harassing me. You've left several messages on my answer phone and my neighbours tell me that police officers have been knocking at my door all week. For someone who's not a suspect, that's extremely embarrassing for me – my neighbours have all been speculating about what's going on. It's very damaging to my reputation and bordering on libellous. But I figured I'd better come in and speak to you first so you can eliminate me from your half-arsed inquiry and let it be known publicly that I am not a suspect.'

'I'm sure we can do that today,' Hollie replied, her hackles well and truly risen. 'Let's get started, then you can be on your way.'

'This coffee is disgusting, too,' McCready said. 'I mean, fine for the scumbags who come in here. They can drink ditch water as far as I care. But it's not very hospitable to people like me who are volunteering their time to assist in your blundering investigation.'

'What was your role at the mother and baby home?' Hollie said, anxious to ask her questions and get this man out of the police station.

'If you don't know that already, officer, then your investigation is in a worse state than it sounds from the news on the radio. I was the social worker assigned to the home. I was a moral welfare officer by title. It was in the very early days of my career—'

'How long have you been retired?' DS Anderson interjected.

'A long time. I went early,' McCready answered immediately.

'Any reason why?' Hollie said.

'Wouldn't you retire if you got half the chance?' McCready replied. 'I like to spend time out in my place in Amsterdam. Social Services are under-resourced and overworked. You know the drill.'

'You never made social services director then?' Hollie pushed. She'd seen McCready's type before and knew that vanity was his Achilles heel.

'You never made detective chief inspector then?' he replied.

DS Anderson shuffled in his chair.

'Okay, let's move on. Why do you think Sister Brennan was murdered?'

'I don't know, detective. Why was Sister Brennan murdered? Or am I now having to do the work of the police?'

'You must have a theory? You knew her, didn't you?'

'I knew of her. She was in the same room as me sometimes, as were many of the nuns who worked in the mother and baby home. I dealt mainly with the church, through Father Duffy.'

'What was your relationship with Father Duffy like?' DS Anderson asked.

'Professional. Why? It was just like your relationship, officers. Two professionals working together. What's more to say?'

'So, there was nothing untoward with any of the adoptions?'

McCready glared at Hollie. She'd blindsided him; it couldn't have happened to a nicer person.

'Excuse me? Am I a suspect now?' McCready asked, blustering. 'Do I need legal representation?'

'No, you don't,' Hollie asserted, 'but you might do if we think you're hiding something.'

'Listen to me, officer, and listen well. The girls in that home were grateful to have their babies adopted. Most of them were silly little teenagers who'd got themselves pregnant. They had no way of supporting themselves, they were a source of deep shame to their families, and it was considered the only solution back then. We were helping them to sort their lives out and get them back on track. It was all for the best.' He sighed. 'These days we give them houses and a cosy life on benefits, but if I had my way, I'm not sure I wouldn't go back to the old methods—'

'Really?' Anderson challenged him.

'Really.'

'And were all the adoptions above board?' Hollie asked. He was trying to seem cool, but she could see he was on the ropes.

'What do you mean by that, officer?'

'I mean, was it all handled according to procedure? Were any of the adoptions off the books? If a rich couple had offered to make a donation to church funds, might they have been offered a baby to adopt before a poorer couple?'

'I don't know what you're suggesting, DI Tierney—'

'It's DI Turner and I'm sure you'll understand why we have to explore every avenue. I'm just confused as to why somebody might want to violently murder a nun and make an attempt on the life of an elderly priest.'

'You and me both, officer. That's why I'm here, trying to assist you in your enquiries like a good citizen.'

'Yet you don't seem very forthcoming,' Anderson chanced.

'I think I'm being very forthcoming. I also know that if I'm not under arrest, I can walk out of here any time I like. So, unless you have any more questions, I think we're done here.'

'Do you recall any of the names of the girls who had separate rooms at the mother and baby home?'

'I was attached to the place for eleven years, officer. You didn't have to have a university degree to sweep the streets back in those days, so I was a young man with a lot of responsibility. I can't remember the names of everybody I dealt with. Can you?'

'Cast your mind back to 1975. A very slim girl. She went to David Lister School. She had a common surname. Watson. Does it bring back any memories?'

McCready gave the impression that he was dredging the recesses of his mind. He was a poor actor.

'Nothing, officer, sorry. Besides, you'll struggle to find records from the seventies. What with the changeover with the councils and everything being on paper, I'd be surprised if there's any paperwork remaining from those days.'

'You don't look too concerned about that,' DS Anderson put it to him.

'I'm neither concerned nor unconcerned about it—'

'What if I told you we'd managed to obtain some paperwork from one of the adoptions?' Hollie interrupted.

'That's unlikely.'

'Why is it unlikely?'

He blustered again.

'I'd be very surprised if any paperwork can still be found—'

'Is that because it was destroyed?'

'Am I under arrest, officer?'

'No, you're not.'

'Then let me say this, off the record. If any of those girls have suggested anything untoward was going on there, good luck proving that after all these years—'

'Are you able to help us identify any of the agencies that were used to manage the adoptions?' DS Anderson asked.

McCready was primed to issue another insult but was obviously caught out by the sudden change of direction. Hollie could see him thinking. He made a meal of pretending to be dredging through the recesses of his mind, then offered his answer.

'Most of them were managed directly through social services,' he began, 'but we also worked with an agency called Brand New Family. It was that or Brand New Families, it was so many years ago now.'

Hollie studied his face. She reckoned he was more likely to be sending them on a wild goose chase than offering up anything useful.

There was a knock at the door. DS Patel entered.

'Is it urgent?' Hollie said.

'Yes, you'll want to know this.'

Had they finally located Bartram? Hollie stood up and left the room. She turned to face DS Patel in the corridor, lowering her voice so McCready wouldn't hear through the door.

'What is it that can't wait, DS Patel?'

'We've just been alerted by uniform that Gilly Hodges was assaulted in her home this morning.'

THIRTY

1975: GILLY'S STORY

'Where are we going?' Mandy asked. She was looking back at the window, apparently still undecided about the night's events. 'I don't know this part of Hull.'

'This is my local neighbourhood,' Gilly tried to reassure her. 'I know where I'm going. We'll just make a couple of calls first, then we can head into town.'

'What if Sister Brennan finds out?' Theresa said. She seemed only marginally more confident about that night's plan than Mandy. 'I'm really scared what she might do if she discovers what we've been doing.'

'She won't find out! She's an old cow, anyway,' Gilly replied, snappier than she'd have liked. 'She can't get much nastier, can she? I don't know why she's so down on life. And what are they going to do to us? We're pregnant. It's not like they can throw us in a dungeon.'

That seemed to encourage the other two girls. Capitalising on her small win, Gilly continued, 'Besides, we're going to have a great girls' night out. This is our final opportunity. Nobody looks in on us after eight o'clock on a Saturday. The nuns are on weekend staffing. And they'll all be at church tomorrow morning until midday. It's the one time of the week when we can do this. Are you in?'

She knew she was playing with fire by giving them a last opportunity to chicken out, but Gilly was prepared to head off into the night alone if need be. She had some plans of her own before they took a taxi into the city centre.

'Okay then,' Theresa agreed, 'but we must be back by midnight.'

'Deal!' Gilly exclaimed, knowing that with Theresa on board, Mandy would surely follow.

Mandy took a look back at the window, the frame propped open by the two pencils. Sister Payne's shadow could be seen through the blinds; she was back after attending to Violet. If they turned back now, they'd definitely be in hot water.

Gilly could almost see the devil and the angel sitting on Mandy's shoulders. She knew that dilemma well; it's what a childhood of going to church had given her. Fortunately, it was the devil who won. Sister Payne's return seemed to convince her.

'Okay, I'll come,' she said at last. 'But like Theresa, I don't want to be later than midnight. I've never even been to a night-club before.'

'Then tonight is going to be an extra special night. But first, we're going to nip into the church—'

'It's a bit early to be praying for forgiveness, isn't it?' Theresa laughed.

'I want to prepare a surprise for all the good churchgoers tomorrow morning,' Gilly said. 'But they'll lock up the church later this evening, I reckon, so we need to go there now. It won't take long.'

The Church of St Mary and the Angels was adjacent to the mother and baby home. Gilly knew there was a small footpath through the grounds that led directly to it, so they wouldn't have to make their way out via the long gravel drive, which might have given the game away. As the three girls headed along the path, Gilly started to gently hum the music from *The Great Escape*. Theresa and Mandy caught on quickly and, by the time they were walking through the graveyard, they were giggling away. That's when Gilly knew that they wouldn't turn back.

She lifted the latch of the church door and held her breath, hoping it wasn't already locked. She'd seen the opening hours hundreds of times at Sunday services, but she still didn't quite believe it would be open. The latch lifted and the door opened, creaking. Gilly was scared at the prospect of an empty, dark church, so she searched the wall to the left of the door, hoping to locate the light switches without too much delay. It turned out they were on the right-hand side, and Mandy found them. The church lit up.

'We'd best just leave one set of lights on,' Theresa suggested, 'just in case one of the nuns comes over to investigate.'

'So, what are we doing here?' Mandy asked.

Gilly dug into her coat pocket and pulled out the copy of *The Joy of Sex*.

'We're going to make Father Duffy's sermon more entertaining.' She grinned, a sparkle of mischief in her eyes. 'Everybody gets a picture page in their hymn book,' she declared. 'Fold them in half so it's not too obvious. I want the service to be well underway before anybody realises.'

Mandy and Theresa looked shocked at first, then after a few seconds, they saw the fun of it.

'I'll tear out the pages. You two slide them into the hymn books.'

Gilly led the way, flicking through the pages, ignoring the text and tearing out the full-page illustrations.

She thought back to her most recent conversations with Father Duffy. He'd seemed wary of her since she'd walked in on him, and whenever he was in the mother and baby home. He always appeared uncertain whether to speak to her or give her a wide berth. She'd sat through enough of his dull sermons and she wished she could be there to see the commotion in church the following day.

'This will test their faith.' She laughed as she made a small pile of images and piled them up to the side of the collection box.

'Do you think they'll work out it was us?' Mandy paused as she placed a particularly adventurous image into a leather-bound hymn book.

'If we get in and out undetected tonight, I think it will completely confuse them,' Gilly laughed. 'They'll see that the book has gone, they'll suspect it's something to do with me, but they won't have a clue how I did it. I can't wait to see the look on the nuns' faces when they all come back from church tomorrow.'

The girls finished their work and looked to Gilly for their next move. She stuffed what was left of the book back into her pocket.

'We've one more thing to do before we go nightclubbing.'

Gilly held up the can of spray-paint from the office, which she'd pushed into her other coat pocket.

'Oh no, I'm not vandalising the church—' Mandy protested.

'I draw the line there—' Theresa spoke at the same time.

'How bad do you think I am?' Gilly said. 'We're not damaging the church, even I know better than that. We're going to pay Eric a visit on the Gipsyville estate.'

'I'm still not getting involved in any vandalism,' Mandy reasserted.

'This is all me,' Gilly reassured her. 'If anybody gets into trouble for this, I'll take all the blame. I just want to make sure Eric has something to remember me by. We'll need to take a bus over, though. Follow me.'

Gilly led the way. They turned off the lights in the church and secured the door. The path through the graveyard gave them direct access to the main road, and that meant they'd clear the mother and baby unit undetected. This was Gilly's home patch, and she guided them through the streets to the nearest bus stop.

'My house is just along that road over there.' Mandy and Theresa glanced over to where she was pointing.

'That's a posh estate,' Mandy remarked. 'You didn't tell us that you're rich.'

'I'd hardly say we're rich,' Gilly defended herself. 'We only live in a semi-detached house. But I know I'm lucky. It is nice here.'

She'd never thought about her two friends and where they might come from. It had never bothered her who came from where or how much money they had. She disliked that about her parents; they always seemed to be judging people. As far as Gilly was concerned, she knew who she liked, and she knew who she didn't like. And she liked Mandy and Theresa a lot.

As they boarded, the driver made a wry comment, noticing the bumps each girl displayed through their unbuttoned coats as they pulled themselves up onto the bus.

'If there's no room at the inn for Mary, I think you'll be out of luck, girls.' He smirked.

Gilly paid their fares and gave a polite smile. The bus wound its way around the estate until, at last, Gilly stood up and gave the cue to get off.

'The maternity hospital is on the other side of the city!' the bus driver called after them as, one by one, they carefully stepped down onto the pavement. The girls ignored him.

'Right then, let's hope Eric is in tonight. His mum and dad go to the working man's club on a Saturday, so he'll probably be staying in with his new girlfriend—'

Gilly stopped dead as she realised that used to be her, whenever she said she was staying over at her friend Helen's. She felt a sharp pang for the loss of the relationship. She'd liked

Eric and they'd had fun. Whenever she thought about him, she pictured them happy, laughing and joking together, and she missed the physical side of their relationship, too. She'd dared to imagine a future together, marriage and children, the whole package, but now she could see that would never happen. He'd broken her heart and destroyed her dreams. But she was angry with him, and that's why she had to pay him a visit before she had the baby.

'This way,' she announced, taking the shortcut through an alleyway. She could see his car the moment they stepped out onto his road. It was Eric's pride and joy.

'We're not knocking on the door, are we?' Theresa asked, suddenly wary about what Gilly had planned.

'No, I'm not paying a house call. You two stay here. I don't want you involved in this, in case I get caught.'

Mandy had spotted a low wall outside one of the houses, and she took a seat. Theresa followed.

'My ankles are sore already,' she complained. 'I'm not sure how much dancing will get done this evening.'

But Gilly was on her way, a woman with a mission now. She strode up to Eric's Ford Escort and checked around the street for any witnesses. She stood there looking over at the house, remembering a time when she hadn't felt wretched and alone. They'd had some happy times in that house – why did Eric have to go and screw it all up? Gilly then took the lid off the paint can and sprayed a message across the bonnet of Eric's car.

Eric Gittens is a cheat.

THIRTY-ONE

'Finish off the interview with McCready, please. I want to drive over to Gilly Hodges's house.'

Hollie had called DS Anderson out into the corridor.

'That man's a complete toerag,' Anderson whispered. 'How did he ever manage to survive so long in social services?'

'Do you think he's implicated?'

Anderson shrugged. 'Who knows? And he's bang on the mark about being able to prove anything.'

He turned to DS Patel.

'Have we had any luck tracing the paperwork for the mother and baby home?'

'Don't hold your breath,' she replied. 'We'd have more luck surfacing Tutankhamun's lost Egyptian scrolls.'

'Could it have been destroyed?' Hollie wondered aloud.

'I'd say there's every chance of that,' Patel continued.

'I've got a possible solution,' Hollie said. 'But it's a long shot. Theresa Morgan may have something for us. Keep everything crossed. I'll let you know if anything comes of it. And check out this place McCready mentioned – Brand New Family or Families. It's an adoption agency from the seventies, follow up on it, will you?'

The interview room door opened, and an annoyed-looking Patrick McCready appeared.

'I take it from all the whispering out here you're undecided about what to do with me?'

At that moment, DCC Warburton and DCI Osmond walked around the corner. Hollie noticed how they doubled back the moment they clocked a member of the public running loose in the corridor.

'You're free to go,' Hollie informed him, 'but please stay in close contact and let us know if you have any plans to leave the city on business or for leisure—'

'Does that mean I'm under suspicion?' McCready wasn't at all daunted by the presence of the three officers.

'You're not under arrest and you're not presently under suspicion. As I said, you're free to go. DS Anderson will escort you through the building to reception.'

Hollie would have loved to throw McCready into the cells for the night, but all she had to go on so far was a whiff of shit. Once she found the source of the stink, she'd be hot on his heels.

As DS Anderson walked McCready towards the staircase, DS Patel leant into Hollie.

'Did you see the speed Warburton and Osmond fled the moment they saw we were dealing with a punter? God forbid they might get caught up with a bit of hands-on police work. I swear, they forget what real policing is the moment they start shuffling papers.'

'It happens to all of us eventually,' Hollie lamented. 'You need the promotions to pay the bills, but the higher up the food chain you progress, the more piles of paper you have to move around. I'm pleased I still get to use my legs occasionally. Speaking of which, I'm going to drive over to check up on Gilly Hodges. Do we have anybody over there?'

'DC Gordon is on-site,' Patel replied. 'You can skip it if you want to.'

'No, I've developed a personal relationship with Gilly Hodges. I want to be sure she's okay. This was a targeted attack. It's connected with the case. I want to see it with my own eyes.'

It didn't take Hollie long to arrive at Gilly's place. She bypassed the pool cars, taking her own vehicle for speed. A single patrol car was still parked outside the house, and one of Gilly's neighbours peered out of the window at her as she walked up the path to the front door. It was already slightly ajar, and there was no sign of forced entry.

'Gilly?' Hollie called out. She could hear the hum of voices inside. She whisked out her ID and showed it to the constable who came to see who'd entered. As Hollie walked into the lounge, she immediately noticed that the picture of the girls was missing from the wall. Gilly was sitting on the same armchair that Hollie had occupied when she'd been drying out after giving chase near the River Hull. Gilly looked shaken and had a bruise on the side of her right eye. DC Gordon was sitting with the second constable on the sofa.

'How are you?' Hollie said, rushing over to Gilly.

'Shaken and stirred,' she replied. 'I have a sore jaw. He struck me across the face.'

'What have we got here?' Hollie addressed Harry and the two uniformed officers.

'A guy knocked at the door and forced his way in when Ms Hodges opened it,' DC Gordon began. 'He struck Ms Hodges across the face and asked her a series of questions about the mother and baby home. He then saw the photograph on the wall, smashed the frame, and took the image. He punched Ms Hodges in the face before leaving the property. He was on foot as far as we can tell.'

'Have you done any door-to-door knocking yet?' Hollie checked.

'Just the neighbours on either side so far,' Harry answered, sheepish.

'What did he want?' Hollie asked Gilly. 'What was he asking you? Did you recognise him?'

'It wasn't Mandy's son, if that's what you want to know,' Gilly said.

Hollie could see that her jaw was still sore. Her words weren't forming properly, like she'd just come out of the dentist's office after a filling.

'You're sure?'

'Yes, I've seen Clive several times. That wasn't him. Besides, I've always found him perfectly pleasant when he's off the booze and the drugs. He's a sweet man really.'

'What can you tell us about him?'

'I've already gone through this with your colleagues—'

'Humour me, please.' Hollie encouraged her.

'His clothing wasn't distinctive, just joggers and a top with a black jacket. Oh, and he was wearing a red cap—'

'It's our killer—' Hollie interrupted.

'Really?'

Gilly seemed suddenly terrified.

'Any prints?' Hollie asked her colleagues.

'I can put you out of your misery there,' Gilly said. 'He was wearing gloves.'

'Of course he was,' Hollie muttered. 'These people watch too much TV. They're far too wise to our methods these days.'

'Shall we knock on some more doors, ma'am?' one of the constables asked.

'Yes, please, officer.'

The two constables left the room. Harry shuffled awkwardly on the sofa.

'What did he want from you?' Hollie said to Gilly.

'He wanted to know about Father Duffy and where he's staying. He was obsessed with the girls in the photograph and who has been reunited with their adopted children.'

'Did you tell him where Father Duffy is?'

'I don't know where he is. He said, *You're a fucking councillor, you know everything.* I told him I could sort out his bin collection if he wanted some help. That's what got me this bruise.'

'That was ballsy.' Hollie winced. 'But the best thing to do is to keep quiet and give them whatever they come for in a situation like that.'

'Yes, I've learnt that lesson now. Next time a psycho breaks into the house, I'll remember that.'

'You made a note of all this, DC Gordon?' Hollie checked.

'Yes, ma'am. It's your standard threaten and intimidate playbook.'

Hollie made a mental note to check that Father Duffy was safe at the nuns' lodgings. It seemed that he might still be a target. She cursed how tight they were on resources; he needed a police guard really.

'He mentioned that McCready guy, too. He didn't seem to like him very much—'

'I'm not sure who does like McCready. I had the pleasure of his company only a half hour ago. What did he want to know?'

'He wants to know who Twiggy is.'

'Really? Did he call her Twiggy?'

'No. He called her the fifth girl.'

'How many girls were in the home at that time?'

'Just seven of us, I think. Me, Mandy, Violet, Theresa and Twiggy and some others that I hadn't met properly. One girl left just as I arrived, and two girls came just as I was leaving. It's hard to say, because Twiggy was on her own—'

'So was Violet, wasn't she?'

'Not by choice. She was in a dorm of three, but that first girl

212

left as I arrived. She'd rather have had company. That's why she made friends with us.'

'So, everybody is anxious to speak to this fifth girl. I wonder why the killer wants to find her, too—'

The crackle of a police radio could be heard from the entrance of Gilly's house.

'Will do, making our way to the scene now, over.'

The officer peered into the lounge.

'We've been called to an incident at the old pier, ma'am—'

'That's just across from The Deep,' Gilly remarked.

'It's that guy everybody's after. The one connected with the death of the nun—' the constable continued.

'Clive Bartram?' Hollie checked.

'Yes, ma'am, we'd better get over there fast. They've got him cornered, and he's threatening to jump into the Humber.'

THIRTY-TWO

'DC Gordon, call DS Patel please, and make sure Mandy Tyson is kept apprised of what's going on.'

'Yes, ma'am.'

'And let DS Patel know about Father Duffy. If this lunatic who attacked Gilly Hodges is still intent on finding him, we need to be sure he's safe. It pains me to say it, but Patrick McCready is also at risk here. He needs to be on high alert.'

Hollie's mind was working in overdrive now.

'May I use your dining room to make the calls?' DC Gordon asked.

'Be my guest,' Gilly replied.

When Harry was gone, she lowered her voice.

'He knew your name,' Gilly began.

'Who? The guy who came into your house?'

'Yes. He wanted to know where to find you.'

'Christ! Did he say why?'

Hollie pulled out her mobile phone. Phoebe hadn't sent over her new number yet.

'No, but I don't think it was a social visit he was after. He threatened me with one of my kitchen knives—'

Gilly began to sob.

'Did you tell the officers this?'

'No. I wanted to tell you personally. I'm so ashamed of how frightened I was. I said something that I shouldn't have. I was scared—'

'You've nothing to be ashamed of,' Hollie reassured her. 'It's terrifying when things like this happen. Did you tell him anything?'

'I don't know where you live, but I saw Pearson Park mentioned on those envelopes of yours that are drying on the radiator from when you were here the other night. I'm sorry, but I did tell him that much.'

Hollie moved closer to Gilly and placed her hand on her shoulder.

'Pearson Park is huge, so that won't give him very much to work from. Don't worry, I'm sure it's okay. Lunatics wanting to hurt police officers is a hazard of the job. They don't usually follow through with it. I've got visitors at the moment. As soon as I'm in contact, I'll let them know. Thanks for mentioning it.'

'I'm sorry. It was all I could offer him. I just wanted him out of my house.'

'Gilly, it's fine, I promise. Look, I'd better get over to the pier. I'll leave you with DC Gordon. I'm sorry to rush off like this. Will you be all right?'

'I'm fine now, honestly,' Gilly replied.

Hollie didn't want to leave her, but they needed Bartram in for questioning as a matter of priority. She left Gilly, brought DC Gordon up to speed, and then exited the house. The two officers had gone ahead in their marked vehicle, so she made directly for her car. Gilly had advised her to head for Nelson Street, so she entered the details into her satnav and let it guide her.

. . .

She found a spot to the side of a statue that overlooked the Humber and abandoned the car, heading for the crowd which could be seen further along the street. If there was an attraction guaranteed to pull in an audience, it was the prospect of a member of the public jumping to their death.

'What's the situation here?' Hollie asked, drawing out her ID. The two officers who'd previously been at Gilly's house were trying to create a cordoned-off area while two foot patrol officers dealt with the incident. Gates had been put up at the flood wall, with a notice warning of a dangerous structure. The second foot patrol officer was on the far side of the floodgate, shouting over to somebody. The officer seemed relieved that someone senior was on the scene.

'We have a highly distressed individual standing on the old Corporation Pier, ma'am. It's been closed because of concerns about its structural integrity. He's threatening to jump, ma'am.'

'Okay, do we have a specialist officer on the way?'

'No, ma'am, there's none available. They're all on a training course in Bridlington. They're on a course about suicide prevention.'

Noting the youthfulness of the officer and the proximity of the public, Hollie resisted the urge to curse. Instead, she reasoned the best course of action was for her to take over. She'd received some training, as had most officers, and she reckoned her connection with Clive's mother would do the job.

'I'll pick it up from here,' she informed him. 'Is there no easier way to climb over?'

'Sorry, ma'am, you've got to hop over the wall or the gate.'

Hollie clambered up, doing her best to appear composed and dignified with such a large audience now looking on.

'Give her a leg-up, mate!' some joker shouted from the gathered crowd.

She ignored it and made it over to the other side. The young officer looked completely out of her depth.

'I'll take it from here,' Hollie said. She heard a siren approaching and the sound of a boat nearby out in the Humber. The foot patrol constables had done well; Humber Rescue was out there ready to catch him if necessary, and an ambulance was on hand to thaw him out if he was silly enough to jump.

'Just stand by the floodgate. I'll try to get closer to him.'

Hollie surveyed the scene. It was a wooden pier with a waist-high white fence around its perimeter. It was stable enough to walk on, but in places there were gaps between the boards, and she could see the water below. The Humber was a lot calmer than when she'd picked a fight with it a few days previously.

Bartram was standing on the first rung of the fence, on the water side, both hands gripping the top railing. It could have been worse; there was what appeared to be a gangway part of the structure that stretched out further into the sea. She assumed this was where the river crossing departed before the Humber Bridge was built.

Hollie walked towards Bartram at the far side of the wooden platform. Ironically, he was no distance from a lifebuoy housing. She might need that if he didn't see any sense. There was no sign of a red cap, and his manner of dressing was nothing like Gilly had given in her description of her attacker.

Hollie shouted over to him: 'Clive, my name is DI Hollie Turner—'

'Don't come any closer!' He was like a cornered animal, simultaneously frightened and hostile.

'It's okay, Clive, I'll stop here. I need to be close enough so we can hear each other over the wind. Is that okay?'

'You come closer, and I'll jump!' He was looking over the edge, weighing it up, trying to find the courage.

'I won't come any closer unless you say so, Clive. I wanted to tell you that I know your mum—'

'You're just lying to sucker me in—'

She caught the sense of victimhood in his voice; this was a man who felt persecuted.

'I'm not lying, Clive. She's called Mandy Tyson. I only just met her. I know she'd do anything to protect you. Did you know she handed herself in to the police because she thought it would help you?'

'You're lying. Leave me alone. I just need some time to think!' He was desperate now. She could see his mind was racing, weighing up the options before him.

'Take it easy, Clive. I know Mandy would be very upset to see what you're doing now. I think after all those years of wondering where you were, it would break her heart if you did something silly.'

'Leave my mum out of this!' His voice quavered at the mention of Mandy, like she was hard-wired into his heart.

'I know she loves you, Clive, despite the difficulties you've had in your life.'

'You don't know anything about me!' He was defensive now, and floundering.

'Why don't you climb back onto the boards, Clive? I won't come any closer. Come over this side in case you have an accident.'

He looked like he was considering it for a moment. Hollie could hear the Humber Rescue boat buzzing about in the distance. They were giving Clive a wide berth, which was good. He'd likely panic if they came too close.

'I'm staying here. I don't trust you. You cops are all the same.'

Hollie didn't know much about Clive, but he seemed damaged and hurt. Is this what the actions of the Church done to the children who were taken from their mothers?

'We just need to chat about Sister Brennan, Clive. You don't strike me as the sort of man who'd hurt someone like that.'

'So why did those cops come to my work, then? Why can't you leave me alone?'

'We just needed to talk to you, Clive. We have to talk to everybody as part of our investigation. It doesn't mean we suspect you. We just have to eliminate you from our enquiries.'

'I've got a police record. I know how this plays out. You get your hands on a man like me and I'm an easy fit-up. I've been trying to clean myself up. I've had some steady work at the docks. And now you and your lot are sniffing around, screwing it up for me again—'

For one moment, Hollie was certain he was going to let go of the railings. He seemed to be inching closer to his final decision as every second passed.

'Think of Mandy, Clive. Think about how ruined she'll be if you go ahead with this. We can clear things up straight away. I don't think you murdered Sister Brennan, Clive. I know you've had your problems, but you don't seem like a killer to me—'

Her words were carried away by the wind off the estuary. Clive seemed to have spotted a third person clambering out onto the wooden pier. In a moment of panic, his foot slid on the fence, and he grasped at the railings to steady himself. But he was too slow. Hollie watched as he lunged backwards, out into the cold, unforgiving Humber.

THIRTY-THREE

'Oh, for fuck's sake!' Hollie cursed as she ran towards the end of the wooden pier. She'd seen the look on Clive's face as he lost his grip. He might have been threatening to jump, but she suspected it was more a cry for help. Hollie reached the white fencing and looked over the side; Clive was flailing in the water. It was difficult to hear him, but she was sure he was saying he couldn't swim.

'Hold on to the supports,' she shouted down to him. The lifebuoy was right next to her. She took a look at it, figured out how to open it up, and threw the buoyancy aid down to him. The coastguard was with him in a matter of moments. Hollie was pleased about that; there was no way she was diving in there.

She thought back to when she and DS Anderson had walked up to the side of the Humber Bridge, looking over the side, and wondering what it must be like to jump into those formidable, grey waters. Clive only had a short drop from the pier and already the sea seemed to be doing its best to swallow him up. Hollie had no intention of doing battle with the currents.

Two police constables had joined Hollie on the pier now. One of them was sending radio updates back to base.

'Is he all right, ma'am?' one of them asked. It was the officer who'd attended at Gilly's house. Hollie peered over the edge again. Clive was being pulled onto the boat by the Humber Rescue team. He looked cold, sodden and miserable, but he was alive.

'Do you have any idea where they'll drop him off on dry land?' Hollie asked.

Both officers shrugged.

'They're going to want to get him into an ambulance for a check over, but I'm not sure how they'll manage that around here. We'll have to leave that one to the experts.'

'Can you check in on the radio and see where they'll take him? We need to put a watch on him, so he doesn't bolt again.'

'Will do, ma'am.'

Hollie spotted a nearby bench and took a moment to think things through. With Clive Bartram as good as in police custody, they'd hopefully be able to eliminate him from their enquiries. He'd brought trouble on himself by doing a runner, but she had little doubt now that he was not involved in the murder.

That left two mystery men. The attack on Gilly meant nobody was safe. She made a call to DS Patel and updated her on the situation.

'I'm going to try to get a word with Clive Bartram before they whisk him off to the hospital, but we'll need to put a watch on him—'

'About that, boss—'

'This doesn't sound good.'

'It isn't, I'm afraid. We're too short on resources to place an officer with Father Duffy or Gilly Hodges—'

'You're kidding me?'

'No, sorry, the brass reckon Father Duffy is safe enough

where he is, and that Gilly Hodges would have been killed already if our man had wanted her dead.'

'Did DCC Warburton sign that off?'

'I couldn't possibly comment, ma'am, but let's just say she had some involvement in the decision-making.'

'We'll be chasing crooks on the local buses soon if they keep cutting our budgets.'

It sounded like DS Patel was drawing breath to make a comment, but she clearly thought better of it and waited for Hollie to continue.

'Well, they won't be able to deny an officer to watch over Clive Bartram until he's in police custody. Can I leave you to make sure that happens? I'm just waiting to see where they're bringing him onto dry land.'

She ended the call with DS Patel and saw one of the officers was waiting to get her attention.

'They're bringing him up by The Deep, ma'am. The rescue team are more confident of the currents there. The ambulance is heading over now.'

'Great, thank you, officer. I'll leave you to finish off here. I'm going to try to get a word with our man before he gets whisked off to the infirmary.'

Hollie headed back along the wooden boards of the pier to where a good crowd had now gathered. She climbed over the flood wall with as much grace as she had managed the last time, then headed for her car.

Before long, she'd made the short trip over the River Hull and was circling back to The Deep, which sat proudly at the side of the Humber, looking out across the estuary.

She shuddered as she drove past the Premier Inn and opposite the spot where she'd followed the man with the birthmark out into the River Hull. The water was much calmer now, but she didn't know what she'd been thinking when she followed him. She passed under the concrete flyover, past the cut-through to Gilly's estate, and parked up as close to the rescue scene as she could manage.

Another small crowd had gathered at the side of the ambulance. Clive Bartram was being moved up to the car park on a stretcher, the Humber Rescue team overseeing the operation while the medics awaited their patient. Clive seemed more embarrassed than anything, but at least he was firmly secured in the stretcher. He wasn't going anywhere while he was trussed up like that. She was pleased to see a uniformed officer waiting to accompany Clive in the ambulance. At least the police budget had managed to stretch that far.

Clive was carefully brought up the sloped bank that ran alongside The Deep, then was lifted over the white fencing that ran all along the car park. The moment he was laid down on the concrete, the medics moved in and ran their checks. Hollie let them do their work, then waited until he was safely strapped into the ambulance. She showed her ID card to the team.

'He's not an emergency case, I take it?' she checked. She already had one complaint pending from an injured Shane Hardy. She didn't want any more for the time being.

The medic gave her the all-clear to have a few words with Clive while they were tidying up at the scene and handing over to the coastguard.

'That was a silly thing to do, Clive. How are you?'

'Cold and embarrassed,' he replied.

'They're going to take you to the infirmary for a check over, then you'll be released into police custody once you've been given the all-clear. But save me some time here, Clive. We're going to have to question you formally, but your mother might be at risk here. Anything you tell me will help to keep her safe.'

Clive was a man chastened.

'Okay,' he said. 'Look, I'm sorry, but I don't have a great track record with the police.'

Hollie noticed the ambulance crew was almost ready, so time was of the essence.

'Is it you who's been dossing down at the derelict mother and baby home?'

She could see by the confusion on his face what the answer was.

'No, why? That's an odd question to ask. I'm staying in a place on Terry Street at the moment. They're helping me get things together.'

'You know we can check that, Clive?'

'Check it. They'll confirm what I've been saying.'

She knew that they already had, after chatting to Mandy. At least he was telling the truth. She caught a taxi pulling up out of the corner of her eye, but ignored it, assuming it was somebody paying a visit to The Deep.

'Is there anything you can tell me about Sister Brennan's murder? Has anybody spoken to you? Has anybody been asking questions?'

'I don't know anything about it. I just saw those cops at the docks, and I knew they were coming for me. I've seen it all before. I panicked and ran. Then when I saw on the newspaper boards that you were looking for me, I got scared. When you're a man like me, you worry about being fitted up for things. I thought you were blaming me. I didn't know what to do. I've only got my mum – my real mum – in this world, and I've pushed her as far as she'll go, with the drugs.'

'Is that why you don't live with her?'

'Yes, she chucked me out. She won't let me back until I'm clean. That's why I'm staying in Terry Street. I'm trying hard this time, officer.'

A familiar voice called over from her side, but she had to look to place who it was. Mandy was walking across the car park, a look of horror on her face as she stared at the ambulance and tried to make sense of the scene in front of her.

'Where's Clive? Is he okay?' she asked, making directly for Hollie. As she came around the side of the ambulance, she caught sight of her son and rushed to his side.

Hollie wondered what it must have been like for Mandy to throw out the son who she'd been separated from for years. She wondered if she could be as tough as those women had had to be. Mandy was half crying, half scolding her son, relieved to see he was all right but angry with him for what he'd done.

'The newspaper tweeted that something was going on at the old pier, and I knew what it was,' she explained to Hollie.

The poor woman must barely have been at home after being released from custody, before seeing the news.

'Can I go with him?' Mandy asked.

'I'm sorry, Mandy, but Clive is still a suspect in a murder case. Until we've had time to question him, he's out of bounds, I'm afraid.'

Hollie hated herself for even having to say the words. A pack of ravenous wolves couldn't have dragged her away from accompanying her own children to hospital.

'Okay, Clive, I'm going to leave you with the ambulance team now. Once you're cleared by the hospital, some officers will want to interview you. Don't run. Tell them the truth and you'll be on your way in no time. Do it for your mother, if nothing else.'

The medics took over. The uniformed officer jumped in the back of the ambulance, and Hollie watched the vehicle drive off.

'Get Mandy Tyson a lift over to the infirmary, will you?' Hollie spoke quietly to the other officer.

She was about to return to her car when she remembered Gilly. Her house was only around the corner if she used the cut-through, and she wanted to apologise that they couldn't post an officer with her to reassure her of her safety. Hollie explained what she'd organised to Mandy, then retraced her steps from the night she'd first encountered the man with the birthmark and knocked at Gilly's door. She noticed that DC Gordon's pool car had gone. She saw Gilly check who was outside through the lounge window. The door opened; Gilly was still pale.

'Oh, Hollie, I'm glad you're here. You know I said I hadn't told that man anything about you?'

Hollie could see from her face that this wasn't going to be good news.

'Yes.'

'Well, you know I put your clothes to dry on the radiators? I had them piled up in the airing cupboard, ready to give back to you—'

'Go on, Gilly.'

'I fished some leaflets and a letter out and left them on the radiator to dry. I didn't notice until after that young officer left. The letter is gone from the radiator. I think that man has your home address.'

THIRTY-FOUR

1975: GILLY'S STORY

Gilly headed out across Tiffany's dance floor, figuring out where in the building the DJ was located. All around her, sweaty bodies gyrated and moved to the thumping beat, and the multicoloured lights left floating rings in her eyes as she pushed her way through. She was struck once again by a sudden sense of loss. Why had Eric betrayed her like that? She thought they were happy. Why hadn't she seen that coming? What was so wrong with her that Eric preferred another woman? As she slipped behind the DJ's console, she tried to push aside an unwelcome sensation of uselessness from her mind. It was not a problem she usually struggled with, but the sight of all those young people having a good time hit her hard.

It was much quieter in the DJ's area, the pounding music being pushed out into the room, rather than towards them. The DJ was speaking to another guy. Gilly noticed immediately what good shape he was in, and she craved Eric's body against hers once again.

'What can I do for you, my dear?' the DJ asked.

'Can I get a couple of requests?'

'Sure, what do you want, beautiful?'

Gilly gave him Mandy's request, and he began to search for the single in his record collection. He pulled it out and let the record rest halfway out of the cover, placing it at his side.

'Don't tell me the other request is for the little one? We don't have Pinky and Perky, I'm afraid.'

The DJ seemed amused by his own joke; his mate shot Gilly a smile behind his back. The second guy had a cheeky sparkle in his eyes, like Eric did when he wanted to kiss her.

Gilly gave the DJ Theresa's request, and he moved away suddenly to fade in the next record. It was Abba's 'Waterloo', a firm favourite since its Eurovision success. There was a collective sound of unanimous approval, and from behind the DJ's console, Gilly was aware of a swell of movement toward the dance floor. Right across the room, momentarily caught by the light of a spinning disco ball, her two friends waddled out from their table for a dance. Good, they were enjoying themselves at last.

'Fancy a dance?' the DJ's mate asked.

'You don't mind this?' Gilly checked, indicating her belly.

'You look gorgeous,' the man replied. 'I don't mind if you don't. Besides, it's only a dance.'

Eric's words echoed in her ears the first time they'd made love in the back of his car.

'It's only a kiss,' he'd reassured her.

Gilly looked him over and gave him a smile.

'Yes, why not? Let's go for a dance.'

Gilly loved Abba, and 'Waterloo' was a great song to dance to. It created a wave of instant positivity among the crowd, and Gilly felt like she hadn't got a care in the world. All thoughts of babies, births and bullying nuns were banished from her mind. The DJ capitalised on his success by fading directly into 'Ring, Ring' and it seemed that the dance floor was even more packed than it had been for the previous song.

She was aware of people pointing at her belly, but she

couldn't care less. Just because she was pregnant didn't mean she couldn't enjoy a night out.

'What's your name?' her dance partner shouted over the music.

'Gilly,' she shouted back. 'What's yours?'

'Barry,' he answered. 'You're very pretty.'

Gilly didn't know what to say.

'I'd better tell my friends that I'm okay—'

'What?'

'I'm just going to see my friends for a minute!'

Gilly pointed in the general direction of where she'd left Mandy and Theresa, and Barry appeared to have picked up the gist of what she was telling him.

Theresa and Mandy were sitting down when she returned.

'My ankles hurt,' Mandy complained.

'I feel so heavy,' Theresa joined in.

'I requested your songs. They'll be on soon. Save your energy for when the DJ plays them.'

'Where were you?' Theresa asked.

'I met a guy. We were just having a dance—'

'Is that him coming over now?'

Gilly turned around and Barry was standing behind her, grinning.

'Are these your friends?' he shouted in Gilly's ear.

'Yes, Theresa and Mandy.'

Barry shook Mandy's and Theresa's hands; the music was so loud it was impossible to hear voices.

'Ring, Ring' ended and the low, growling voice of Barry White boomed through the sound system. Mandy was straight up on her feet, and Theresa rushed after her.

'Fancy another dance?' Barry asked.

'Why not?' Gilly grinned back at him. 'I get two helpings of Barry for the price of one!'

He took her hand and walked her out to a part of the dance

floor that was some distance away from her friends. She gave them a wave to let them know where she was going. As the song worked its way through to the chorus, Gilly became aware that Barry was an active dancer, using a lot of space and gradually working them towards the DJ's console. Immediately after Mandy's request, the DJ segued into The Rubettes, and Gilly knew that Theresa would be up dancing away with Mandy, despite any physical discomfort. Barry was nice; he was a better dancer than Eric, and he obviously fancied her. At the end of the song, Gilly felt suddenly light-headed and a little faint.

'Are you okay?' Barry asked. 'You look really hot.'

'Do you mind if I pop out for a bit of fresh air? It's so stuffy in here.'

'Of course not.' Barry smiled, offering his arm for support.

As they walked over to the doorway, Gilly caught the attention of her friends and made a couple of gestures to let them know she was heading outside. As they stepped into the street, the cool, fresh, night-time air was glorious, and Gilly felt instantly better.

'Shall we take a walk around the block?' Barry asked. 'I'm sure you'll feel much better.' Gilly's hand was still resting on his arm, so when he led the way, she followed. They turned down the side of the street. There were several couples there, some taking refuge from the traffic noise on Ferensway, others kissing and cuddling.

'That's better,' Barry said. 'I can hear you speaking at last. So, what do you do, Gilly? I mean, when you're not having babies.'

'I used to work at the Cecil Cinema.'

'Oh, I go there a lot. I might have seen you. I'm sure I'd have noticed a girl as attractive as you.'

'Maybe,' Gilly replied. They'd stopped. It was quieter here.

'I thought it would be nice to spend a bit of time alone, away from the music. I'd like to get to know you better.'

Gilly wanted to return to the club. Somehow, he'd taken her to a dark area of the street. There weren't any couples there. She began to pull her hand away from his arm, but he grasped it with his other hand.

'Not so fast,' he said. 'I thought I might at least get a little kiss while we're out here—'

'Oh, no, I don't think so.' Gilly tried to pull her hand away again, but he gripped it tightly.

'It's okay, Gilly, no need to rush back. I know the sort of girl you are. I'm sure you won't mind giving me a small kiss before you go.'

'Barry, no, I don't want to. I have a boyfriend already—'

'Well, he's not here now, is he? And you're obviously a bit of a tart if you're out on the town with your slapper friends—'

'Barry, that's enough!' she shouted at him. She tugged at his hand again, and this time it came away. She turned to rush back up the side street, but he grabbed her shoulder and pushed her against the wall.

'Why be in such a rush, Gilly? It's not like you can get pregnant again.'

Barry had seemed so nice, but his tone had changed completely, and Gilly was scared now.

'I want to go back to my friends,' she protested, but Barry wasn't listening. He pushed his body against hers so that she was pinned against the wall. He was pressing on her stomach; he didn't seem to care about the baby. His right hand moved up towards her breasts, and she froze as he pushed his lips towards her face. His breath smelt of beer and cigarettes. She raised her knee and hammered it into his groin. Barry shot back as if he'd just got an electric shock.

'You stupid fucking cow!' he screamed at her. 'Why did you do that?'

Gilly didn't wait to answer. She turned and began to make her way towards the main road. She'd almost got as far as a kissing couple when Barry spun her around and slapped her across her face.

'We're not done yet,' he cursed at her.

Gilly was rooted to the spot, stunned at how fast he'd moved to violence.

'Just a bit of girlfriend bother.' He grinned at the man nearby, who'd broken off from his kissing to check what was going on. 'You know what birds can be like!'

The man looked like he was about to say something when Barry cut him off.

'You'd best move along, mate. I think we got to this spot before you.'

Gilly was unable to speak as she watched the man shrug and encourage his girlfriend along the lane.

'We'll let you sort it out between yourselves,' he muttered.

'Right, now we're alone,' Barry said, taking her by her left wrist.

Gilly struggled, but he was too strong for her, and she was tired now. The baby was spinning somersaults inside her; she didn't know what to do.

'It's not like you don't like it, I can see that already. If you want to play hard to get, that's fine with me. But you can't lead a man on like that and—'

'I wasn't leading you on! I just danced with you—'

'Same thing,' Barry said as he pushed Gilly against the wall again and moved his hand up her dress.

'Leave her alone!' came a voice.

'Fuck off!' Barry shouted.

A bottle bounced off Barry's head, then into the wall, shattering at Gilly's feet. She jumped, but Barry released her. Mandy and Theresa were standing there. Mandy was holding Gilly's coat, and Theresa had a full bottle of Babycham in her hand.

Barry was rubbing his head, as shocked by the attack as Gilly was. She stepped over to her friends.

'Leave her alone,' Theresa said, 'or I'll throw the other bottle at you.'

'Oh, boo-hoo,' Barry jeered. 'Look, Gilly, your two whore friends have come to save you. Well, I wouldn't touch some other guy's sloppy seconds. Who wants to shag a fat bird, anyway—'

He stopped dead in his tracks. Theresa had thrown the second bottle of Babycham at him. It was only small, but it was enough to make him break his stride.

'You crazy bitch!' He rubbed his head.

'That's enough, mate.'

The man who'd been canoodling with his girlfriend had returned with a friend. His mate had a bodybuilder's physique. The man's fist went flying into Barry's chin, and Barry crashed to the ground.

'Thank goodness for that,' Gilly said, relieved her ordeal was over.

But it wasn't finished just yet. Theresa stood in front of them, with her legs slightly apart and a look of shock on her face.

'I think my waters just broke.'

THIRTY-FIVE

In the instant Gilly broke the news about the misplaced letter to her, Hollie's phone sounded. The number was identified, but she didn't recognise it. Was it the man with the birthmark?

'Excuse me one moment, Gilly.'

Hollie answered the call.

'Hello.'

'Hollie, it's Phoebe. I've lost Noah.'

Her stomach tensed and she thought she was going to be sick. Her heart began to pound feverishly, and she could barely speak.

'What?'

'We'd been playing in the park. I turned my back, and he was gone.'

Hollie's mind raced furiously. What had he done? Had he wandered off? Had he got into trouble? She pictured her little boy and she wanted to scream at what might have happened to him.

'Where are you now?'

'I'm waiting at the play area.'

'I'm heading over now. Stay there with Lily in case he comes back. I'll check at the flat first, then come over to you.'

'Okay. I'm sorry, Hollie.'

'It's all right, Phoebe, he's a sensible kid. He'll probably have made his way back to the flat. Give me ten minutes. I'm on my way.'

She ended the call.

'Is everything okay?' Gilly asked.

'I hope so,' Hollie replied. Her mind was burning hot with the possibilities.

'You're certain the letter is gone? It hasn't fallen down the back of the radiator or something daft like that?'

'I'll check. Do you want me to call you?'

'Yes, immediately, as soon as you're sure. You've got my number already?'

Gilly nodded.

'I've got to go. Lock the door and take some time to rest. You've had a terrible shock. We'll get this guy, I promise. Sooner or later, he'll make a mistake.'

Hollie turned and ran towards the cut-through. She was out of breath by the time she reached her vehicle, but she didn't care; her sole objective now was to find Noah. She raced off in the car, thanking her good fortune that she was so close to home. It took ten minutes to get there. She didn't bother locking the car when she arrived; she flung the door open and ran across the road to the flats. She trusted Noah to have the good sense to wait on the doorstep if he'd got separated, but he wasn't there. She searched in her pocket for her door keys.

'Shit!'

Phoebe had one set of keys; Jenni still had the spares. They'd been working together throughout the day, and she'd forgotten all about them. Her colleague was probably walking about with them in her pocket. She knocked on the front window of her flat.

'Are you in there, Noah?'

There was no sound and no movement. She slammed her hand on the window, and it vibrated. Hollie stared across the park. The play area was on the opposite side, and it suddenly seemed like a vast space. She tried to sweep across the entire area, scanning for boys of Noah's age, trying to recollect what he was wearing. Her heart pounded fast, like the ticking hand of a clock, marking out the seconds since he'd last been seen.

Hollie's hand hovered on her phone. It was clammy, so she wiped it on her clothing. Should she alert her colleagues? She wanted every patrol down at the park, straight away, with no delay. It didn't matter what else was going on in the city, this was her son.

She wrestled her escalating fears to the ground, waiting a while to make sure they were in check. She couldn't sound the alert, not yet. In all likelihood, Noah had wandered off. She'd sound like a neurotic mother if she demanded they send out teams to search for him. But what if he hadn't got lost and was in danger? These crucial seconds would be vital to his safety. The competing voices in her mind were all shouting for attention, and she didn't know which to listen to; she just wanted to scream and let it out. But the kids had wandered off so many times when they were younger; it was an everyday hazard for a parent. They usually turned up with a staff member, or a call over the Tannoy resulted in a swift reunion. No, she'd wait. They'd do a quick search, and then she'd alert her colleagues.

Hollie ran over to her car, her legs unsteady and her hands trembling. She climbed inside and had barely released the handbrake when she shot off towards the perimeter of the park. As she drove, she scanned the pavements and the park, glancing around furiously, not wanting to miss an inch.

The play area arrived soon enough, and she pulled up the car on a double yellow line, not caring much about finding a proper parking space. She paused for a moment, her mouth dry, her hands shaking as they gripped the steering wheel.

Phoebe was standing with Lily close to the gate, looking out of her mind with worry.

'Thank God you're here,' Phoebe said as Hollie walked through the gate.

'It's okay. He won't have gone far,' Hollie tried to reassure her. 'Now, tell me where you were when he disappeared.'

'Lily and I were messing about on the outdoor gym equipment, and Noah said he was going to sit on the swings. I told him we'd come over when we finished. It's all fenced and gated for the tiny kids who play there anyway. He's ten. I thought he'd be okay—'

Phoebe looked like Hollie felt. There was only space for one of them to fall to pieces; she had to keep her shit together.

What would you do if you were still a beat bobby and a parent with a lost child came up to you?

She repeated the words in her head. The park covered a large area; there was so much ground to cover and so many places he might have gone.

'We've got to get organised. Lily, I want you to come with me. I'm going to ask that lady over there to look out for Noah. If he comes back here, he can wait with her until we get back. Don't go anywhere. Phoebe, we're going to circle the pond. Once we've done that, we'll sweep the rest of the park—'

'And what if we don't find him?'

Phoebe looked like she was on the verge of tears.

'We give it fifteen minutes, then I call in my colleagues.'

Hollie checked in with the woman on the bench who was watching her two children playing in what looked like a cross between a swing and a hammock. She showed her the photo she'd taken of Noah earlier when they'd been sitting on the sofa.

'If you see this boy, please tell him to stay here with you. We'll come back for him—'

Oh, Noah, where are you?

'Right, Phoebe, you take that way, we'll take this way. Meet back at the play area. Call me if you see anything.'

Hollie grabbed Lily's hand and she seemed happy to be led. Hollie had intentionally taken the route with more of the distractions that might tempt Noah away from a play area. She started to jog, anxious to cover as much ground as possible, but Lily was struggling to keep up, so she slowed down a little. She checked the outside gym area, but there was just a retired couple there, laughing and chatting as they used the equipment. She made a circuit of the tearoom and toilets, then headed to the bandstand. She'd taught the kids to look for a responsible adult or stand somewhere visible, where they'd be found easily. The bandstand seemed a likely place to find him, but he wasn't there, so she checked the nearby statue.

Hollie scanned the park ahead of her, looking for a child on their own. She daren't even imagine him being taken; she refused to let her mind go there.

'Do you see him, Lily?'

Her daughter was growing tearful now, picking up on her blind panic. It was unfair to drag her around so frantically; they needed help.

Hollie took her phone out of her pocket and rang the office, asking to be put through to DS Patel.

'Hi, it's Hollie. I need your help.'

DS Patel seemed to pick up on the urgent tone of her voice.

'Go ahead, boss.'

'My son's gone AWOL in Pearson Park. I need a bit of discretion, please. Can you see if there are any foot patrols in the area? I could do with some extra pairs of legs searching the park. It's so big, I don't remember it being this vast. I don't want a big deal making out of it, in case he's wandered off.'

'You sound like it's more than that, boss.'

'It might be. There's a chance our killer has my home address.'

'You don't think—?'

'I can't even consider it, or I'll have a nervous breakdown. Just see who's in the area and tell them to meet me at the play area if you would. Once we've done a full sweep of the park, I'll put out an official alert.'

'I hope you find him, boss, I really do.'

Hollie couldn't count the times she'd had to search for lost kids while she was a beat officer in Morecambe. They'd get separated from their families at the arcades, in the Arndale Centre, and all manner of other places. She knew the drill. But he had her home address, which made this more threatening.

From the statue, Hollie jogged over to the large, greenhouse-like structure further along the path. Lily tried to keep up but was tiring. Hollie opened the door, rushed inside, searched it as fast as she could, then made her exit. As she stepped outside, Phoebe called out to her. She was on a small bridge that crossed the pond.

'Anything?' Hollie asked.

'No sign of him,' Phoebe answered. She'd been crying. Hollie felt a surge of guilt. She'd abandoned Phoebe with her two kids while she was rushing around at work. Phoebe had only asked if she could stay overnight for a university interview, and she'd dropped childminding duties on her from a great height. Léon's voice sounded in her head.

You're always at work. You can't care for the children. They're better off with me.

'Come with me, I've got us some help.'

Phoebe took Lily's hand, allowing Hollie to lead the way back to the play area. She could have kissed the two Specials who were waiting there. They were talking to an old lady who was out walking her two dogs. Hollie took out her ID card and made herself known to them.

'This lady thinks she might have seen your son,' one of the officers began. 'Please tell DI Turner what you told us, madam.'

'I came to tell the officers immediately,' she said, a look of concern across her face. 'I saw a young boy being pulled along by a man on the other side of the park. The boy was crying, and the man called over to me and said he'd been misbehaving so he was being taken home. It didn't look right to me. I got a bad feeling about it.'

THIRTY-SIX

'Which way were they heading?' Hollie asked, desperate now. The calm police-officer exterior was long gone; hers was now the face of a frantic mother.

The woman pointed vaguely into the distance.

'I'm going to need more detail than that,' Hollie urged, doing her best not to scream in frustration at the woman. She knew how this worked. Every second counted. If this man had got her address from the envelope at Gilly's house and had somehow found her son, Noah was in terrible danger. Every minute they wasted was an opportunity for his abductor to get further away. If he was in a car, he could be leaving the city by now. Hollie had been through this as an officer so many times in her career. But there was nothing quite like being involved first-hand to sharpen the mind.

'You see that group of cars over there?' The woman signalled.

'Yes, where the white van is, next to the motorcycle?'

'Yes. He headed over that way.'

'Phoebe, wait with Lily please—'

'I want to come with you, Mum.'

Lily looked terrified, her face blanched. She was picking up on the tension and was old enough not to have the wool pulled over her eyes. Hollie forced herself to calm down. She'd told members of the public to do it in similar situations: she had to get a grip. She'd lose her mind if she didn't.

'Lily, I need you to stay here with Phoebe, okay? It's really important because if Noah comes back, he'll return to where he left you. Or he'll find the flat again. Can you do that for me?'

Phoebe took Lily's hand and knelt at her side.

'Your mum's right, Lily, this is a really important job. We have to be here if Noah comes back. He might not speak to these police officers, but he will be looking for us. He'll get scared if we're not here for him. Once we've found him, we can go to that KFC that's just up the road. How does that sound?'

Lily nodded. Hollie could have kissed Phoebe; she was growing up to be an impressive young woman. Phoebe led Lily back to the bench where they'd been sitting previously, giving Hollie a small nod before turning.

'I need you to radio Control and make sure there are more officers on the way to support the search. This entire park needs to be swept and I want to know all the CCTV points that circle this place. If he's driven off, we need a vehicle ID and number plate ASAP,' Hollie said.

'Right, ma'am,' the first officer replied.

'When backup arrives, make sure they're organised in a methodical sweep of the park—'

Hollie pulled out her phone. She found the photo of Noah they'd taken sitting on the sofa earlier that day and held it up for both the officers to see.

'That's my son. That's who we're looking for. Do you have anything on you that I can send this to?'

The officers drew out mobile devices and Hollie sent the image over via text. Her hands were shaking as she tapped in the numbers and she cursed her mistakes, knowing that every mistyped number was time wasted.

'I'd like you to come with me.' Hollie addressed the second special constable. 'I want to check out those vehicles, then I'm going to ask you to walk around the perimeter of the park and note down any CCTV locations, especially anything the council has that we can access quickly.'

She took a pause.

'Have I missed anything obvious?' she asked.

The officers looked at each other. They were special constables, volunteers and part-timers; they'd likely have limited experience in situations like this. She was in charge, the experienced officer. For the sake of her son, she prayed she was bringing her best game.

'Let's go,' she said, heading off in the direction of the white van, then stopping to address the woman with the dogs.

'Is there anything else you can tell us about this man? Was he carrying anything? Was there anything else distinctive about him?'

The woman appeared to be searching her mind. Her facial expression changed; she'd clearly recalled a detail.

'He had a rucksack on his back. It was old and worn, but it had blue panels on either side. Is that helpful? Oh, and he was wearing a red cap. And sunglasses.'

Hollie froze for a moment. It was all she could do to hold herself together.

'Thank you, that's very helpful. I don't know what we'd have done without you. Officer, please make sure we have this lady's details recorded, if that hasn't been done already.'

'We did it straight away,' the second officer replied, with a beaming face like a dog that was just about to be handed a bone.

'Excellent work, both of you, thank you,' Hollie replied.

From the smiles on their faces, the two Specials looked like the case had been resolved and wound up already.

'Let's keep it up now. We've a boy to find. My son. We all need to focus on this.'

Hollie led the way across the park, with her full attention on the white van. There were four vehicles in the small cluster indicated by the woman with the dogs. A motorcycle, the van and two cars: one an SUV and the other a small Fiat. From experience, she knew vans were often used in abductions, though some SUVs had tinted glass, which was useful for concealing dubious activities. At least the van was still parked up. If that was where Noah was concealed, they'd get him back in no time.

When they were close enough, Hollie drew her phone and took photos. She knew that makes and precise colour palettes were essential for identifying vehicles, but she was not such an expert that she could identify them from their look and shape alone.

'I want to check the van first.' Hollie remembered that despite the uniform, it was unlikely such a young officer would have much experience under their belt. 'You take a look at that camera over there. If it has a reference code on it, jot it down. Radio Control and see if we can get images pulled off. We also need to note the plate number and the make and model. Okay? Once you've done that, come and join me again.'

The officer headed to the tall CCTV post positioned in a clearing well away from the trees. He looked like he was having the best day of his life. This was her son they were looking for; it was not a training exercise. She forced down her annoyance, knowing that she needed this man's assistance. And, if it came to an altercation, he looked like he'd be a handy guy to have on her side.

Hollie couldn't see anybody at the front of the van. They were close enough to be seen and heard now. The remaining officer's fluorescent jacket possibly wasn't the best attire for a stealth move, but she'd have to make do. She pointed at the back of the van. The officer took the near side, and Hollie walked around the back. She listened for sobbing. There was nothing. Then she heard movement. She immediately moved for the rear doors, placing her hand on the lever, and then giving it a tug. It was locked.

The van's engine started up and engulfed Hollie in a black cloud of diesel fumes. The driver swerved the vehicle out into the road, without a signal or caution, almost striking an elderly woman with a walking frame who was crossing over to the park.

Hollie slammed her hand on the back of the van, urging the driver to stop. He'd paused for long enough to check the old lady was all right and was now moving the vehicle to the side of the road. Hollie ran behind him, shouting at him to stop. The engine sounded like it'd seen better days, and she could barely hear herself over its moaning mechanics. She moved to the side of the van so the driver would be able to see her in his wing mirror, but he seemed more intent on what the pensioner was up to rather than being aware of what was going on around him.

The van pulled out into the road and Hollie ran for the passenger-side door, lunging at its handle. She missed it the first time, but the second time she caught it, just as the driver began to pick up speed, having now cleared out of the old lady's path. She flicked it and it clicked open, but it didn't swing open fully.

'Stop!' she shouted, but the driver revved the engine and picked up speed along the road. She ran after him, knowing already that she'd never keep up. Before he'd got too far away from her, Hollie photographed the number plate and noted the model.

'Fuck!' she shouted out. 'Fuck, fuck, fuck!'

A woman was walking on the pavement nearby and tutted. The officer was running up behind her.

'You should have a word with her, officer, swearing like that in front of young children!'

'I'm so sorry,' Hollie called over, but the woman was having none of it.

'It's difficult enough bringing up young children in this day and age. And people like you don't help—'

She appeared to have no appetite for further confrontation and continued along the pavement.

'Are you all right, ma'am? Was that him?'

'It might be,' Hollie replied. 'I've got the registration plate. Get this over to Control and let's get this bastard stopped before he has a chance to get away.'

The officer got straight onto it. Behind them, a motorcycle revved up and drew away, heading in the opposite direction to them. He was behind trees before she knew it, but it was the motorcycle that had been parked close to the white van. Hollie cursed for a moment, then cut herself some slack. The motorcyclist was alone and there was no way of concealing a young boy without him being seen. She could at least be thankful for that.

THIRTY-SEVEN

Hollie's uniformed colleagues had moved fast. Across the park, she could see high-vis vests. At least six officers fanned out, covering the entirety of the space. If Noah had simply wandered off, they'd find him. If he'd been abducted in the white van, the driver would be pulled over in no time. Her legs felt suddenly weak, and she looked for a bench.

'I have to sit down for a moment,' she informed the young officer. There was a place to sit nearby, and Hollie was grateful for that. She'd been hit by an overwhelming wave of fear and anxiety. The thought of any harm coming to Noah was unbearable.

Her phone rang, and it was out of her pocket in a moment. She checked the screen. It was Léon. Of course it was.

For a moment, she considered ignoring it. That wouldn't be unexpected on a regular workday. Instead, she decided to answer it and lie.

'Is everything all right? I haven't heard from Phoebe.'

Hollie hadn't considered that. With Phoebe's phone lost, there was no way for her to update Léon after they arrived in Hull.

'Everything is fine. We're in the park at the moment—'

The young officer who was standing at the side of the bench gave her an inquisitive look.

'Phoebe left her phone on the train. I met them at the station and picked them all up as arranged. Everything is fine here. Léon, you should get off and do whatever it is you and Veronique like to do.'

She hated herself for lying, but what else could she say? *Sorry, the kids have barely been here for a couple of hours, and we suspect one of them may have been abducted already.* If she hadn't been fighting so hard not to have a complete mental and physical breakdown, she might have laughed at the sheer ridiculousness of the situation.

'I know you, Hollie. Your voice is slightly shrill. That means something is going on. Can I speak to the kids?'

'I'm on my own right now. I just needed to head over to the loo—'

The officer glared at her this time. She knew she was overcompensating in trying to calm her voice.

'My voice is so shrill because I'm busting for a pee and you're stopping me from going by speaking on the phone. This is a middle-aged woman's bladder emergency!'

She could sense Léon's doubt at the other end of the phone, but she had to push through the lie. There was no way she could cope with his accusations and shaming right now. He'd be right to throw every bit of negativity he had at her, but she couldn't deal with it at this moment. The only way she could cope with what was going on was to lie.

As she sat there, waiting to see how he'd respond, Hollie saw that she was going to have a fight on her hands to keep the children with her. The only way she could do that was to leave the police. It would be like removing the safety net from her very existence. If she wasn't a police officer, she wasn't sure what she was. She knew what Léon's answer would be.

You're a mother! A mother to two children.

She loved her children as much as any mum, but that alone wasn't enough. There had to be something else in her life: her career. Policing to Hollie was like having another lover. She was as wedded to the job as she was to her family, or at least what was left of her family.

'Okay, but I'd like to chat with the children this evening before they go to bed. I want to catch up with their day and see how they're doing. I'll call after seven, okay?'

'Of course, and now can I go for my pee?'

'Go for your pee, we'll speak later.'

Léon ended the call, and Hollie started to breathe again. The officer busied himself with his radio, but she knew he'd heard the full conversation.

'I'm not proud of what I just did,' she announced to him as if she owed him an explanation. 'But I can't face dealing with their father at this moment.'

'It's fine, ma'am. I think we all do it. If my girlfriend knew some of the situations we get into as Specials, she would have insisted I never left my day job to try to become a salaried police officer. It kind of gets you, doesn't it?'

It kind of gets you, doesn't it?

That was exactly it, and it was something Léon would never understand, what with his laptop and kitchen table working life.

The officer's radio crackled, and Hollie caught the update. They'd apprehended the van driver before he'd even had time to leave the road that circled the park; he never made it as far as one of the city's arterial routes.

'Is Noah in there?' Hollie asked, standing up, the power now returned to her body.

'They've literally just got him,' the officer replied. 'They're by the Beverley Road exit.'

Hollie scanned the area and got a fix on where they were.

'That's across the grass over there, isn't it?'

The officer nodded, and she was away. That was the exit closest to her flat. Her legs were steady again now, so much so that she ran across the grass. She could see the white van already. It had been pulled over to the side, and three fluorescent vests were darting around the vehicle. She thanked her lucky stars that she was in a position to get such fast action from her uniformed colleagues. Hollie knew that members of the public would be subjected to much more scrutiny before getting so many resources deployed to search for a child who may just have wandered off.

'Is my son in there?' she asked, out of breath, to nobody in particular. Two of the officers looked at her, as if to say, *Who the hell are you?*

It was an occasional hazard of being plain-clothed, so she pulled out her ID card and they checked it over, immediately tensing when they saw her rank.

'Just paint pots, plastic sheets and brushes, ma'am. He's been painting the living room in somebody's house all day.'

Hollie could see that the third officer was speaking to the van driver on the far side of the vehicle, so she walked around to join them. The painter had a hangdog look about him. There was no doubt he was genuinely a painter from the state of his hands and overalls and the smell of turpentine that was coming off him.

'The vehicle isn't insured,' the third officer informed her, after inspecting her ID.

'This is all I need,' the man said, on the verge of tears. 'I haven't been paid for a couple of jobs and so I let my insurance slip for a few days. And now you're accusing me of abducting a kid. I'll never work again after this.'

The moment he spoke, Hollie saw this wasn't their man.

'Didn't you see me in your wing mirror?' Hollie asked.

'There's no glass in that offside mirror unless you hadn't noticed. That's another thing I need to fix as soon as someone pays me. Bloody vandals smashed it two weeks ago. I'm just trying to make a living here.'

Hollie felt her body slump; it was like every drop of hope had just leaked into the road. This man was as desperate as she was, in his own way.

'Make sure he didn't see anything, take his contact details, then let him go.'

'Really?' the painter asked, like it was the first break he'd had in a very long time.

'Even the insurance, ma'am?' the officer checked.

'Make it the next thing you do before you go home tonight. Is that clear?'

The painter nodded. She reckoned he couldn't believe his luck.

Hollie walked off in the direction of her flat. She needed a moment alone to collect her thoughts. She'd gone from case lead to victim in an hour; she wasn't sure she could hold it together much longer.

'Thank you! Thank you!' was all the painter could say.

'Give me a minute,' Hollie said to the special constable who'd become stuck to her like a loyal pet.

'Yes, ma'am. I'm here when you need me, ma'am.'

It was all Hollie could do to walk along the road towards her flat. She just wanted to close the door for five minutes, to shut out the noise and figure out what to do next. As she neared the flats, she saw something on the doorstep. It looked like a sack from that distance, but something told her it was more than that. Her heart began to pound, like it had just received a blast of electricity. She was running now. She could see what it was: Noah, curled up in a ball, motionless and silent.

'Over here!' she called over to the officers along the road. 'He's over here.'

They moved in unison as if a general had just given the

battle charge. Hollie pictured Noah, cradling him in her arms, swearing to him that she'd keep him safe.

She rushed up to her son, kneeling down, desperate to know if he was still alive. Her hands were trembling, her mind rushing to take it all in, to work out what had happened to him and to ascertain if he was hurt. It felt amazing to touch him and hold him again, but he was not moving.

Hollie's heart felt like it had stopped momentarily, like a car engine about to stall. She looked for blood or bruising, frantically trying to work out what had happened to him.

She turned him over, desperately searching for a pulse in his neck. She could barely stop her hands from shaking, her entire body was gripped by paralysing fear, and she felt like she was about to crumple, like a paper cup under a heavy boot.

'Call an ambulance!' she shouted. 'Get an ambulance here now.'

Hollie wanted everything to happen at once, but she didn't know where to begin.

She caught his pulse. It was like a half-lit candle, struggling to stay lit in a breeze, but it was there.

'He's alive!' she shouted out, inspecting his body for blood, a wound, a bruise. Anything that might suggest he'd been hurt.

Her tears were flowing freely now, both with relief and frustration. She kissed his head over and over, as if touching him would prove it was real.

There was an envelope at Noah's side. His body had been concealing it. It had her name on it. She tore it open and read the handwritten, capitalised message inside.

BACK OFF OR HE WON'T BE ALIVE NEXT TIME.

THIRTY-EIGHT

1975: GILLY'S STORY

'You stay right there, sunshine,' said the man who'd thrown the punch. Barry had calmed down in the face of superior physical force. The man's foot was resting on his chest; Barry's face was bloodied and sore.

'Are you sure the baby's coming?' Gilly asked.

'It feels like I just wet myself. It was like a small pop,' Theresa explained.

'Does it hurt?' Mandy asked.

'No, but it felt a bit weird,' Theresa continued. 'What should we do? I'm worried, I'm not ready for this yet. I thought I'd have more time—'

For the first time that night, Gilly considered that her actions might have been irresponsible and potentially dangerous to her friends. The three of them looked ridiculous with their bellies hanging out and coats that wouldn't fasten. They were gathering a small crowd from the nightclub. Most of the girls there were slender and well-dressed, whereas they looked like a bunch of waddling ducks out on a coach trip.

For the briefest moment, Gilly wanted to cry. This was supposed to have been their big night out, a final fling before they became mothers. She saw now that she'd gone too far. Theresa was having her baby, they were stuck in the middle of the city, and they were in a whole lot of trouble. She thought of Sister Brennan waiting for them back at the home and imagined her checking the room and finding the girls gone. She might threaten Violet and even push her. She should have thought it through better.

'Do you want to go to the hospital, or should we sneak back into the home?' Gilly asked.

'How long will the baby take to come?' Theresa replied. 'I know the doctor told me about this stuff, but I wasn't really listening. It all seemed so far away. I didn't want to think about it. I'm feeling really frightened now.'

'It could come in a couple of days,' Mandy suggested. 'Just because your waters break, it doesn't mean you're about to have the baby.'

The blue flashes of a police light lit up the side street.

'Oh hell, the police are here,' Gilly remarked, pleased that they hadn't deafened everybody by using the siren.

Two police officers got out of the car and walked over to where Barry was pinned down on the pavement.

'Should we run for it?' Gilly suggested.

'It won't be much of a chase at the speed we can walk!' Theresa exclaimed. 'Besides, we'll have to take our medicine now, however bad it tastes.'

One of the police officers walked up to the girls, a slight smirk on his face.

'Shouldn't you be at home knitting booties, girls?'

He seemed pleased with his joke.

'Now, we've been told that one of you got into a scrape with this lad. Which one of you was it?'

'It was me.' Gilly stepped forward. 'He tried to attack me.'

The police officer gave her a doubtful look.

'He did, he tried to force himself on me—'

'She's a fucking liar,' Barry called out. 'She was practically begging me to kiss her!'

'That's not what happened!' Gilly protested.

The policeman looked her up and down, giving a knowing nod as he did so.

'It looks like you enjoy a bit of attention from the boys, luv, if you get my drift—'

His mate stood by his side, chuckling.

'It sounds to me like you might have bitten off more than you can chew, sweetheart,' he added.

Gilly was about to protest to them, thinking of the vandalism that had been scrawled on the sign at the mother and baby home. *Home For Whores*, it had said. Did they all think the same thing?

She looked at her friends. Theresa appeared exhausted and on edge, Mandy looked like she'd rather be any other place but here. She'd already caused enough trouble for one night, and there was still the inevitable fallout from vandalising Eric's car and the rude pictures in the hymn books to deal with.

'Can you have a word with him and let us go home?' Gilly asked, cutting her losses. 'I don't want my friends to get into trouble.'

'That's a good choice, my darling,' the officer replied. 'It looks to me like you've all got more pressing things on your mind. How are you getting home?'

The girls looked at each other, and then Mandy replied.

'Taxi, I think?' she said.

'I tell you what, we'll give you the VIP treatment, seeing as you all look like you need it. I'll run you back home in the police car, and we'll get another patrol vehicle to pick up your male friend here and give him a free night in the cells. How does that sound?'

It was sorted. The police officer explained to his colleague what was happening, and they pulled Barry up from the pavement and cuffed him.

'Fucking slut!' he called over to Gilly.

The guy who'd punched him moved his knee into Barry's balls and Barry doubled over in agony.

'He just assaulted me,' Barry complained when he was able to speak again.

'Sorry, mate, I was looking the other way,' one of the cops said.

'Me too,' his colleague added.

'You all saw that, didn't you?' Barry appealed to the small crowd of onlookers.

He was met with a flurry of denials.

'No, mate, I didn't see it.'

'You got what you deserved.'

'Give us two minutes to get these girls shifted, then let him go,' the first officer called over to the men who had Barry restrained. His next comment was quieter, but Gilly still heard it. 'These young lasses have got a bit of an imagination on them, it's probably their condition that's doing it.'

The three girls were escorted over to the first police car. It was a squeeze to get in the back seat, but they managed it and were relieved to have a ride back to the home.

'Where are we heading, ladies?' the driver asked.

'The Church of St Mary and the Angels,' Gilly replied.

'I think it might be a bit too late for prayers, girls.' The second officer laughed.

'If you drop us there, we can all walk home easily—' Gilly began, rapidly covering her tracks.

Mandy was about to chime in when Gilly stopped her with a gentle nudge to her side.

'Are you sure you'll be okay?' the second officer checked. 'Only I hear there's no more room at the inn.'

The two officers couldn't stop laughing. Gilly was beyond

caring. They'd got them out of a scrape, and it wasn't anything they'd not heard before.

They were dropped off outside the church soon enough and, as the police vehicle drove off, the girls made the brief pretence of heading in different directions. Once the police car was out of sight, they gathered outside the church gates.

'What did you nudge me for?' Mandy asked.

'You were going to tell them we lived at the mother and baby home, weren't you?' Gilly replied.

'Yes.'

'I didn't want them getting all serious with us. I thought they might insist on handing us over to the nuns, if they knew.'

'I think they probably worked it out for themselves, don't you?' Theresa suggested.

Gilly thought about it for a moment. She was probably right. The mother and baby home was right next door to the church; it wouldn't take a detective to figure out what they were up to. Still, she was grateful they didn't make a big deal of it. They might have got some cops who weren't looking for such an easy Saturday night on patrol.

'What now?' Theresa asked.

'I want to take those naughty pictures out of the hymn books,' Gilly answered. 'But only if you're not about to have your baby. I've lost my nerve now.'

'I'm okay. I'm sure it's not coming yet,' Theresa reassured them.

'In that case, let's get those hymn books sorted out and get back to our beds.'

Gilly led the way up the path to the church. She placed her hand on the iron handle, but it wouldn't move.

'Damn, they've locked it up for the night,' she cursed.

'It looks like we're committed now,' Mandy replied.

The girls headed back over to the home via the side path.

'I'll take the blame,' Gilly offered. 'It's all my fault. They'll think it's me, anyway.'

She imagined what Sister Brennan might do and she felt foolish and small. Gilly was relieved to see the home so quiet and dark; there was a good chance now they might pull it off. She fumbled about for the pencils that she'd left to prevent the window frame from closing. Her fingers found the gap, and she quietly pushed the frame upwards so they could get back into the building. The moment the frame clicked into place, the office light was turned on. The blinds were drawn back swiftly, and, to the girls' horror, Sister Brennan was standing there.

'Good evening, girls,' she began, a sneer on her face. 'I think you've got some explaining to do.'

'Urgh,' Theresa said, her knees bending slightly and her hands moving to her stomach. 'I think the baby's on the way. I think it's coming right now.'

THIRTY-NINE

Even in the heat of that moment, Hollie pushed the note deep into her pocket. She'd decide what to do with it later, her mind was all over the place now. The killer had just made this personal. He'd threatened her son and intruded into her domestic life. He'd shown her that he could extinguish one of the most precious things to her. Whoever he was, wherever he was hiding, and whatever his motive, she would track him down and see justice served.

The ambulance was there in minutes. She knelt at the doorstep, tightly clutching Noah's hand, hanging on to him for dear life and not wanting to ever let him go.

'You'll need to let us get to him, my darling—'

She'd tuned out completely. She was aware of the blue lights flashing, the approaching siren of the ambulance, and the flurry of activity and urgency around her. But she'd been alone in her head, thinking things through, determined to make sure her son was okay and then to hunt down his assailant with the single-minded monomania of a pack of hounds that had scented blood.

'We've got him now. We'll take care of him.'

Hollie looked up. It was a middle-aged ambulance worker wearing the distinctive green overalls, her male colleague standing immediately behind her. She had a kind face, but Hollie could see she was eager to take over.

'I'm sorry, I'll let you get to work—'

She knew the medic was right, but Hollie didn't want to let go of her son, in case he slipped away from her again. She squeezed Noah's small, limp hand and allowed a tear to run down her face. This was her worst nightmare. All she could think of was Noah opening his eyes and it all being over at last.

Slowly, she kissed Noah's head, got up off her knees and stood up, stepping aside so that they could get to him. In what seemed like moments, they were all over him, running checks and asking what felt like a hundred questions. She began to panic, her mind suggesting a million things that might have happened to harm him.

What were they doing to her child? She'd been at so many scenes like this, but now it was her son, every check they made caused her mind to run out of control, petrified at what they might tell her at any moment.

'Is he on any medication? Does he have any medical conditions? Does he have an adverse reaction to any drugs?'

Hollie answered the questions as they came, a barrage of requests that only a parent could answer. And she could answer them. She was not so far removed from the lives of her children that she couldn't recall every detail about them.

Then a question came that jolted her.

'Has he ever taken drugs or solvents?'

She stared at the medic.

'I beg your pardon?'

'It's important, madam—'

'No, not to my knowledge. Look at the age of him. Do you think he's ever taken drugs?'

'We think he's been given a drug, madam. We won't know

for certain until we can run some tests. It could be GHB, Rohypnol or ketamine. I can't be certain right now—'

'They're date rape drugs. He wasn't—'

Hollie repeated the words to herself in her head: *date rape drugs*.

Her head began to swim, and she thought she was about to pass out. This couldn't be right. The medic's voice brought her back out of her head.

'No, there's no sign of any assault—'

Hollie began to breathe again.

'None of his clothing appears to have been tampered with. These are not good drugs to use on a child, but it looks like whoever did this wanted him compliant.'

Hollie wanted to scream. Who the hell would do this to a child? She was angry now, too, furious that this despicable thing had been done to her boy.

This is what Léon was always talking about. However hard she tried, the job always intruded on their home life, even if it was just her being preoccupied with the details of a case rather than engaging in a conversation at the dinner table. But it was the psychos who did things like this. What he'd done to Noah was not her fault, she knew that. But someone was sure as hell going to pay for it.

Everything was a blur for some time after that. Noah was bundled off into the ambulance. Hollie travelled with him. She remembered to mention to one of the Special Constables to alert Phoebe and Lily as to what had happened. She said she'd call Phoebe from the ambulance, and she did, but she had no recollection of it afterwards. Her mind was elsewhere; she could only think of her son now.

Noah was attended to swiftly at the hospital, and Hollie cried when they informed her they'd need to check him properly for signs of sexual assault.

'No, he can't have—'

She knew they might be right.

Thoughts of what might have happened to him tormented her. Her experience in the job told her it might be true, but she was unable to confront that possibility; if he'd been hurt in that way, she could never forgive herself.

The sense of failure came crashing down on her once again. He was supposed to be in her care and look what had happened to him. No mother should allow that to happen to a child.

At last, she fell asleep in Noah's room, at his bedside, exhausted, drained by everything that had happened. She held his hand as he slept, thankful just to be at his side, listening to his gentle breathing, feeling the warmth from his body, and touching his skin.

The lighting had been dimmed, and she'd been overcome with relief and exhaustion after the attending doctor gave her the update. It was ketamine, but only a small dose. There were no early signs of harm. He had not been physically or sexually assaulted. He would be fine after a good night's rest, though it was likely he would feel very groggy for some time afterwards.

Hollie woke with a start and couldn't work out where she was. Her neck was stiff, and the lighting was still dim. She saw Noah, peaceful in the hospital bed.

'Sorry if I woke you.'

She looked up to see DS Anderson standing just inside the door. Hollie rubbed her eyes and sat up, moving her head from side to side to ease the discomfort in her neck.

'It's fine. I'm pleased to see you.'

Hollie sat up in the chair and looked around for a place where her colleague could sit.

'I'll perch at the end of the bed, if that's all right with you?'

'Yes, but none of that nonsense you pulled on Shane Hardy, please. I've seen what your bedside manner is like.'

They laughed and she was relieved to have some normality.

'Is he going to be okay?' Anderson asked.

'Yes, he'll be fine.'

'I know I said my son and I don't get on, but I'd be in pieces if something like this happened to him. I'm so sorry this came to your own doorstep.'

'You know all the details by now, I take it?'

Anderson nodded.

'Yeah, it's a warning shot from a bully. We checked for prints and DNA. We've drawn a blank. We've also pulled the CCTV off already—'

'Did you find anything?'

'Not much that we didn't know already. The CCTV is facing the park, not the road. We've got a clear view of him walking your son across the grass, towards your flat. He's wearing a cap and dark glasses; he clearly knows the CCTV is there. He doesn't have any facial hair, he's of normal height, and has no distinguishing features. A copper's nightmare—'

'This man knows what he's doing. Was there any suggestion of ketamine being used on Sister Brennan?'

The idea had just occurred to her. Doctor Ruane hadn't mentioned it, but she wondered if his tests had checked for it.

'Not that I recall. I'll mention it to Doctor Ruane and let you know. Oh, there was one thing—'

'Yes?'

Hollie was ready to pounce on any scrap of information that would lead her to this killer. She wanted to see him now before he entered the formal legal process. She had a few words to say to him – off the record.

'We think he was riding a motorcycle.'

'Shit! Near where we saw the white van?'

'Yes. Why?'

'I must have been metres away from him.'

'Did you see anything?'

'No, I was concentrating on the white van. Have we got a plate number?'

She could see what the answer was on Anderson's face.

'No, as I said, the CCTV is on the park, not the road. I'm sorry. There's a short flash of a motorcycle passing by in the distance. It fits the timeline, and the attire is the same, only he's wearing a helmet.'

'We've got all this damn technology and these buggers can still slip right under our noses.'

'I know, it's frustrating as hell. We'll get him, don't worry. He stepped out into the open to give you a warning. He's getting braver. That was a risky thing to do.'

'I'd say throwing a nun over the side of the Humber Bridge is a risky thing to do, too, and that's what he did for a warm-up. Do we have anything else to go on? I can't believe we're no further forward.'

Hollie's hand moved to the note that the man had left at Noah's side. It was pushed deep into her pocket, where she'd almost forgotten about it in her panic over Noah.

Should she hand it over to Anderson? It was written in capital letters, there would not be much of a clue in terms of handwriting. Would there be DNA on the scrap of paper? Possibly.

She handed it over to Anderson. This was something she didn't need to keep to herself.

He examined it and sighed.

'Personal threats now – you've really caught this guy's attention.'

'Log it back at HQ, would you? I picked it up in the heat of the moment, it's probably got my DNA all over it by now, but it might be useful.'

'Shane Hardy is dropping his allegations—' Anderson said, placing the note to his side.

'Really?' Hollie checked. 'Surely the gobshite hasn't seen the error of his ways?'

'Let's say he was given some encouragement. It came from Warburton, interestingly. Hardy has a pending case for shoplifting. Warburton made it go away. She wants your path cleared, according to Osmond.'

'Wow, I have friends in high places,' was all Hollie could say. 'I wonder what that's all about.'

'Maybe she wanted to cut you some slack after what happened to your kid.'

'Look, I appreciate you coming to see me, DS Anderson. I really do. You know you're going to have to take more of a lead while I sort out my son? I guess you'll relish that.'

'I'm happy to take more of a lead, but I wouldn't want it this way. I prefer things fair and square. If it helps, though, I'm happy to pick up the slack while you take some personal time. You certainly deserve it.'

Hollie studied his face. They appeared to be cutting through the bullshit at last. Anderson's initial bravado and cockiness were all but gone for the time being; they were conversing like professionals now, like adults.

'Are you staying here overnight?' Anderson asked. 'I'm happy to give you a ride home if you want it.'

'I need to get home, but I don't want to leave him—'

It was the same old problem; Hollie needed to be in three places at once.

'I'll check with the nurses, but I'm going to have to call back at my flat. My daughter is there, and I have to make some arrangements for tomorrow. I can't just abandon her.'

Hollie closed her eyes for a moment. The lighting in the room was soothing and it was late enough at night for the corridors to be quiet. Suddenly, her phone interrupted the silence. It was Léon.

FORTY

'I'm taking legal advice on securing sole custody of the children.'

Léon hadn't taken the news well. It had become so uncomfortable that even DS Anderson, a veteran of domestic disputes, left the room to let her get on with it.

'I'll wait outside,' he said, making a hasty retreat.

'You can't do that,' Hollie protested.

'I think I can,' Léon fired back at her. 'You've actually put our child in mortal danger today. He's only been with you a couple of hours!'

Hollie opened her mouth to reply, but she had no words. She broke down, sobbing, unable to find an answer for him.

'But then it never happens to me, does it, Hollie? None of the clients I work with ever bundle the kids into a car and hold them hostage. It's because of your job. Why can't you—?'

'What? Stay at home and get the dinner on? Is that what you were going to say?'

'No, you know I don't mean that, Hollie. It's just that—'

'It's just that you would rather I took some boring job and played housewife all day.'

'No, that's not what I said. I just think you do the job because you've got some unresolved issues in your life—'

'That's below the belt, Léon—'

'You don't have to prove anything to anyone, Hollie. You're great as you are—'

His tone had softened. He was right, she knew it, but she couldn't bring herself to acknowledge it just yet. It was true, but it hurt to admit it.

'Mum, are you and Dad arguing again?'

Noah was awake. Hollie started to cry, partly out of relief that Noah was awake and speaking to her, but also at the horror of realising that Léon was right. She simply couldn't walk away, because she was intent on trying to prove herself.

She rushed to the bed and held Noah tight, stroking his head and kissing him over and over. She could hear Léon at the end of the phone, asking what was happening.

'Dad's on the phone,' she said. 'He wants to chat with you.'

Hollie handed it over to Noah and let them speak. Léon asked the same questions that she was going to ask. The man had been friendly and fun; he'd said Noah's mum wanted him at the flat and had sent him out to find Noah. He'd had a drink in a carton and had offered it to him. He told Noah that Phoebe and Lily had already gone ahead. Noah had checked that the man had known the number of the flat and he had, so he'd assumed it was okay to walk across the park with him. After that, he couldn't remember anything, other than a couple of flashbacks: being carried by the man, being placed on the ground, Hollie shouting when she found him, and a few glimpses from the hospital. He felt tired and confused, but otherwise, he was okay.

'Can you hand me back to Mum now?'

She heard Léon's tinny voice over the phone's speaker. Noah passed it to her and snuggled down in the bed, pulling his sheets up around his neck.

'I'm tired now, Mum,' he said.

Hollie stroked his head as she picked up the call with Léon.

'I know you love them, Hollie, I never doubt that. But we can't do this anymore. We can't expose the children to danger like this. It has to end.'

Her hackles rose, but she checked herself; he was right. It would help nobody if they ended up rowing over the phone, least of all Noah. She stood up and moved over to the corner, lowering her voice.

'Look, Léon, can you just slow down a bit on trying to dismantle the marriage? We can talk about it properly, I promise. But I have to put this case behind me first. It's been a lot to deal with, a job change, your bombshell about the marriage, and what just happened to Noah. I need a moment to catch my breath. I don't even know who this woman is that you've taken up with, or if she's suitable to be around my kids—'

'Our kids, Hollie, and that's a bit rich coming from you.'

She deserved that; she knew it. Noah was asleep again and she could see a nurse hovering with DS Anderson outside.

'Can we park this again, Léon? I promise we'll talk it through, but not right now, okay?'

To her relief, Léon agreed, and they ended the call. She promised to keep him up to date with their son's progress. She sent him a photograph of Noah sleeping in the hospital bed, looking calm and peaceful. If that didn't reassure him, nothing would.

She noticed that an email notification had come in while they'd been talking, but she prioritised speaking to the nurse first.

'He'll be out cold for the rest of the night by the look of him,' the nurse reassured her. 'Why don't you go home and get some rest? You look exhausted.'

Hollie looked back at Noah. He'd always been a good sleeper, and they'd had an early start with Phoebe for the train journey. Besides, Lily would need some reassurance back at the flat and she'd abandoned Phoebe, too, whose university interview was tomorrow. It made sense to go home.

She thanked the nurse and was reassured that her son would be safe in their care. She made sure they had her contact details then went back into Noah's room to say goodbye and kiss him goodnight.

DS Anderson guided her through the hospital corridors to his car and drove her back to Pearson Park. As they made their way through the city, she checked her emails. Acting DI Burns had got back to her from the police station at Lancaster. She opened up his email, eager to see if he'd dredged up anything useful on DCC Warburton.

Hi Hollie,

I'm not sure how useful this will be, but this is what I got.

It didn't sound promising, but she read on.

Rose Warburton was the daughter of a wealthy businessman in Hull. There's a gap in her CV; she seems to have been off the radar for a couple of years around the time she'd have been taking exams at school. Sorry, I can't find anything about that time without an illegal search of the database. She makes a reappearance as a police cadet in Bracknell of all places. She started there in 1980. She transferred from Bracknell to West Yorkshire and then to Humberside, moving up the ranks all the time. She's a career copper and could have retired several years ago in terms of pension years. Her father's name was Harold Watson, he was a bit of a big shot in Hull, by all accounts. That's it, sorry I can't help more!

There was something about the name Watson that was troubling her.

'Do we know a Watson in this case?' she asked.

DS Anderson was in a world of his own; she'd caught him off guard.

'What? Watson?'

He drove on, mulling it over.

'Isn't Watson the name Violet Farrow gave you?'

'Shit, yes! She said she'd seen a name on the file at the mother and baby home. It was Watson. Theresa said the same thing. It can't be the same though, surely? That would be far too much of a coincidence?'

'You'll have to bring me up to speed. I don't know what you're talking about.'

Hollie remembered she'd been reading an email; there was no way Anderson could read her mind. She'd need to protect Acting DI Burns as her source, too. She brought him up to speed but didn't tell him where she'd got her information.

It took a moment to dawn on him what the implication was, but he got it soon enough.

'So, if Twiggy's surname is Watson, and DCC Warburton's maiden name is Watson—' he began.

'Yes,' Hollie confirmed. 'It might also imply that Twiggy was DCC Rose Warburton.'

FORTY-ONE

1975: GILLY'S STORY

It was strange, Theresa not being in the dorm. Gilly felt lonely, even though Mandy was still there with her. She was desperate for somebody to talk to about her fears over the birth, but her parents wanted nothing to do with her. It had fallen on her to reassure Theresa and Mandy, yet all she craved was a bit of kindness and comfort for herself.

She thought back to Saturday. For the second time on that night, Gilly genuinely thought she was going to come to serious harm when they arrived back at the home. Sister Brennan had launched at her when she'd climbed through the window, and it was only because Sister Payne showed up that she escaped physical harm.

Sister Brennan had sent them to bed early. She'd warned that if she heard a sound out of them, there'd be hell to pay. Gilly believed her. The fire in her eyes, she looked like it was all she could do not to start beating the two of them.

'Are you asleep yet?' Gilly whispered across Theresa's empty bed. Mandy had been still since the light went out. There was some kind of commotion going on downstairs, and they were dying to know what was happening.

'No, I can't sleep. The baby's moving. It knows something's up.'

'Mine too. Whose baby will come next, do you think?'

'I'm scared, Gilly. I thought I would be all right about it, but seeing Theresa like that, I don't know if I'm ready.'

'I'm coming over,' Gilly said.

She tiptoed as quietly as she could manage to Mandy's bed. The floorboards creaked anyway, and she hoped that whatever was going on downstairs would distract Sister Brennan from coming to scold them. Gilly slipped into bed next to Mandy and they started to giggle.

'Two of us can't fit in here,' Mandy laughed. 'We're far too big.'

'Shove over,' Gilly urged her. 'If we lie on our backs, we'll be fine.'

'They lay side by side. Gilly reached out her hand in the darkness. Mandy's hand was already there, waiting. Gilly gave it a squeeze.

'We'll be okay,' she reassured her friend. 'It'll be a couple of hours of discomfort, and then we'll have our babies. Women have been doing this for years. We'll be fine.'

'Do you ever regret getting pregnant?'

Mandy's voice sounded young and innocent in the darkness of the room.

'I wish things had gone differently with my relationship, I can tell you that much. I know it's not the best thing to happen to me right now. But I'll have a baby of my own. I know I got the order wrong, and I was supposed to get the husband first. But I'm excited. It feels special. I'll have something – somebody – of my own.'

'I never felt that my parents loved me,' Mandy continued, out of the blue.

Gilly gave her hand another squeeze and snuggled close, as

best as she could manage. The baby stirred in her belly. It would be her turn soon enough.

'I'm sorry,' Gilly sympathised with her. 'It's been hard on you being here. I can't imagine what it's like feeling that way. My parents love me, I know that, but they have a screwed-up way of showing it. Fancy being ashamed of your own daughter. I'm exactly the same person as I was before I got pregnant. I didn't suddenly change.'

She realised she was talking about herself when Mandy reached out to her. She was bad at that, she knew. She was about to encourage her friend to say more when she heard the sound of a hand gently clasping the handle on the other side of the door.

'Shit! It's Sister Brennan.'

The door opened, and somebody stepped in quietly and left the door ajar enough to let a decent amount of light in from the landing.

'Are you awake, girls?'

Gilly started breathing again. She'd been holding her breath, like that would do any good.

'Sister Kay, I'm so relieved it's you.'

'I heard the ceiling creaking from downstairs. I thought I'd better warn you. Sister Brennan is still on the warpath after your antics. If you're going to chatter, please keep it quiet.'

'What's going on down there?' Gilly asked.

Sister Kay sat at the end of the bed. In the semi-darkness, Gilly could see the nun's smile.

'You look like two overgrown peas in a pod. Not long for you now.'

'We were just talking about that,' Mandy replied, pulling herself up in bed. She was so awkward in her movements that she almost squeezed Gilly off the bed.

'What's going on, though?' Gilly pushed. 'You can always

tell when something's up. The atmosphere floats up the stairs and creeps under the gaps in the doors.'

'It's a busy night. I can't stay long,' Sister Kay whispered. 'We're getting two babies back tonight—'

'Two! Who?' Mandy exclaimed. 'Is it Violet?'

'Shhhhh,' Sister Kay warned. 'No, it's another of the girls.'

'Can we see the baby?' Gilly asked.

'Not tonight, girls, I'm sorry. If you hadn't got up to all that mischief, then yes, I'm sure I could have arranged it. But not now, I'm sorry. Wait until tomorrow morning. It'll keep until then.'

Gilly wasn't so sure about that.

'Whose is the other baby? It has to be Twiggy's, doesn't it?' Mandy said.

'Twiggy?' Sister Kay asked.

'The girl in the room downstairs,' Gilly added. 'The mystery girl. She who remains unnamed.'

Sister Kay laughed.

'She is a bit of a mystery, I'll give you that. It happens some-times. She'll be from some well-to-do family. They'll be making a nice donation to the church for a private room and a bit of discretion. I do know her name, of course, but I can't say. Just in case.'

'Pleeeeease,' Gilly and Mandy both asked.

'No, girls, I can't. But she's back tonight, too. She won't be here long now—'

'Why?' Gilly questioned. 'Is she going somewhere?'

'Her baby was breech.'

Sister Kay had changed the subject.

'The doctor told us people don't usually have problems like that,' Mandy said.

'Well, sometimes they do, and this girl you call Twiggy did. It wasn't for turning. They had to help turn the wee mite.'

'Ouch!' Gilly grimaced. 'I hope I don't have one of those.'

Gilly felt a wave of anxiety sweep over her. There was so much she didn't know about what was going to happen when the baby came.

'I'm a bit scared now,' came Mandy's worried voice.

Sister Kay reached out and touched her leg over the bed sheets.

'Don't you worry, Mandy, you'll be fine. The doctor was right, it doesn't happen very often. Your baby will fly out of you, no problem, I'm absolutely sure of that.'

Gilly knew better, but there was no way she was going to scare Mandy at this stage.

'I'd better get back now. I'm certain you'll be able to see the babies tomorrow.'

She stood up, wished the girls goodnight, and then slipped out of the door as quietly as she'd arrived.

'Mandy, look.'

Gilly was looking towards the door.

'I want to go downstairs and take a look.' Mandy ignored the cue.

'We can sneak out quietly. Look.'

Sister Kay had left the door slightly open. That would spare them the risk of daring to open it themselves. And strictly speaking, they weren't letting themselves out of the room; it was already open.

'Let's sneak down and see the babies.'

'Maybe we shouldn't,' Mandy protested. 'Not after our antics. I'm so scared Sister Brennan will get us. She seems to have eyes everywhere.'

'What are they going to do to us?' Gilly challenged. 'Take away our babies? Come on, follow me, I'll take the blame. Sister Brennan already thinks I'm the devil in a female form.'

Gilly moved slowly off the bed. The baby wriggled inside her. She'd miss that feeling once it was born. Mandy followed, as Gilly thought she might.

They pushed the door open slowly. The landing was quiet. There was movement downstairs in the hallway. Gilly could hear Sister Brennan's whispering voice, as well as Sister Kay and Father Duffy.

'She's in her room now. Is the baby still asleep?'

'The second taxi is here.'

'Already? Come on, Sister Kay, we'd better help her in.'

Gilly put her finger to her lips.

'They're going outside,' she whispered. 'If we're quick, we'll be able to see who's coming back. And we'll get a peek of the baby.'

'I'll go and check on the mother,' came Father Duffy's voice.

The front door was opened and, suddenly, the hallway was quiet.

'Quick, now!' Gilly instructed.

As fast as they could, the two girls made their way down the ornate staircase. The moment their feet touched the tiles, Sister Brennan came through the door.

'I'll leave him in the hall for now. I'll help you with her bags.'

Gilly and Mandy crouched behind the banister on the far side of the staircase. Sister Brennan had barely glanced inside the building; she'd just been dropping off a bag of baby paraphernalia.

'There's a carrycot over by the office.' Gilly pointed. 'There must be a baby in there. If we're quick, we'll have time for a look.'

'Whose baby though? Twiggy's?'

'Who knows?' Gilly answered as she started to move towards the carrycot. 'Did you hear who's arriving now? Anyway, we'll find out soon enough. Let's take a look at the baby, then we'd better get upstairs again.'

The two girls crept across the tiled hallway; Gilly was well aware they were playing with fire. If they got caught, they were in danger of being separated. Gilly wasn't sure she'd feel so brave if she was on her own.

They'd reached the carrycot now, but it sounded like the taxi driver was about to be sent on his way with his fare.

'We'd best be quick,' Mandy urged.

They peered into the carrycot.

A tiny baby was fast asleep. There were no clues as to its gender: the sheets were neutral, and the baby was so tightly wrapped up that none of its clothing was visible.

'I want to know if it's a boy or a girl,' Gilly whispered.

'I'm going back upstairs,' Mandy said. 'Come on, Gilly, we'll get caught.'

'One moment,' Gilly replied, gently tucking her fingers into the sheets so she could pull them back a little and see if the child was dressed in girls' or boys' baby clothes.

'Oh,' she said, louder than she wanted to.

Mandy stopped by the staircase and turned.

'What is it?' she asked.

'The poor thing. Look, it has a bright red birthmark all along its neck.'

FORTY-TWO

'Do we tell anyone?' Anderson asked as they drove back from the hospital.

It was the first occasion that he'd deferred to her in the short time they'd been working together.

'No, we can't. Not yet. It seems so unlikely. It can't be true; it must be a coincidence. It's quite a common surname. She'd have declared her interest in the case, wouldn't she?'

DS Anderson seemed shocked at the prospect.

'We'll have to try to stand it up. How the hell do we do that?'

'Isn't the photographer back from his holidays tomorrow?' Hollie said.

'Yes, but how likely is it that he'll be able to give us a name after so many years?'

'I agree,' Hollie continued. 'But it's our best chance at the moment, other than having a quiet word with the DCC. It can't be her, that would be crazy.'

'We'll have to ask her, if the photographer can't help us,' Anderson replied. 'I mean, we can't sit on this. It's potentially explosive.'

'Keep it quiet for now. We could get shit all over our shoes if we let this out. And for the DCC's sake, too. Jesus, if it is her, if she's Twiggy, it's going to be a nightmare to pick through.'

DS Anderson had pulled up the car.

'This is just between you and me, yes?'

'Yes,' Anderson agreed. 'I'll say nothing. I'll get straight on to the photographer tomorrow. Are you okay on your own?'

It was dark outside now; he'd kindly dropped her directly outside the flats.

'I've got people inside, thank you. I appreciate this, Ben—'

It seemed like the right time to start using his first name. They were, after all, conversing like friends now.

'I feel like we may have got things off to a rocky start. I hope we can move on from that now, though. I'm very grateful for this.'

He seemed embarrassed and gave a small nod of acknowledgement.

She got out of the car, and he waited to watch her safely to the front door of the flats. Perhaps she wouldn't have to have a difficult conversation about behaviour with this man after all. He'd gone some way to redeem himself in her eyes.

'Did DC Langdon catch you, by the way?' he called across the road to her, having lowered the car window. 'She's been trying to return a set of house keys to you all day apparently. She said she'd drop them in on her way home if she didn't run into you beforehand.'

Hollie had forgotten all about the keys, so it was a good job Phoebe was inside the flat to let her in.

'Thanks for letting me know, I'll listen out for her.'

Hollie gently tapped at the flat window to be let in. Phoebe checked who was there, then came out to let her in. Hollie quietly entered, uncertain if Lily would still be awake at that time. She was snuggled up on the sofa watching something on Phoebe's laptop; it sounded like *Love Island* or something similar. It was not normally the kind of TV she'd want Lily exposed to, but she wasn't going to begrudge the two of them some mindless viewing. After the day they'd all had, it was the least of her worries.

She joined them on the sofa, sitting at Lily's side and cuddling in.

'Is Noah all right?' Lily asked.

Hollie brought them up to speed, omitting some of the details that she didn't want Lily to know about. *Love Island* was quite enough for one evening without introducing her to the shady world of ketamine.

'Are you all fixed for tomorrow?' she asked Phoebe.

'Yes, all sorted. Are you fine with the kids?'

'Yes, I'm not going into the office tomorrow. My colleague will pick things up. I'll need to make some calls, but I can stay at home. It'll do all of us the world of good.'

Lily yawned and Hollie chased her to bed.

'You've been up since before dawn, no wonder you're tired,' she said.

Lily sorted herself out and Hollie settled her down in her sleeping bag bed. The tags were still attached; she'd barely had time to take them out of the cellophane. More feelings of shame. It was the best she could do, given the circumstances.

After waiting with Lily until she was asleep, Hollie returned to the living room with Phoebe. She was yawning, too, and looked like she was also ready for her bed.

'I can't tell you how grateful I am for everything you've done—'

'What, letting your youngest child get abducted right under my nose?'

Hollie hadn't considered that Phoebe might feel responsible for what happened.

'Listen to me, that man would have got to me somehow, whether it was snatching Noah from the park or some other way. It's not your fault. Noah knows not to walk off with strangers, but from what he told us in the hospital tonight, this guy was convincing. He'd got my address after all—'

'I think I led him to Noah,' Phoebe blurted out, crying now.

'How could you have done that?' Hollie comforted her. 'It's not your fault.'

'When we left the house to go to the park, this guy was hanging around outside. He had a red cap on. He was holding an envelope in his hand which had your address on it. He asked if I knew you and I stupidly told him I was staying with you and that these were your kids—'

'It's not your fault, Phoebe.'

'But it is, isn't it? If I'd just kept my mouth shut, he'd have been none the wiser. But he had that envelope. I thought he was a delivery man or one of the residents who'd picked up some of your post by mistake.'

'What did he do?'

'He asked if I'd let him in so he could put it in your mailbox as it was confidential. I didn't see any harm in letting him into the shared hallway, as your flat was locked up. I just didn't think anything of it at the time.'

Hollie drew Phoebe close to her. She looked like an adult and behaved like an adult, but she was really still a kid.

'It's okay. Anybody would have done the same thing. I'd have thought he was a delivery guy with that red cap on. Did you notice anything about him that might help us identify him?'

Phoebe shook her head.

'He was just a guy. I barely even looked at him. I'm sorry. I don't mean to be rude, but men of his age are invisible to me. Unless they're my dad, I don't really look at them.'

They sat for a while, with Hollie reassuring Phoebe and trying to convince her that none of it was her fault. They fell asleep like that, on the sofa, with Phoebe's head resting against her shoulder.

. . .

Hollie awoke abruptly to the sound of a phone ringing. It was muffled in her pocket; it hadn't disturbed Phoebe, who'd removed herself from Hollie's shoulder and was now resting her head on the arm of the sofa. At first, she checked her personal phone, then she realised it was the burner phone that was making the noise. Hollie's finger shot to the volume control, and she reduced the sound to a whisper. The clock on the display screen informed her that it was still the middle of the night. Why the hell was her contact calling her at this time?

She lifted herself off the sofa as gently as she could. Phoebe stirred a little but was in a deep sleep. Hollie darted into the kitchen and pulled the door closed behind her. She picked up the call.

'Yes?' she asked, annoyed at the intrusion, but apprehensive about what might follow.

'It's me. We need to talk.'

'Who's *me*?' she snapped. 'You still haven't identified yourself. You're not the prick who took my son this afternoon, are you?'

'No, it's me, the man at the river. I can't tell you my name yet, I'm sorry. But I need to speak to you.'

Hollie had had enough.

'For fuck's sake. What is this to you, a game of Cluedo? What are you going to tell me? That it was the nun, on the bridge, with the rope? I know that already. It's been a long, testing day. Come up with something useful or piss off and leave me alone.'

There was silence at the end of the line. She immediately regretted her tone.

'Look, I'm sorry, it's been a terrible day. It's really late, and I'm exhausted. Can't this wait?'

'Can we meet to speak in person?'

'What, now?'

'Yes, now.'

'It's almost four o'clock in the morning. Can't we do this another time?'

'No, not really. Nobody's going to know where you are at this time of day. This needs to be in confidence.'

'Can't you tell me over the phone?'

'I'd rather not. I have to know that only you hear this.'

'Why me?'

'Because I think I can trust you.'

'You don't even know me.'

'But I know of you. And I think you're a good cop.'

'Who are you protecting?' Hollie pushed.

The man sighed at the end of the phone.

'It's... difficult,' he began. 'I can't tell you, not yet. But I'm as interested as you are in getting this murderer safely in police custody. You have to trust me, I promise. It will all make sense, eventually. But I have to keep out of sight for now.'

'You know we can trace the phone—'

'It's a disposable, non-registered phone. Don't you watch the telly? Everybody knows that nowadays. Besides, you'll only find it connected to a city centre phone mast if you dig deeper. Good luck with that. It's like finding a needle in a haystack.'

That's exactly what Lance from the tech team had told her in the update email he'd sent over to her. This man seemed to have a lot of technical knowledge. Was he a cop?

'Okay, okay, tell me how you want to do this.'

'I'm going to text you a location in ten minutes. Get in your car. Head for the city centre. I'll tell you where to go.'

'This is very cloak-and-dagger. How do I know you're not going to kill me?'

He laughed.

'You've been close to me already. Do I seem like a murderer to you?'

'No. All right, I'll come.'

'Come alone. No tricks. Make sure you're not being followed. I don't want anybody placing us together.'

'I get it. I'm leaving the house now.'

The man ended the call. Hollie opened the kitchen door and checked that Phoebe was still sleeping. She slipped on her shoes and coat and grabbed her keys. As she did so, she hesitated, wondering if Jenni had called to return the spare set of keys while they'd been sleeping. She hoped not – after a long day at work, she didn't want her colleague calling round on a fool's errand.

She crept out of the flat, through the front door, and gently clicked the lock closed. As she looked ahead out into Pearson Park, she couldn't shake the feeling of being watched. Hollie glanced around to check; her mind was playing tricks on her, she thought she saw movements everywhere. She was being ridiculous, just spooked by the day's events.

The car door was still unlocked, but it was untouched. She climbed into her seat and a message came in on her phone. This was it: she was heading out on some crazy mission on her own. She activated her phone screen and checked the message.

> Land of Green Ginger. Take Bowlalley Lane,
> enter The Pathway. 10 minutes. Come alone.

FORTY-THREE

The Land of Green Ginger: it sounded like something out of a fairy story. It was part of a nightmare for Hollie; she knew she was playing with fire accepting this meeting. What choice did she have? She was up to her ears in domestic and work shit and in danger of drowning. It had to be done. If the man with the birthmark reckoned he had something worth knowing, she had to take a leap of faith. It had worked for her before in her policing career, so why not now?

She pulled up the handbrake and turned the key. There was something comforting about the running engine, like she'd got company at that time of night. The streets were quiet; there was not even a drunk to punctuate the silence. Half past four, what a godforsaken hour for a meet-up. Most night shifts wouldn't be clocking off for some time, and the early starters didn't usually get active until six o'clock or thereabouts. They had the city to themselves, though Hull never truly slept.

She wished she'd paid more attention as a student. She'd heard of the Land of Green Ginger but hadn't a clue why it was called that. All she remembered was that it was in the city's Old Town, and they used to go drinking there. She seemed to recall throwing up in the doorway of some historic-looking building in her fresher's week, not because of alcohol, but due to a dodgy kebab she'd consumed earlier that day. It had been lying in wait until she was out with her new university friends before making its reappearance. She suspected that story wouldn't be retold by any local historians as they trod the cobbled streets and regaled tourists with tales of the past.

She was looking for the Bowlalley Lane entrance. Well, it was just around the corner according to her phone app, but it wasn't showing up. She got out of the car and clicked the locking button. She clicked a second time, this time to unlock the vehicle. It would spare her precious seconds if this meeting turned sour and she had to make a run for it. In a worst-case scenario, if she could make it to the car, she could lock herself in until help came.

Hollie closed the map app – it was useless. She'd have to go old school and use her eyes.

It seemed to her just like any other city's historic quarters. It was full of solicitors' offices, mainly, though she did spot a tattoo shop in a very old-looking building before she turned into the lane. It seemed incongruous in that historic setting, but she figured it didn't much matter considering the present state of UK high streets. Even history buffs wanted tattoos. Who was she to judge?

Hollie was more nervous than she had been for some time. She passed a pub and a recruitment agency on either side, her gaze crisscrossing the narrow street as she looked for the entrance. It was still and dark, with just a couple of early rising seagulls squawking in the cool air of the early morning. Or was it still the middle of the night? She wasn't sure where four o'clock belonged on the night-time spectrum.

There were cameras on the pub, one facing down the lane, the other down the Land of Green Ginger. Hopefully, they were switched on. If she ended up chopped into pieces and floating out in the Humber Estuary, at least they'd have a record of her last movements. If only the man with the birthmark had chosen this entrance, she might have been able to get a few still images pulled off one of those cameras.

She passed what looked like a residential property, though she couldn't be certain. At least there was a door to bang on if she needed it. At the end of the building was a recess, which she assumed was a side alley, the sort where residents placed their bins out of the way of the wind and the seagulls. As she got closer, she saw that it had some wording on the wall. She cursed the absence of streetlights; it was precisely the type of place she'd be telling her own daughter not to frequent late at night when nobody was around. She opened up the torch on her phone and shone it into the mouth of the alley. This was the place. The Pathway. It was marked in small black tiles attached to ageing brickwork in what seemed to Hollie to be a long and dark passage. It was the perfect place to get mugged, assaulted or robbed. And she, a senior member of the local police force, was going down there alone, contrary to a lifetime of warning young women how to stay safe at night.

The Pathway was poorly lit. It had a couple of low, tradi-tional-looking streetlights, no doubt the council's best effort to combine safety with historical integration. She'd have liked it a lot brighter.

She walked through a low, arched tunnel that ran under a building. It was only short, but it opened out into a wider paved area, lined by the end walls of buildings constructed more recently. Hollie was pleased to emerge from the narrowness of that claustrophobic passage; it felt sinister to be in such poor light. She looked ahead but could see no sign of the man she was meeting. She could hear a motorbike revving in one of the adjacent streets and wondered if it might be a late night or early morning fast food delivery. Either way, it felt reassuring to know there were other people around.

Meet by the iron posts, under the streetlight, he'd instructed in a second text. She carried on walking until she found the place. It was at the back of another anonymous office building, with a small recess. She wondered if he was waiting there for her. It would be a good place to pounce on her, taking her by surprise, assaulting her well out of sight. She scanned for security cameras. It was doubtful they'd show up anything useful in that semi-darkness, even if they were recording.

'Hello,' she ventured.

Hollie was suddenly aware of movement from the end of the alley, where she'd entered. She blinked and tried to focus, but it was too far off now and the light too poor. Surely nobody else would be walking down that passage at that time of night.

'I'm here,' came a man's voice.

Hollie jumped, surprised that she could have been so close without spotting him. The motorbike was revving again; it seemed to be hovering somewhere beyond the alley. Perhaps the delivery man couldn't find the address.

'I'm not going to hurt you,' he continued.

His voice was calm and educated. He was older, too: fifty or sixty, maybe. The last time they'd spoken, they had been yelling at each other across the waters of a deadly River Hull.

'I thought this might be a little safer than the river,' he said, as if reading her mind.

'You can say that again.'

Hollie was on high alert, her mind intently focused on this man now.

'Why did you leave it so long to make contact again?' Hollie asked.

'I had to be certain. There are a lot of people who'd rather this information didn't get out. I'm trying to protect somebody. That's why I have to be careful—'

'Can you hear that motorbike?' Hollie interrupted.

'You weren't followed, were you?' he asked, suddenly jittery.

'No, I checked. I didn't tell anybody. I promise. This is possibly one of the worst decisions I've ever made in my policing career, but this is just between me and you. Please convince me I'm not making a terrible mistake.'

'You're not. I'm taking a risk, too, you know. I just feel you're the right person for the job. I've read about you online. I've seen some of the things you did in Lancaster. I hope I can trust you, too.'

'If you help me find this damn killer, you can rely on my discretion,' Hollie reassured him. 'Now, why are we here? What's so important that you can't send it over in an email?'

'I can't have this in any electronic form. There can't be any evidence that I helped you out here—'

'That bloody motorcycle. That's disturbing the peace at this time of day... shit!'

Hollie was looking up the far end of the alleyway, on the side she'd entered. A motorcycle had pulled into the narrow entrance, its front beam on full and the rider revving the engine hard.

The engine sound changed suddenly, and Hollie could see the motorcycle rider was driving directly at them.

'Hollie, get out of the way!'

A familiar voice was shouting from the other side of the iron posts. It was Jenni. What the hell was she doing here? She was supposed to be off-shift and at home.

'He's been watching you in your flat,' Jenni shouted. 'I came over to your flat late last night to drop off your spare keys. He was sitting on his motorbike, just watching and waiting. I've been keeping an eye on him all night from my car—'

'You told me you came alone,' the man cursed, looking along the alley at the approaching motorcycle and seeking the source of the voice in the darkness.

'For God's sake, Jenni, what were you thinking? Get out of here—'

The motorcycle was almost upon them now. The rider was wearing full leather, his face concealed by his helmet. It was a big bike, too. It must have taken some manoeuvring into the narrow entrance of the alley, but he was confident on the wider paved area. And he was aiming directly for them.

Hollie and the man were standing in the path of the motorcycle now, but the rider showed no sign of slowing. Jenni was behind them with no way to duck aside.

'Get out of the way!' Hollie screamed at her, leaping into the recess as the motorcycle flew past. The man with the birthmark was not so fast and was clipped by the side of the bike. He fell to the side, catching his head on the edge of one of the posts.

Hollie's mind was working furiously. This was all going terribly wrong. She was operating outside the police investigation. For some reason unknown, a young detective constable had followed her to the alleyway. And now her secret informant was injured.

She rushed to him on the floor. The motorcyclist had turned the bike and was racing up the far side of the alleyway, from where he'd made his entrance.

'Put pressure on it,' Hollie urged. 'I don't think it's serious.'

'Where are you going?' he asked.

'There's a girl out there who shouldn't be here—'

'Look, if I don't make it—'

'You'll be fine.'

'You need to look into the connection between Father Duffy and Sister Brennan. There's something – or someone – who binds them. I'm convinced of it. I just don't know who yet.'

Hollie stood up and rushed back out into the alleyway. The motorcyclist was revving for a second try. Hollie searched the path for Jenni. At first, she thought she'd got out, but at a closer look, she saw the young DC on the ground, struggling to get up.

'Jenni, are you all right? Are you hurt?'

'The bastard pushed me,' she called over. 'Let's get this prick.'

She pulled herself up to her feet and stood defiantly in the path of the motorcyclist, who was now approaching at a speed that made Hollie's legs feel like they were about to give way under her.

'He can't go through me,' Jenni shouted. 'He won't do that.'

'Get out of the way, Jenni!'

The bike was almost upon them. Jenni was really going to face him down.

'For fuck's sake, get out of the—'

Jenni didn't seem to realise until too late that the man on the motorcycle had no intention of stopping. As Hollie ran towards her, Jenni turned to avoid him, but her ankle gave way and she collapsed onto the paving, letting out a scream of pain.

Hollie was too late to reach her. The motorcyclist put his head down and ploughed directly into her. Jenni's body was hurled into the air, her head giving a terrible thud as she landed on the cold, hard slabs. The motorcyclist braked suddenly, just before the end of the narrow passageway. He raised his visor and looked back.

'Fuck you!' he shouted over. 'Back off or it'll be your kids next time, bitch!'

He pulled his visor down and exited the alley.

Hollie rushed over to Jenni.

'Oh, Jesus Christ. Jenni, what were you thinking?'

Her face was bloodied and torn. Blood was pooling out of her mouth. She lay still, and Hollie checked for a pulse.

'For fuck's sake, don't you die on me, Jenni Langdon. Don't you dare die on me.'

Jenni coughed; a spatter of blood appeared on the slabs at her side.

'I figured it out. She had a baby...' Jenni whispered. 'She had a baby, Hollie—'

'Who did? Who did, Jenni?'

'That's what she doesn't want us to know.'

'Who? Who did? Oh, Jenni, why did you get involved? Why couldn't you stay out of this?'

'I was bringing your key back... I saw someone watching the flat... I followed you... I was just trying to be a good cop...'

Hollie was sobbing now, fumbling for her phone. Jenni needed an ambulance. Her informant needed help. It was a bloody mess. What had she been thinking?

Jenni was about to say something when she coughed and spluttered more blood.

'What is it, Jenni? I'm getting help. You'll be okay.'

But Jenni had slumped onto the slabs, her body still and lifeless.

Hollie stopped dialling and screamed out into the dark alleyway.

A LETTER FROM THE AUTHOR

Thank you so much for reading *Her Last Cry*. If you want to join other readers in hearing all about my latest releases, you can sign up for my newsletter at the link here:

www.stormpublishing.co/paul-j-teague

Or sign up to my personal email newsletter on the link here:

www.paulteague.net/storm

I'd appreciate it very much if you would leave a review for this second title in this DI Hollie Turner trilogy, as this helps other readers to discover my stories.

Let me start with an apology for what just happened at the end of the book. I know it's going to be unbearable waiting for book three to come out to discover the outcome, but I was resolved from the start of this trilogy to build a special kind of shock into the story.

In the UK, there's a TV series called *Line of Duty* and I recently signed up for a writing masterclass by the writer of that series, Jed Mercurio. One of Jed's core philosophies is that you insert shock scenes throughout a story, so that's what I wanted to do. The scene in *Line of Duty* that I like best is where a key character, who we'd been encouraged to like and gun for, got pushed out of a window with no forewarning whatsoever. It's the type of scene that leaves you open-mouthed, staring at the

TV. I wanted to try that technique in this book so, sorry, that's why it ends like that.

I always promise at this stage in a trilogy to pull together all the loose ends, and I will do that; all the strands of the case will tie up into a neat little bundle by the final page of the next book.

It was great for me to return to some familiar settings in this story, having worked and reported for radio in the city of Hull. I'd almost forgotten several of the locations used in this book, but writing this story has brought back a lot of reporting memories for me. Take David Lister School, for instance, which is where the sports team photo of the mysterious Twiggy was taken. I was hunting around for a school that I could use, making sure they were open in the seventies and checking if they're still around nowadays when I stumbled across the name of David Lister and the memories came flooding back to me.

When I was a radio producer and presenter at BBC Radio Humberside, we broadcast a School's Day from David Lister School, with various radio shows dropping in throughout the day. It was a long time ago now, so my memories are vague, but I broadcast a breakfast show live from that location and recorded several reports from staff and students who were based there. I also recall hosting a debate about education issues with a panel of representatives on that topic. I had to use that school in the story, even though it's now been demolished to make way for a new national health service building and what looks like a very nice housing estate on Google Maps.

As ever in my books, everything is entirely fictional, the characters are not based on real life, and none of the events took place. I like to mention that early in the day, just in case somebody thinks they recognise someone or something!

The Cecil Cinema was another Hull city centre location that I had to mention. The cinema was easy walking distance from where BBC Radio Humberside used to be based, so it was a great place to go to catch a film. My wife and I lived in Hull just before we started a family, so we spent many an evening watching films in the city. My wife assures me that we went to see *Reservoir Dogs* at the Cecil Cinema, but I have no memory of that now, even though its release year was 1993, which would be perfect timing for that. I have no reason to think that isn't correct, but my memories of cinema-going in Hull involved going to the UCI (which was my favourite), the Odeon, and the cinema that was based in the city library.

One of the perks of working on the radio station in those days was that we got free passes to the Odeon Cinema, presumably in the hope that we'd mention it on our radio shows, which we did, of course. The afternoon presenter once convinced the cinema manager to give a small group of us – my wife included – a preview showing of the latest *Star Trek* film. Now that was a treat.

I used to finish my shifts on BBC Radio Humberside's breakfast show, after a week of getting up at 5.00 a.m. or whatever time it was that my alarm went off in those days, and head over to Hull Cinema's Friday matinee films, which were usually non-mainstream or indie movies. There was a chap who used to fall asleep in the front row in every film and start snoring. It was only by a hair's breadth that wasn't me, and my week of earlies usually left me ready for my bed by that time.

The Gipsyville estate, where Eric lives, is also another part of Hull that I'd almost forgotten until I did my location research for this book. In the case of Gipsyville, the then HRH Prince Charles was making a royal visit and as the breakfast show presenter at the time, I was wheeled out to do a preview breakfast show from the estate and then live commentary later in the day for the actual visit. Now, I'll freely admit, I was no Jonathan Dimbleby when it came to royal commentary and my broadcasting strengths lay elsewhere.

When you do a live commentary, you're able to talk off-air to the team back at the radio station. The idea is, when the royal person appears, you alert the radio station, they whisper in the presenter's ear, and the presenter crosses over to the reporter. When Prince Charles (as he was then) visited, we were broadcasting our daily phone-in show, so it was a bit of a nuisance to the presenter being interrupted. Unfortunately, Prince Charles would suddenly appear from whichever house he'd been in, I'd alert the radio station, they'd cross to me, Prince Charles would go back and continue his chat, and I'd then have to send the radio presenter back to his show because nothing was happening. We weren't the only people who he was messing about. There was a big group of school kids waiting for the prince on a nearby playing field, and every time it looked like Prince Charles was going to show his face, they were instructed to start playing. Whenever he disappeared again the gameplay ceased, and they waited for the next false alarm. That was my one and only royal commentary; I think it was a mercy to the listeners that it was a task I succeeded in avoiding for the remainder of my radio career.

It was another trip down memory lane for me when Hollie goes on her night out along Hull's Beverley Road. We lived in that area when we first moved to Hull, and Hollie's stomping ground used to be ours. Incidentally, the poet, Douglas Dunn, wrote a famous poem about Terry Street, which gets a mention in this story. It was influenced by the poet Philip Larkin, under whom he worked at the University of Hull in the library. I like to add a touch of culture when I can.

We drank in the Banks Harbour; I remember a very drunken night in The Welly, and we used to walk our first child around Pearson Park for fresh air and recreation. The Welly is famous in Hull, having hosted bands such as U2, The Specials, Pulp, and Hull band, The Housemartins.

The club we had the most fun in was a venue called the Silhouette Club, which was a gay club when I lived in the city. Several of the guys I worked with at BBC Radio

Humberside were gay, so that's where we tended to end up on work nights out. On a New Year's Eve out in Hull with my sister and brother-in-law, which started at the Banks Harbour and concluded in Silhouette, we ended up gyrating on the dance podiums while our spouses looked on in despair. In my defence, I was a lot younger then and hadn't yet become the responsible adult I would become when we started our family.

The other location I must mention to you is the Land of Green Ginger. It sounds like something out of *Lord of the Rings*, but it does exist, I promise. You'll find it in Hull's Old Town, on a narrow street at the bottom of Whitefriargate. It boasts the world's smallest window, which is just a slit in the wall used by the gatekeeper at the George Hotel to keep a lookout for stage-coaches.

There are several theories as to how the area got its name, but I'll leave that to historians to sort out between themselves. Instead, I'll tell you that there's a marvellous shop front on the corner of Manor Street and the Land of Green Ginger which looks very similar to the shop front that was used in *Bagpuss*. And knowing that the Land of Green Ginger isn't fictional, you'll also understand that Bowlalley Lane is equally real. If you ever get a chance to go to Hull, this is definitely an area that's worth checking out. I remember the Old Town most fondly for its pubs and eateries. In the days before we started a family, many a Friday and Saturday night was spent there.

My final revelation in these author notes is that I have actually broken out of a nunnery to go drinking with some fellow escapees. I was on a week-long summer drama course in Lincoln, and we got to stay in a nunnery nearby. A group of us climbed through a window at night and went drinking at a nearby pub. I can't remember what age I was now, but I know we shouldn't have been doing any of those things. So, when I tell you that much of the content in my books is based on personal experience, I really mean it! Even I was surprised by that one.

Before you go, please connect with me on social media.

I'll share more Hull memories at the end of book 3, but for now, we've got Jenni to fret about and we still haven't figured out who killed Sister Brennan. Oh, and things are going to get a lot worse for Hollie who's going to have to decide if finding a killer or caring for her children is her main priority. I won't hold you up any longer. Instead, I'll let you get on with the final book in this trilogy. Once you've read *The Fifth Girl*, you'll find out who's up to no good and who's completely innocent. Enjoy!

Paul Teague

paulteague.net

facebook.com/paulteagueauthor

x.com/paulteagueuk

linkedin.com/in/paulteague23uk

Printed in Great Britain
by Amazon

45533634R10172